# A COMPROMISING SITUATION

Mirabella Prey was still naked when the heavy polished doors opened abruptly. Two figures burst in, dressed in anoraks, hoods, and stocking masks. One of them pointed an automatic pistol unwaveringly at Prince Ferdel. Mirabella, although not directly threatened by any weapon, stood still, holding her position of lascivious Eve, her clothes in a black and glittering heap at her feet.

"Prince," the taller of the intruders said in a muffled voice, "you will now do what we say. Stand beside the lady." Ferdel hesitated an instant, noted the unaltered position of the gun, and walked slowly and coolly, sauntered as it were, in the direction of Mirabella.

"Take her hand."

The Prince picked up Mirabella's hand with its many glittering rings in his. There was a sudden radiant flash as the diamond bracelet with the puma's head slid like a falling star along her naked arm.

The short man then stepped forward, loosened the Prince's knitted silk tie and undid the top button of his shirt. Then he removed Ferdel's dark-blue jacket. It joined the heap of Mirabella's clothes on the floor. The pair of them, the Prince in his dark formal trousers and white shirt, the woman naked, had the air of some corrupt painting.

"Do it," the tall man said. "Do it quickly." Mirabella began to tremble slightly. The short man backed away from the pair of them and produced what was only too clearly a camera.

Books by Antonia Fraser
Coming soon from Bantam Books:

YOUR ROYAL HOSTAGE
JEMIMA SHORE'S FIRST CASE AND OTHER STORIES
OXFORD BLOOD
COOL REPENTANCE
A SPLASH OF RED
QUIET AS A NUN
THE WILD ISLAND

# YOUR
# ROYAL
# HOSTAGE

*A Jemima Shore Mystery*

## ANTONIA
## FRASER

**BANTAM BOOKS**
TORONTO • NEW YORK • LONDON • SYDNEY • AUCKLAND

This edition contains the complete text
of the original hardcover eidition.
NOT ONE WORD HAS BEEN OMITTED.

YOUR ROYAL HOSTAGE

A Bantam Book / published by arrangement with
Atheneum Publishers

PRINTING HISTORY
Atheneum edition published February 1988
Bantam edition / March 1989

Bantam Books are published by Bantam Books, a division of Bantam
Doubleday Dell Publishing Group, Inc. Its trademark, consisting of the
words "Bantam Books" and the portrayal of a rooster, is Registered in
U.S. Patent and Trademark Office and in other countries. Marca
Registrada, Bantam Books, 666 Fifth Avenue, New York, New York
10103.

*For Tasha*
princess over the water
with love

# CONTENTS

# YOUR
# ROYAL
# HOSTAGE

# ONE

# Innocent?

"We don't want to hurt her. We must remember that. All of us. She is, after all, innocent." There was a brief pause. Then the man who called himself Monkey repeated firmly: "She is innocent."

He raised one eyebrow—the right, a familiar habit—and then smiled at them, lifting the left side of his upper lip as he did so to exhibit a flash of long slightly yellow tooth. It was as though he was willing them to agree.

The girl who called herself Lamb found that she was becoming increasingly fascinated by these physical tricks on the part of Monkey. No one was at first sight less like his chosen code name than Monkey (any more than she herself resembled a lamb); yet the more Lamb studied him, the more she found something significant about the choice. Monkey, for all his bulk, had something simian about him, with his long upper lip and flat splayed nostrils: a friendly monkey of authority who gazed at you calmly from his cage until you wondered which of the two of you dwelt in the outside world.

Similarly Fox was at first sight a somewhat languid young man, with a pale complexion and of slight build, most unfoxlike; closer inspection revealed an oddly sharp nose and bright, small deeply set eyes. Even his slight build was belied by his surprisingly long and muscular arms. Also Fox could be cunning, as Lamb had learned, cunning as—well, cunning as a fox. As for Beagle: but it did not do to think about Beagle. So Lamb stopped herself thinking about Beagle, stopped thinking anything at all about him as she promised herself to do, and concentrated once more on Monkey.

"Well, isn't she? Of course she's innocent." Monkey happily answered his own question as one delighted at solving a difficulty. That was another familiar trick; Lamb imagined Monkey had used it to effect in innumerable committee meetings in the past. And after all, what was this except a committee meeting? If a committee meeting in rather an odd place of rather an odd sort.

Nobody else had spoken or showed any signs of doing so. So Monkey went on: "Quite a pretty story in the *Standard* this evening, by the way. Anyone read it?"

Lamb looked down automatically at the evening paper which lay on Monkey's lap although she had in fact seen the lunchtime edition. The original headline had been moved to the second half of the page. All the same, she could still read the words: PRINCESS: WEDDING SCARE.

The story itself, as Lamb knew, having studied it earlier, was fairly insubstantial. Something to do with the route the wedding cortège would take. But since no one yet knew officially what that route would be, it could hardly amount to a serious scare. There had been numbers of similar stories—or non-stories, if you like—recently: PRINCESS: WEDDING SNUB (some ex-

treme Labour councillors who had refused to sub-
scribe to a local wedding present).

PRINCESS: WEDDING HOPES (Some extremely loyal ten-
ants on a grand country estate who believed the
young couple would spend their honeymoon
nearby).

PRINCESS: WEDDING EXCITEMENT—what on earth had that
been about? Certainly nothing which was actually
very exciting. The arrival of an unusually large number of American tourists in the capital perhaps. Just
as PRINCESS: WEDDING FEARS might refer to the fact that
exactly the same unusually large number of American
tourists were staying at home. . . .

All that these numerous headlines went to prove
was that any combination of the two words "Princess" and "Wedding" was deemed, probably rightly,
to sell larger numbers of newspapers than for example a similarly recurring combination of, say, "Government" and "Spending"; the public appetite for
weddings having grown rather than diminished with
the most recent example, that of the Duke and
Duchess of York. In short, Princess Amy was News.
Or rather, when in the process of getting married,
Princess Amy of Cumberland was News.

Up to this point, to be frank, the media had been
strangely unaware of the potential news value of this
particular twenty-two-year-old girl. The Cumber-
lands were after all not a particularly important
branch of the Royal Family. Although the Duke of
Cumberland himself, as a king's son, had retained his
place in the succession, his marriage to a Catholic
princess meant that his three daughters were actually
outside it. None of this had seemed to matter very
much at the time. The Duke, a bachelor soldier as it
seemed, had surprised everyone by marrying at the

age of fifty, and surprised himself even more by producing three daughters; the youngest, Amy, being born when he was already scurrying toward the end of his uneventful life. The children of the Duke's royal siblings being already grown up when the Cumberland Princesses were born, the latter had in effect skipped a generation.

As a soldier the Duke had once referred to a previous holder of the title—"Butcher" Cumberland of Culloden—as "a damn fine general who understood how to deal with the natives"—remarks which caused a sensation in Scotland where he happened to be at the time. Otherwise he had led a life of almost total obscurity so far as the Press was concerned. As for the Duchess, the fact that she had been a French princess, related to half the royal families in Europe, had somehow never cut much ice with the xenophobic English Press.

Ah, but a wedding! And the wedding of a princess who was in effect an orphan (never mind the continued existence of her mother)! And the wedding of a princess who was not only an orphan, but also the youngest of three sisters. . . . What was more, a Catholic wedding—in Westminster Cathedral—made a nice change, it was generally agreed, from the Abbey and St. Paul's; as well as providing excellent opportunities for interdenominational tolerance to be paraded in these ecumenical days. Already the possibilities so far as the Press was concerned were infinitely exciting, with words like "Cinderella" produced in all sorts of hopefully tactful combinations: if you could not after all exactly term the Princesses Sophie and Harriet of Cumberland "Ugly Sisters," you could somehow hint that poor little Princess Amy had been neglected since her father's death;

surely she must have been neglected, since she had been so signally neglected by the Press. . . .

It was fortunate from the point of view of contrast that Princess Sophie, pop-eyed, lively and rather bossy, had married an unnewsworthy Scottish landowner. Then Princess Harriet, melancholy, wraith-like, bonily beautiful like her mother but not particularly photogenic, had married a French businessman without a title (where did she *find* a Frenchman without a title? In any case, title or no title, a French businessman was if possible less newsworthy than a Scottish landowner). All this made Princess Amy's match with a real live prince, admittedly European, but a genuine prince for all that, shine yet more brightly.

What was more, Princess Amy, little (she was 5'3"), unpretentious (well, why not?), stay-at-home (she had no job that anyone could remember) Princess Cinderella-Amy, had captured a prince who could by a little stretching of the imagination be described as the richest young man in Europe. The fact that Prince Ferdinand, being thirty-three, was also a Prince with a Past, was almost too much joy.

No wonder that AMY MEANS I LOVE YOU, according to one enterprising if inaccurate newspaper headline, and a lot of enterprising if inaccurate T-shirts and buttons subsequently. (Curiously enough, it was the combination of Amy's blameless past and her poverty, together with Ferdinand's blameworthy one and his wealth, which had suggested the match to certain ageing royal relations in the first place; thereafter at various Royal Family gatherings and other weddings, a certain amount of discreet promotion had taken place.)

Lamb sighed and fingered the AMY button on her

own brightly coloured handknit jersey. Beagle had described wearing the button as a cynical gesture when he pulled the jersey quite roughly over her head that famous night, the night she had temporarily decided not to remember.

"But I do love Amy," Lamb had protested, "I love her in my own way for what she's going to do for us—"

"Us?" queried Beagle, touching her; he was delighted and she thought surprised to find that she was naked under the thick garishly patterned wool.

"Us. Innocent Rights."

"I love her in my own way for what I'm going to do to her—no, that's a joke, Lambkin. Believe it or not I've loved little Amy from a respectful distant for years."

Monkey had finished speaking. He picked up the *Evening Standard* and turned to the City pages.

"As a matter of principle, I don't think she's innocent and nor does Pussy here." It was quite unexpected for Tom to speak like this. He did not generally say much at meetings, having been introduced comparatively recently by Beagle.

Pussy was a distinctly large middle-aged woman. Her code name was actually Cat, but they had all given in lately and called her Pussy since she insisted that she preferred it. Certainly "Pussy," with its comfortable overtones of fireside and hearth, suited her appearance. That meant that Beagle's friend, introduced to them as Tom, had been able to adopt the code name of Cat. Except that he had, slightly humorously, announced that if the previous Cat was a Pussy, he was undeniably a Tomcat. So that Tom was how he was generally known.

"No real names, if you please," Monkey had put in

on this occasion. "Sorry to be tiresome but if Tom's your real name—"

"Oh but it's not," replied Tom blandly, "just a *nom de guerre*."

"All the same, I believe Beagle did call you Tom." In his charming way Monkey could be very persistent.

"Cut it out, Monkey." Beagle used the slightly crude tone he tended to adopt towards Monkey as if determined, however pointlessly, to shake him from his chairman-of-the-board composure. "Supposing we say that Tom's real name is double-barrelled? Will that satisfy you? And let's say his Christian name is hyphenated. Will that do?"

"Hyphenated as in Tom-Cat. But not actually Tom-Cat, of course." Tom smiled with a charm equal to Monkey's own.

Now Lamb turned her attention back to the argument concerning the innocence or otherwise of Princess Amy. This particular argument had occurred once previously (before Tom joined them). Lamb wondered what Monkey felt about the subject being thrashed out all over again, especially since time was on this occasion short. And they had to decide on the next meeting before they parted.

Of course they had all discussed the subject of Amy herself, discussed it very thoroughly at the first of their regular meetings. It was the other middle-aged woman in their group, the one known as Chicken, who raised it. (And Chicken did have something suitably scrawny about her appearance: even if, in view of her age, Hen might have been even more appropriate.)

Lamb knew more about Chicken than she knew for example about Tom. Something in Chicken's man-

ner, a mixture of diffidence in the details of everyday
life and confidence when on her own subject, reminded Lamb of one of her teachers at school. And
sure enough, Chicken had revealed herself to be a
retired teacher, if from a very different kind of school
from the one Lamb had attended. What a thoroughly
nice woman, what a reliable person, that would be
the first reaction of most people to Chicken. As it had
been to Lamb's teacher, known as Miss Ursula. Yet
Miss Ursula had contained something oddly desperate inside her outward shell of responsibility; witness
the fact that she had got into the papers for assaulting
the woman with whom she lived not many years
after Lamb left school. Was there then something
desperate struggling inside pleasant, slightly didactic
Chicken?

"Of course some people would reckon us *all* to be
desperate, especially since—" But once again Lamb
stopped herself thinking along those dangerous
lines. Instead she cast her mind back to the previous
argument about Princess Amy. Monkey had been
cheerfully patient with them all, although Lamb
suspected that he had intended to bring in an "innocent" verdict all along. Chicken had delivered
herself of a well-turned little historical lecture on the
attitude of the British Royal Family to animals. In the
course of it, she mentioned King Charles II: "A lover,
as we know, of spaniels."

Beagle interrupted: "And a few other things too,
ho ho." That had mercifully leavened the serious
atmosphere—and equally mercifully, cut Chicken
short.

Without Tom, Pussy had merely clicked her tongue
over a Press story, unproved, that Princess Amy had
commissioned a coat of rare white Arctic fox. Other

than muttering: "She may be innocent but she's a spoiled brat," she had not played much part in the discussion.

It was Fox who, for all his bonhomie, had proved quite persistent in his personal condemnation of her, whom he termed "our little Royal Madam"; until Monkey cozened him out of it.

Lamb had said little or nothing on that occasion. So that now she thought she would come to the aid of Monkey.

"After all she's never hunted; Princess Amy."

"And she loves dogs. How sweet. She loves all animals. Even sweeter. We *know* all that, Lamb." Tom was becoming uncharacteristically vehement. "But surely you realize that a princess is more than just a nice little girl. She's a *symbol*, Lamb, ever heard of a symbol? And a symbol, Lamb, is *never* innocent." Lamb felt quite alarmed by Tom's expression: why was he looking at her in that particular way? Lamb was increasingly frightened by Tom, even if he was Beagle's friend.

"This is all quite unnecessary, Tom." It was remarkable how Monkey could pull a meeting to order, even by a gesture like putting a *Standard* beneath his arm, even a meeting as weirdly placed as this one. "I merely mentioned Princess Amy's innocence in the context of the fact that we have to be careful, extra careful, not actually to harm her. Or harm anyone for that matter. It would hardly do for us, my dear Tom, who oppose all violence and mean to say so publicly in our own way, to be accused of any form of real violence ourselves. It's especially important in view of the radical nature of the Plan, critical in fact. . . . But we've been through all that, haven't we? After all we're not *petrol*-bombers!" exclaimed

Monkey in a voice of disgust although the subject of petrol-bombing had not actually been raised. "So that the general question of Princess Amy's innocence is surely irrelevant."

Monkey stood up. "This is my stop."

The Tube train shuddered slightly as it came into the station.

"Next week same time but on the Northern Line between Golders Green and Leicester Square. It's a good long line; we can use it right down to Kennington if necessary. Usual procedure for joining each other. I'll get on the train at Golders Green station. One stop each in reverse alphabetical order this time which starts with you, Tom, at Hampstead and ends with Beagle at Euston. Watch for me in the last carriage as the train enters the station. We'll work down if we have to, once we're all gathered. Follow my lead. When I judge we're safe, I'll open my *Standard* at the City pages."

"What about Mornington Crescent?" questioned Fox plaintively; he was studying his Tube map. "I see I'm to get on at Mornington Crescent—"

Monkey smiled at him. "Follow the map, my dear Fox, that's all."

"Actually, I get on at Mornington Crescent," remarked Chicken to no one in particular. As so often with Chicken, she sounded politely superior.

The Tube doors slid open.

In stately fashion Monkey descended from the train. The others watched him go, a heavily built man in a dark-grey pin-stripe; the sort of man you would not be surprised to see wearing a bowler or at least carrying a furled umbrella. But Monkey had never so far carried an umbrella since the presence of an umbrella was the emergency signal to abandon the meeting. As for the bowler, that was the final signal for the disbanding of the group.

The others watched him go and remained silent. It was against the rules for anyone to speak to anyone else once the meeting was over, except for Chicken and Pussy, who used their agreed cover as a couple of middle-aged ladies to continue to chat.

In this way it was not breaking the rules, only breaking the spirit of them, for Pussy to remark aloud to Chicken in a small defiant voice: "I still think I'm right. Of course she's guilty. Youth is simply no excuse."

# TWO

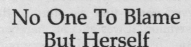

# No One To Blame
# But Herself

PRINCESS: WEDDING SCARE—Jemima Shore was relieved to find that headline in the *Standard* which she bought at Tottenham Court Road Tube station. She did not bother to read any further. Another made-up tale about these tiresome nuptials. All the headline meant to Jemima was that the story, her story, was not yet out.

For Jemima Shore Investigator had just been sacked by Megalith Television. That was the plain truth of the matter, however much lawyers, spokespersons and purveyors of official statements might attempt later to wrap it up, for one reason or another. Undoubtedly Jemima Shore, the star reporter of Megalith, was News (much as Princess Amy getting married was News). Television companies like Megalith were also on the whole News, especially when enjoyable things were taking place, like management coups, or the arrival of so-called hard-faced businessmen and the abrupt disappearance of household names from the company's employment—household faces might be a better phrase under the circumstances. The combination was liable to prove irresistible to the Press: thus Jemima was under no illusions but that her peremptory dismissal would make the headlines when it emerged.

By the time the train reached Holland Park station, however, Jemima was wondering just why she had been relieved not to find the story in the *Standard* lunchtime edition. It was after all merely postponing the evil hour. The story had to come out sooner or later. So she bought the late edition from the wooden booth outside the station just to show that she could face it, whatever it contained; it also occurred to her that her flat in Holland Park Mansions might by now be ringed by Press and though that too had to be faced, it was just as well to be warned.

PRINCESS: WEDDING SCARE had now been moved to second place in the *Standard* but there was still no sign of the headline she expected. What form would it take? Could she expect something as mild as JEMIMA QUITS? Unlikely. Fleet Street had its sources inside Megalith as well as everywhere else. TV STAR "SACKED" was the best she could hope for, the inverted commas round the word "sacked" being a delicate protection against the possibility of Jemima suing them just in case the story was not true.

But the story *was* true. Jemima Shore spared a wry thought for Cy Fredericks, the recently departed Chairman of Megalith Television. O Cy, O Tempora, O Mores. . . . O Cy, O Cy's mores which were not always absolutely open to ruthless inspection. Yet in spite of this, Jemima could not rid herself of a certain fondness for her former Chairman, despite the manner of his abrupt departure from the board which had led indirectly to her own dismissal. It was a dismissal brought about directly by Jemima's public declarations of loyalty for Cy. In short, as the hard-faced businessman had pointed out, more in sorrow than in anger (for he had studied Jemima's ratings on the eve of the interview) Jemima had no one to blame but herself.

One way and another, Jemima was inclined to agree with that verdict. Why on earth had she agreed to speak up for Cy—at his own urgent request— without paying more attention to the dark, and not-so-dark hints dropped by his knowledgeable secretary Miss Lewis on the subject of Cy's future plans? She had even told the board that she would not continue to work for Megalith if Cy was ousted, believing Cy when he assured her that this was purely a formality, and would enable him to defeat the powers of hard-faced darkness threatening him, without delay.

And now where were Cy Fredericks and Jemima Shore respectively? Cy Fredericks was somewhere in America with an enormous golden handshake to arm him in a future life which turned out to be remarkably well organized in advance, considering the apparent suddenness of his fall at Megalith. Jemima Shore was trudging back from the Tube to her flat in Holland Park Mansions (dashing white Mercedes sports car, like Megalith, a thing of the past, because, in some mysterious way, like everything else it turned out to belong *to* Megalith). Redundancy payment if any was certain to be the subject of long, long argument between Megalith's lawyers and her own, just supposing she could afford such a thing. In short, Jemima Shore, like a good many of the rest of England, was out of a job.

She turned to the inside page of the *Standard*. Yes, it had to be the day when she read about something else she had been dreading, dreading proudly in

silence for several weeks. She found herself gazing at
a wedding photograph. But this was no royal wedding, no bride in white tulle and diamonds on the
arm of a chocolate soldier in Ruritanian uniform.
Where the groom was concerned, Jemima Shore was
gazing into the face of a man she knew, no newspaper creation, in fact until recently had known very
well indeed.

"I wonder what happened to his spectacles? He
must be wearing contact lenses," she thought irrelevantly.

The bridegroom was one Cass Brinsley, a barrister
who had been Jemima's steady lover for a period not
long enough in her opinion, too long in his. The
bride, who was called Flora Hereford, was also a
barrister and had once been a pupil in Cass Brinsley's
chambers. Jemima angrily reflected that Flora Hereford, wearing a dark high-necked dress with a small
white collar, looked *extremely* pleased with herself. As
well she might. After all, she'd been after Cass for
years. And now she'd got him.

LAWFUL MATRIMONY ran the witty caption under the
happy couple. Really, the Press these days and their
headlines; what with PRINCESS: WEDDING SCARE almost
daily, and now this. . . . Furthermore: "What a dull
dress to wear at your wedding! I wouldn't dream of
wearing anything quite so lacking in style as that,"
was Jemima's next uncharitable thought. And then
something most unpalatable occurred to her: "How
on earth would I know? I've never been married."

Immediately after thinking this, in spite of herself,
Jemima found a wave of horrible emotion sweeping
over her as she walked down the broad silent street,
still clutching the paper folded back at the fatal
photograph.

Unhappiness? Yes, perhaps. Jealousy? Yes, definitely.

Oh Cass, thought Jemima, Cass, you should have waited. At which point the honest unpalatable voice spoke again in her ear: but he did wait, didn't he? He waited for months, almost a whole year after his declaration in the direction of marriage, and what did you do? You wouldn't say yes, you wouldn't say no. Cass's very own words.

It was only after that that Flora Hereford got him. That one-off programme about child-brides in Sri Lanka, the trip he begged you not to make—"not *another* eight-week stint without a telephone call"— she could hear Cass's voice now, and her own defensive reply: "Is it my fault if you're always out when I'm in?" "But I'm always in while you're away," retorted Cass grimly. Added to which the programme had never even been shown, concluded Jemima ruefully, and now it never will be. Ah well, no one to blame but myself.

Jemima Shore decided that these were definitely the most depressing words in the English language. As they resounded in her ears, she took another peek at the photograph, as a result of which honesty once more made her admit that Flora Hereford was really a very pretty girl wearing rather an elegant dress; she was also several years younger than Jemima.

No one to blame but herself. She had a ghastly feeling that this was turning out to be what Cherry, Jemima's former aide at Megalith, a nubile but tearful lady, would term a crying situation. Was she going to manage to get up the stairs and into the flat before the gathering tears flowed? Jemima reached the flat. As she put her key in the lock, she could hear the telephone ringing.

For one wild moment—it was something to do with the sheer unreality of *that* photograph—she thought: "Cass!"

Midnight, Jemima's sleek muscular black cat, a smaller version of a leopard, purred raucously at her ankle. In attempting to reach the telephone, Jemima stumbled over Midnight who squawked pathetically and then knocked over a vase of flowers left by Mrs. Bancroft, her cleaning lady, to cheer her up.

The telephone stopped just as she reached it. At which point Jemima Shore finally burst into tears. Midnight had just forgiven her, in token of which he leapt heavily on to her lap, claws out, when the telephone rang again. It was Cherry, speaking from Megalith. Jemima gulped as she answered.

"Jemima, you're *crying!*" Momentarily Cherry spoke in a voice of astonishment that anyone bar herself could dissolve into hopeless tears; above all, that legend of invulnerability, Jemima Shore. Then, being a person of much good sense when not in floods of tears, Cherry reverted to her usual brisk tone: "Good news and bad news. Which do you want first?"

Jemima gave another gulp.

"All right, here comes the bad news, and it's not all that bad, because it's what you expected. The story is out about you being given the push, this place is like a madhouse, telephones never stop ringing, etc., etc. You can imagine it all for yourself, general flap on about what you will say, and as to that, you can expect the hounds of Fleet Street baying at your door any moment, I fear."

"Thanks for the warning, Cherry. You're a brick, as usual. I'll call you when—"

"Don't you want to hear the good news? Here it

comes anyway. You know the Royal Wedding? How could you not know the Royal Wedding? How could any of us not know the Royal Wedding? Well, whatever you may feel about the Royal Wedding, it's an ill wind, because Television United States, no less, TUS, that is, are doing a special on it, imagine that, a whole special on our very own British royal nuptials, and they want you to be the anchor person. One of the anchor people. Rick Vancy will be the other."

"And you call this good news?" enquired Jemima in a cool voice from which tears had however noticeably departed.

"Jemima, think of it! Dollars, delights, coverage, work, and *Rick Vancy*. Don't you *adore* Rick Vancy? If not, pass him on—"

"What interests me far more than Rick Vancy, and he interests me only mildly, is *why* TUS is making a special on the Royal Wedding. Any clues?"

"Oh, I think they imagine there's going to be an incident, you know what Americans are like. An assassination or something like that," said Cherry airily, "nothing serious, nothing to bother you."

"Cherry, what on earth gave you that idea?"

"Only that the man I spoke to, some London-based chap with a boyishly enthusiastic voice, kept asking if you had a cool head and could guarantee to keep that same head in a crisis."

Jemima burst out laughing. "Really, Americans! They are absurd. The idea of anyone, anyone at all, wanting to assassinate poor little Princess Amy, or even the chocolate soldier, unless some aggrieved husband takes a pot-shot. I mean, it's a wedding, don't they realize that? Just a wedding, a perfectly ordinary wedding, dolled up in fancy clothes, dolled up in its details mainly by the Press. After all, we've had two of them, royal style, recently, without any trouble at all. Weddings! Really!"

"Mmm, weddings. On the subject of weddings—"

"It's all right, Cherry, I saw. Nice photograph. Nice girl."

"She has bad legs," said Cherry loyally. "Now getting back to the other much more important wedding, Jemima, I really think—"

"No, Cherry, definitely no. I'm going to have a rest period, a long, long rest period. Then I'll probably become a probation officer, if they'll have me, and end up Dame Jemima, deeply worthy, with her wicked past in television long ago forgotten. Look, forgive me, we'll talk, there's someone at the door. Pressing the bell *and* banging, by the sound of it."

Actually, there were three people at the door. One was pressing the bell, one was banging and one was leaning so eagerly forward that he fell into the room as Jemima opened it. All three were male. All three were smiling. Jemima took a deep breath.

Then the telephone began to ring again. More to avoid talking to her three new knights than for any more positive reason, Jemima picked it up. The voice was, in Cherry's phrase, boyishly enthusiastic. The accent was American. The voice had been talking for a few minutes with Jemima making automatic responses, as she wondered exactly how much whisky she (a non-whisky drinker) had in the flat for this particular Press emergency, when she heard the words: "exclusive interview."

"Why me?" Jemima, once again acting automatically, did not repeat the words "Cumberland Palace" to the waiting ears of the knights of the Press. What she did say was: "Fifty-five minutes. That's a hell of a long time for anyone, let alone . . ."

More enthusiastic boyish confidences. Then: "Both of them?" Jemima paused. "Just her might be better. Or one at a time. It *is* exclusive? Perhaps you'll tell me just how you worked this magic when we meet."

Some time later as Jemima poured the last drops of the whisky into the glasses of her knights, now installed quite cosily in her flat, with no sign of leaving, she was able to remark quite innocently: "As for myself, I think I'll open a bottle of champagne. If there's one in the fridge. No, I'll keep the one you kindly brought for another day, when it's cold, thank you very much. . . . After all, I really do have something to celebrate, don't I? . . . No, not *freedom* exactly, more like a new life. I'm working on the Royal Wedding. For TUS. With Rick Vancy. Didn't you know? Well, of course I had to keep it absolutely quiet from Megalith. This is all strictly off the record, I need hardly say, please keep it to yourselves, at any rate till the public announcement. It would be so embarrassing if it leaked out. You will promise I won't read all about it in the papers tomorrow morning?"

There *was* some cold champagne in the fridge. After the first knight had opened it with a flourish, Jemima sat sipping it with a most innocent expression on her face. It crossed the mind of the second knight that her expression was in fact not unlike that of the elegant black cat purring loudly on her lap. The third knight was busy wondering how soon he could get away and telephone his paper from the call box he had noticed on the corner of the street.

He tried to imagine the headline.

ROYAL WEDDING SENSATION? Yes, why not?

# THREE

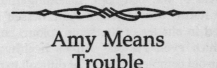

# Amy Means
# Trouble

Princess Amy, breakfasting in bed at Cumberland Palace, read the heading ROYAL WEDDING SENSATION with an agreeable quickening of interest and was correspondingly annoyed to discover that the story actually concerned rival television companies.

She pouted. When she was alone Princess Amy's pouts made her look sulky if sensual; her full lower lip extended and drooped, and her nostrils—perhaps already a little too wide—flared. In public, however, Princess Amy had quickly learnt how to transform "the pout" into something not so much sulky as sweetly disappointed, and thus rather delightful.

The Princess was wearing a short cotton nightdress in the form of a man's shirt, trimmed with white lace. The nightdress itself was her favourite colour, known to the Press as Amy Blue ("Amy Loves Blue—and so will you" promised one feature in a woman's magazine). In fact the colour was nearer to turquoise or even green. The open front of the nightshirt revealed Amy's surprisingly large and full breasts—surprising, that is, only because they did not accord with the girlish image the Press were busy imposing upon her, and thus even when discreetly covered up by day or safely moulded in evening dress, generally took observers by surprise.

The rest of the bedroom, including the narrow wooden four-poster in which Amy herself lay, was decorated in shades of the same colour, something with which even Princess Amy's healthy twenty-two-year-old complexion found it difficult to contend. On the walls, a set of watercolours in oval frames showed a series of eighteenth-century princesses—Amy's relations—in white muslin and blue sashes. Their costumes acted as an unintentional reminder of how much more flattering this kind of garb was to a young girl than a turquoise nightshirt.

There was a quick low knock at the door and a dark-haired girl who looked to be some years older than Amy, poked her head round the door. The Princess dropped the paper and gave a shriek.

"Ione, don't tell me you're here already—what on earth's the time?"

"Good morning, Ma'am. No, it's early, honestly it is, I thought I'd get on with all those letters, and then something came up—"

Amy interrupted her with a groan. She had just looked at the pink enamel and gold clock by her bed. "Oh God, Ione, I *know* I promised to be down. We were going to plough through them together, I *know* we were. For God's sake, don't tell Mama when she wakes up, please, please, please— "

"The Duchess has gone to Plymouth, Ma'am, to the naval base."

"Goodness gracious: she actually went! No headache?" The Duchess of Cumberland's inability—through sudden "illness"—to carry out public engagements was celebrated in her family.

"Well, what would *you* do if you were a royal widow with nothing to do?" charitable Princess Harriet had once asked of her more critical younger sister.

"I'd take a lot of lovers," replied Princess Amy bracingly. "It's so *wet* of Mama to be boringly faithful to Papa's memory. With the aid of the bottle."

"Her Royal Highness went by helicopter at six o'clock this morning," confirmed Ione, to whom all these facts were well known; she spoke without expression. "From the lawn. I'm surprised you didn't hear it."

"Of course I didn't hear it, Ione, you coot. A helicopter would have to land on my *bed* at six a.m. to wake me, as you perfectly well know." Amy stretched so that her breasts half fell out of the open nightshirt; she did not bother to button it up.

"Ione, my angel, my good angel, listen, I've *got* to telephone Ferdel. Then I promise I'll be right with you. All morning."

"No problem," said Ione Quentin easily, "I'll be downstairs." She turned and stopped. "There is just one thing, Ma'am—"

But Princess Amy had already turned to the telephone.

"It can wait," said Ione after a moment, seeing that the Princess was already chattering away.

"ROYAL WEDDING SENSATION" she was reading from the headline of the *Daily Exclusive*. "And then nothing about *one* at all. Quel drag, Ferdel, yes?"

Her fiancé, corralled for the pre-wedding season in the Eaton Square flat of an absent aunt—an aged foreign Royal who had played some discreet part in the promotion of the marriage—laughed in what he hoped was a sympathetic manner and did not pursue the subject. He was wondering whether Amy had noticed the latest instalment about his previous relationship with Mirabella Prey in the gossip column of the same newspaper.

"Don't forget—AMY MEANS I LOVE YOU," Amy was saying now as a light farewell, quoting the familiar text of the buttons (although she had quite failed to make Ferdel himself wear one).

"Nothing about one at all." Prince Ferdinand sighed. That Amy should be so fortunate. . . . It was all very well for Amy, cast as the public's favourite virgin (although that certainly wasn't true in private as Ferdel had every reason to know, Amy having admitted to one lover, with Ferdel suspecting at least one other). But Ferdel, aged thirty-three, was somehow expected to exhibit the man-of-the-world allure derived from an exciting past, without actually having lived this past with any specific individuals. These kinds of ridiculously unreal expectations could only be harboured by the British public, he reflected mournfully.

Ferdel sighed again and thought of Mirabella Prey. *Hélas.* He would miss her. That is to say, he would miss the nights, all of them. He certainly would not miss the days, hardly any of them. No one could possibly want to spend their days with Mirabella Prey, except as a prelude to the nights: Mirabella, with her well-publicized passion for wild animals, Mirabella who was inclined to stock her house with pets some of whose mating habits were even more savagely exotic than those of Mirabella herself.

That confounded cheetah, for example: It was the cheetah which was the peg for this morning's story in the *Daily Exclusive* (generally, but not always accurately, known as the *Clueless*). TROUBLE ROYAL it read. WILL FERDY CHEET-HER? ran the second headline. The writer then went on to enquire with pseudo-innocence whether foreign Prince Ferdinand intended to bestow a second cheetah on his young English bride Princess Amy, following that first cheetah so generously bestowed upon the foreign film star Mirabella Prey, she of the noble passion for the animal kingdom. For most people, however, the headline with its nasty implication of post-marital betrayal on the part of sophisticated Europeans, would be the point of the story. Ferdel hoped that his young English bride had failed to notice the item.

Naturally Princess Amy had noticed it: this was because she read the gossip column of the *Clueless* (as well as those of the *Mail* and *Express*) sedulously each morning. She had done so since her early teens, relying on this method of keeping up with the doings of her friends, much as a stockbroker might turn to the *Financial Times* for the movements of the market. But Ferdel would have been interested to discover that Amy, far from being shocked, was actually in a curious way rather turned on by the Mirabella Prey saga.

That is to say, it was the actress's amorous connection with Ferdel which excited Amy (after all, she had been watching Mirabella Prey's films since she was *so* high, as she put it with a little bubble of malice to Ione, never dreaming that one day . . .). Amy found the actress's public posturings and declared warm love for the animal kingdom, on the contrary, slightly irritating. Where animals were concerned, Amy thought there should be lots of nice ones about, preferably dogs, just as she thought there should be a lot of nice servants about, preferably of dog-like devotion. Towards both dogs and servants, Amy was demonstratively and genuinely affectionate—in private. She just did not think this a proper subject for boasting about in the newspapers.

Here then was Mirabella Prey on the subject of her famous cheetah: "I'd die for him," she was quoted as saying, "I'll never give him up."

"How fatuous," thought Amy. (For Amy, unlike most readers of the *Daily Exclusive*, assumed Mirabella Prey was actually talking about the cheetah.)

"I'd certainly never give you up, you silly old dogs. I just don't need to tell the whole world about it." Princess Amy patted the grizzled snout of one of the two middle-aged cocker spaniels lying huddled beside her bed. "You darling, darling old doggies." Happy stirred and snuffled; Boobie did not move. Years ago they had been enthusiastically christened Hapsburg and Bourbon by Amy's historically minded governess, a woman much moved by the thought of Amy's grand European ancestry. In view of Amy's future grand European marriage, it was perhaps just as well that the dogs' original names, like the dynasties themselves, had receded effectively into history.

Sitting, still at breakfast, in the gloomy dining-room of the Eaton Square flat, Prince Ferdinand read to the end of the cheetah story and gave yet another sigh, the third of the morning; where Mirabella was concerned, he had a feeling there might be more sighs to come. Unlike Amy, he picked up the message of the piece—from "cheet-her" to "I'll never give him up"—perfectly well. It was bad news, not so much that Mirabella was talking to the Press, something she had never been averse to doing, her career in a manner of speaking demanding it, but that she was now condescending to gossip columnists. Unlike Amy again, Ferdel had never heard of Little Mary, she of the *Daily Exclusive* who was alleged to double as Miss Mouse of the Mousehole column in *Jolly Joke;* but he recognized trouble when he read it.

Trouble. Royal Trouble, to adapt the words of the gossip column's headline. There was more than one kind of royal trouble this morning. Ferdel took a letter from the pocket of his silk dressing-gown and then put it back. Where women were concerned, he decided that he was inclined to suffer from a sense of guilt first thing in the morning, a kind of emotional hangover; it might therefore be better to ponder this particular missive a little later on, say after the first Bloody Mary of the day at noon. Besides, threats were so tiresome, especially threats from women, when Ferdel was precluded from stifling them—the threats, that is—by a well-established method. This consisted of a quick immediate telephone call, a short passionate declaration, a more prolonged passionate embrace at a date to suit both parties, followed by a handsome gift bestowed by Ferdel. By the time this ritual was completed, the subject of the threat was quite forgotten; so that the threatener seldom noticed that Ferdel had not actually succumbed to it.

He could not carry out any of these steps now. Could he not? No, he really could not. Not even the first one? Not even the third one, followed discreetly by the fourth one? No, he really could not. Under the circumstances it might be better to throw the letter away, after the others, and forget about it. Probably Amy was too busy chatting on the telephone to her innumerable English girlfriends to read this diatribe from the so-called Little Mary. Ferdel took the letter out of his pocket and threw it, barely crumpled, into the wastepaper basket. He gave no thought as to what might become of the letter; that would have been as uncharacteristic as wondering who washed up his breakfast things, still standing on the heavily polished table before him.

"Trouble," said Taplow, the English butler/chauffeur of Ferdel's absent aunt, when he later retrieved the letter from its resting place and flattened it again without difficulty. (It was Taplow who had cleared the Prince's breakfast table and repolished the heavy table.) "She's still writing to him. That's the third this week. Horrible, the things she says. I told you there'd be trouble."

"She's foreign," commented Mrs. Taplow without looking at him. She was polishing the silver, a task which traditionally fell to the butler; but in the case of the Taplows, it had sometimes been commented upon by employers that Mrs. Taplow was really the more masculine of the two. Although she referred on occasion briefly to "Jossie," most people assumed unthinkingly that the Taplows were childless. Certainly Taplow, a big, soft, stately man, had something of the feminine about him; there was thus an impression, only a vague one, but vaguely disquieting, that there was some kind of sex reversal in their relationship.

"A foreign spitfire," added Mrs. Taplow after a pause.

"Spitfires aren't—"

"I was quoting the paper, Kenneth." Mrs. Taplow narrowed her eyes and inspected her handiwork.

"She loves him, that's all. She has a foreign way of putting it."

"She loves him, does she? God knows why."

"He's got what it takes. I'm quoting the papers again, Kenneth." There was something disagreeably coy about her expression. "Did you read the *Sunday Exclusive*? What *she* said, Mirabella. 'All night passion'; that was the story." Mrs. Taplow picked up another fork and jabbed it gently but firmly into the green baize cloth. "Again and again and again. That's what she said." Mrs. Taplow jabbed the fork in time with her words. Taplow looked away.

"I'm thinking of the security angle, Lizzie, you do appreciate that," he said after a while, fingering the letter. "Gossip has never interested me, I can say that with my hand on my heart. You should know that, Lizzie: gossip writers and sneak photographers, I've no time for them." He paused. "But security, yes. We have a responsibility here. I've been asked, *we've* been asked, to report anything odd. They're jittery about this wedding, it's obvious. So we have to report anything odd."

"Is it odd for a woman scorned to write that kind of letter?"

"Well, what do you think, Lizzie?" Taplow abandoned the letter and looked directly at his wife.

"I've never been a woman scorned, Kenneth," replied Mrs. Taplow equably, "so I wouldn't have the least idea."

"Well then, look at this now—all this about blood for example. Isn't that odd? If it's not odd, I tell you I certainly find it quite disgusting."

Mrs. Taplow put down her cloth and took the letter. She adjusted the small spectacles on her nose, which had hung round her neck on a cord, low enough to give the impression of a chatelaine's keys.

"This blood to which you're referring is the blood of animals," she said at last; she sounded very patient. "Not his blood, Kenneth, but the blood of innocent animals. Innocent animals which have already been slaughtered. She, Mirabella, is not threatening to shed our Prince's blood. It's a matter of fact, Kenneth, that she is not."

"It is a matter of fact, Lizzie, as you put it, that she is threatening to come and daub him, and anybody near him, including HRH, with buckets of animals' blood, innocent animals' blood or not, that is disgusting, Lizzie, which we have discussed before—in a certain connection—" He stopped.

"It hasn't happened yet." Ignoring his last remark, Mrs. Taplow spoke with an air of unshaken patience.

"I'm telling the police. Before it happens. Yes, I know what that will mean, Lizzie. Believe me, I do. Detectives all over the place. It's bad enough when HRH pays us one of her little visits. I am well aware of all that, Lizzie. And when I drive him, that detective always sitting in the front, making small talk as if it was *normal* him sitting there!" Taplow snorted. "But then again, they might move him. Have you thought of that?"

"Move him?" For the first time Mrs. Taplow sounded a little surprised.

"Move him to CP. There's masses of room at the Palace since the old Duke died. Self-contained flat, etc., etc. No suggestion of impropriety, naturally. The detective who spoke to me was in two minds about the whole thing anyway; thought our Prince might well be better off all along at CP."

"And how will you explain the fact that you read his letters?"

"I'm going to tell the truth," replied Taplow loftily. "Find me that number, Lizzie. I don't trust these professional animal lovers, I don't trust them one inch. A violent lot. Are you going to disagree?"

"And what is that supposed to mean, Kenneth?" enquired Mrs. Taplow, her composure restored.

"I was thinking of the Trooping the Colour. And the Opening of Parliament last year. Was that or was it not violent? Talk about blood—there was enough blood about then, the horses' blood, innocent horses, Lizzie."

"If you're referring to Innoright, Kenneth, as I believe you are, Innoright had nothing whatsoever to do with the Opening of Parliament incident. You know perfectly well that Innoright is non-violent." Mrs. Taplow, with deliberation, drew out a small poster from the drawer beneath the table, on which the word "INNORIGHT" in red was clearly visible. A variety of animals' faces peered out of the letters, amongst which a tiger and a monkey could be distinguished.

" 'Innoright abhors all violence.' Did you hear that, Kenneth? And here it is again: 'Innoright specifically does not seek to correct the violence which humanity shows towards innocent animals by violent means towards humanity itself, in so far as humanity itself is innocent.' "

"Whatever that means, which to me, frankly, is somewhat obscure, give me the number. I'm ringing the police. We are here to serve, Lizzie."

"We have paid the price for that," murmured his wife.

But before Taplow could touch the receiver, the

telephone began to ring. In spite of the perturbation of moments before, Taplow's voice was automatically grave and gentle as he answered it. "Yes, Ma'am, I'll put you through to His Highness straight away." Taplow turned to his wife with a raised eyebrow.

"Trouble?"

"HRH sounded quite hysterical. Unlike her. Maybe *she* got a letter."

What Princess Amy was in the process of repeating frenziedly to Prince Ferdinand on the telephone was not however on the subject of letters.

"It's disgusting," she was saying over and over again. "Disgusting, Ferdel, I can't tell you how disgusting it is."

"My poor little darling," began Ferdel once or twice. "Poor little Amy."

"No, but it's disgusting. Blood everywhere. Animals' blood! Ugh! It stinks. It's like living in a slaughterhouse."

"But your guards, my darling, the police, all those detectives—"

"They did it at night from the park side. It wasn't found till Mama set off in her helicopter this morning. They managed to stop her seeing it, thank heaven. They're whitewashing it now."

"Amy, what does it say?"

"What does it matter what it says?" Amy almost shrieked down the telephone. "It's just so disgusting. Oh, it's that thing for animals. No, not the usual one, this is another one, INNO-something or other."

"Ah," Ferdel breathed a long sigh, which might almost sound like relief.

"Anyway what's it to do with me? I love animals," Amy went on. She added quite sharply: "She's not the only one who loves animals you know." It was the only reference made by either of them to the entry in the morning's gossip column.

It was left to a Chief Superintendent from the Royalty and Diplomatic Protection Department (generally known as the RDPD) to inform Prince Ferdinand later in the day that Innoright's bloody message on the Palace wall had actually read, in a grim parody of the AMY MEANS I LOVE YOU button: AMY MEANS TROUBLE—AND SO DO WE.

# FOUR

# Underground
# Plan

The heavy-set man—perhaps something in the City?—who got on the Tube at Hampstead, waited for several stops before he took the evening paper from beneath his arm and glanced casually at the headline. The letters were black and enormous: PALACE OUTRAGE, and then PRINCESS IN DANGER?

"Dreadful!" exclaimed the pleasant-looking woman sitting next to him. She nudged her companion and pointed to the paper's headline, now virtually in her face since the heavy-set man had opened the paper somewhere at the start and was reading it. The respectable-looking woman sounded pleasurably indignant.

"Tch," went her companion, also a woman, also middle aged.

The train stopped at Old Street. Some people got out—one woman from the opposite end of the carriage—but the train as a whole was not full. It was that short lull in mid-afternoon before the office workers started scurrying home in their hordes, and after the comparative intensity of the lunchtime movements.

Once the train started again, Monkey turned to the
City pages at the back of the evening paper. The
meeting had begun, which meant that Chicken and
Pussy no longer enjoyed their privilege of talking to
each other as though they were friends (in reality
Chicken and Pussy had never met until Innoright
brought them together and never now met outside
"working hours" for reasons of security).

Tom, who was lounging by the doors, sat down in
the empty seat next to Monkey. Beagle, already
seated by the small door at the end of the carriage,
moved up until he was next to Lamb, who was on the
other side of Monkey. Fox came next. Before he
moved, Fox had gazed anxiously out of the window
at the departing platform, as though worried whether
he had missed his proper stop; he also consulted a
small paper map of the Underground and then
looked up at the map on the upper side of the
carriage, as though comparing the two. Fox sat down
with an air of relief.

It was all standard practice. The routine had been
laid down several months earlier when this particular
cell of the main Innoright Group had been founded—
by Monkey, who had handpicked the members from
Innoright protest meetings, studying their record
cards for suitable biographical details. In view of the
nature of The Plan he wanted a special mixture of
daring, practicality and imagination: plus true commitment to the cause that held them together. In
theory, of course, any member of Innoright should
possess such commitment. But in practice Monkey (a
founder of Innoright to which he had privately devoted much of his City-made fortune) discovered that
members differed radically in their particular angle of

interest; this meant that they also differed radically in what they were prepared to do for Innoright.

Members who were particularly horrified by vivisection for example could not easily be induced to lobby food shops, regarding them as very much secondary objects of attack so long as laboratory conditions remained iniquitous. Other members believed with equal passion that the animals used for scientific research were at least living in conditions over which some control was exerted by law, whereas the lives of battery hens . . . But the six people Monkey had picked to be part of his team were all of them more persuaded by the general nature of Innoright's philosophy than by any particular part of it. The innocent should never suffer at the hands of the guilty, guilty in the first place because of their torture of the innocent. In that cause, Monkey's team, he was convinced, would do anything, anything that might be asked of them by Innoright, as represented by Monkey. It was an awe-inspiring thought. It was a good thought. Monkey liked being in control of things.

Because Monkey was in control, it was Monkey who had laid down the necessity for a constantly changing meeting-place so that they could not afterwards be easily identified as knowing each other. To avoid suspicion.

"'Afterwards?'" asked Lamb. "What do you mean by 'afterwards'? I thought we were going to declare ourselves. That was the whole point."

"Finally, yes. But you don't imagine, my dear Miss Lamb, that there will be no *hue and cry*." Monkey had a way of putting words in italics with his resonant voice. He looked around and raised an eyebrow. "We want no eager landlady coming forward with information about our constant meetings, no one afterwards to connect the seven of us. After all, we are sufficiently disparate, are we not, for such a connection not to be immediately suspected."

They were certainly disparate, in Monkey's phrase. Although the second thing those members picked by Monkey had in common was a certain convenient flexibility of employment, if not actual lack of it, the reasons for this varying considerably with the members' different ages and classes.

The cell had held its first rendezvous at the National Portrait Gallery, gathering on Monkey's instructions by a huge royal portrait (that appealed to his sense of humour). He chose the study of King George VI, Queen Elizabeth and the two young Princesses over a family breakfast table, hung at the head of a staircase, garishly coloured, impossible to miss. On Monkey's instructions also, at this first encounter they divided into plausible groups; that is to say, Lamb, who might have been Monkey's docile daughter, stood close by him; while Chicken and Pussy chatted animatedly to each other.

"Look at Princess Margaret Rose! What a little poppet! To think that now her own children . . ." The words flowed happily.

Beagle, in baggy grey cotton trousers (in spite of the spring cold), loose whitish T-shirt, camouflage jacket, trainer shoes without socks, lounged alone. The trouble with Beagle was that he looked not so much implausible as subtly menacing in the context of the National Portrait Gallery. He even attracted the attention of one of the uniformed attendants, who spoke to him.

"I'm unemployed, right? And it's free here, right? Any other questions?" was Beagle's response.

"You're asked not to touch the frames of the pictures," said the attendant pleasantly. "That's right," said a young man with a rather high voice standing next to Beagle, self-importantly. "There's a lot of history here, you know, and it belongs to everyone." It was Fox. Beagle glared at him. Lamb, close to Monkey, felt the older man stir angrily.

"Just what we don't want to happen," he muttered, "calling attention to us. Beagle mustn't do that. And what Fox said was unnecessary."

It was then that Lamb came up with the idea of rendezvousing on the Tube, "where you sit next to absolutely anybody without thinking twice about it," as she put it and then blushed (although Lamb rarely blushed). She blushed because Beagle looked at her, a hard, slightly mocking look. Afterwards Beagle told Lamb that was when he first decided to have her.

"You were so sweet and innocent, Lambkin, so polite. One of these days, Beagle to have a taste of Lamb. That was the resolution."

At the time Lamb corrected her statement to "where everybody meets everybody." And so—after an appreciative hum, hum, a raising of the upper lip and eyebrow from Monkey, the Underground Plan was born.

It proved strangely easy to carry out, given that Lamb's original unguarded remark—"you sit next to absolutely anybody without thinking twice about it"—was undeniably true about the London Underground system; even if opinions might vary as to who "absolutely anybody" was. The seven members of the cell were all of them physically common or unremarkable types—which was in fact the third principle on which Monkey had selected them originally.

Beagle for example was, to the outward eye, an apparent loafer of vaguely aggressive demeanour; a prejudiced observer might put him down as unemployed "and happy with it; the sort who doesn't even want to work." But there were after all many such travelling by Tube. In essence, Beagle's medium height, his neat features, lightish-brown hair, lightly tanned skin all combined to make him unremarkable: a common type. It was Lamb who knew that the body beneath the T-shirt and baggy trousers was hard, muscular—and scarred.

Pussy on the other hand had an air of silent self-righteousness, the air of one waiting for someone to light up a cigarette in order to ask them to extinguish it, which made her a common enough type too. She was also the mistress of the uninteresting-looking plastic shopping-bag, providing herself with an extraordinary variety of them as the weeks passed; what the logos of the bags had in common was that you could not possibly want to know more about the contents of any bag emblazoned with them. Pussy, although fat, was not so fat that you would remember her for exceptional obesity; just heavy, in the way that some women over a certain age are inclined to spread in the hips and bosom so that the waist is gradually eliminated.

In the same way, Fox, although on the short side, was certainly no dwarf; his lack of height was not even particularly noticeable unless he was standing side by side with a girl, say, Lamb. Slender as Lamb was, she topped Fox by an inch or two. The most noticeable thing about Fox originally had been his habit of bringing his mongrel dog, an aged bulldoggish sort of animal, to Innoright meetings. The hairless dog, with its crushed apologetic face, had made an odd contrast with the neatly dressed young man.

The dog, called Noel—"for Coward, because as a result of my training, he doesn't get into fights"—had caused some dissension at early Innoright meetings; his continued presence being in the end responsible for the Innoright rule that meetings were, "without prejudice," for human beings only. This was because some Innoright members had strong views on domestic pets—"no better than Negro slaves on plantations"—and others equally strong views in the opposite direction. Monkey, while assuring Fox that Noel's presence at meetings had been perfectly acceptable to him personally, had delicately persuaded him to leave Noel behind for the cell meetings also, on the grounds of Noel's noticeability.

Tom was vaguely foreign looking—but the foreignness was sufficiently unspecific for him to merge into the vast confluence of youngish foreign-looking men on the Underground who might be students or at least carrying students' cards. His complexion was darkish—but it was olive-dark, not brown, and might even be the product of a recent holiday in the sun. Spanish or Portuguese blood? Possibly. Not Asian, at least probably not Asian: Tom was tall. Iranian or an Arab of some sort? Could be. Something Middle Eastern was certainly plausible. In general Tom might have been the kind of actor who plays foreign parts on television, minor characters in established series, never more than half seen or half remembered by the general public. It was the fact that Tom could vary the racial impression which he gave, which had persuaded Monkey to enrol him when he was produced by Beagle (Monkey had had to reject the idea of recruiting a handsome black from East Ham, of

Nigerian descent, a founder member of Innoright, because his ethnic origin was too easily identifiable).

As for Monkey, Chicken, Lamb, their particular types, the City gent, the neatly if drably dressed woman of a certain age, the nice girl in her thoroughly Sloane-Ranger clothes, these types reproduced themselves endlessly around them.

"Nothing exceptional about us." It was Monkey's theme song.

"Except what we're going to do, darling," murmured Tom.

"No connections between us." It was Monkey's other constantly reiterated cry.

"Except that we're all members of Innoright." This time Tom spoke louder.

"Correction. We all *were* members of Innoright. Beagle resigned in protest against current policy, on my instructions. As a matter of fact, Lamb never joined, only went to a couple of meetings and met Beagle. I'm a member, so is Pussy."

"I was a very early member, a founder member, I think you'll find, unlike Pussy," put in Chicken in her comfortably firm voice, the voice of the teacher who will not be overlooked in the midst of the class. "I have consistently voted *against* the amalgamation of Innoright with other groups on the grounds that—"

"Absolutely, my dear Miss, or should I say Mrs., Chicken." Monkey interrupted her hurriedly; this was no time for that hoary old Innoright issue concerning its links with other groups.

"Absolutely. And Fox here was, like myself, a founder member. But he too has resigned. On my instructions."

"The treatment of Noel—" began Fox in a mutinous

voice; he had been becoming visibly restive during Chicken's speech.

"Provided the perfect excuse," finished Monkey neatly. "So you see, Tom, no secrets about it, all carefully worked out, except we don't hand about our membership list in the first place. And you? It's news to me that you are a member. *Are* you a member? Under what name?"

"I vouch for Tom." Beagle, leaping to Tom's defense again.

At recent meetings these frictions had been stronger than ever, as the date on which the Plan had to be carried out drew closer and could not of its very nature be postponed. And yet, as Lamb said privately to Beagle afterwards, these arguments, these niggling disagreements were ludicrous, really. She wished she could tell Beagle her worry about Tom, the way he kept looking at her and other things. But she had to remember Tom was Beagle's friend.

Instead she said: "We all want the same thing."

"Innocent Rights," said Beagle, and he took the lobe of Lamb's delicate ear in his fingers and gave it a little sharp nip.

This afternoon Monkey was angry. Lamb could tell by the way he sucked down his lower lip.

"What's all that about?" he asked Tom in a low voice, pointing to the headline on the *Standard*, PALACE OUTRAGE (although Tom had actually asked him if he could look up the time of a film—another agreed code).

"It was fun, darling."

"*Fun*? Fun for who?"

"For us."

"And the blood? Fun for the animals? You know

how careful we are. We simply cannot afford to fall
into *their* trap of violence— "

"It wasn't animals' blood. Cool down, Monko."

"It wasn't *human* blood! Are you crazy?"

"It was paint, Monkey, paint. Oxblood, I think it's
called. I'll get you the name if you want to repaint
your posh dining-room."

"Yes," Beagle chipped in impudently. "We thought
we'd give the little Princess an early wedding
present. Anything wrong with that? And advertise
our presence, as it were. A trailer for the big show."

Monkey was silent. Lamb supposed that he did not
trust himself to speak. He turned over the page of his
newspaper and then turned it back.

"Any luck with the shoes, dear?" Chicken spoke to
Pussy in her adopted character, which she was not
supposed to do during a meeting.

"Nothing in beige leather at all," Pussy responded
gallantly, scuffling in one of her plastic bags. "Not a
real beige anyway; plenty of cream and canary. I
settled for taupe."

Actually Pussy, like many of the members of
Innoright, avoided leather in all its forms and thus
her shoe shopping took rather a different form as she
searched for synthetic footware, made in large comfortable sizes for her heavy feet. The avoiding of
leather was not however mandatory for members of
Innoright (it was not considered in the same light as
fur, for example). Monkey's polished shoes looked
like leather as did Lamb's; one could not be quite
sure about Chicken's classic shoes, possibly patent
leather, possibly imitation.

Just as Pussy had not in fact been searching for
beige leather, so Pussy was not actually the harmless
if slightly fussy woman she appeared to be. Pussy,

together with her only child, a daughter called Caro (otherwise known as Otter) had been responsible for some of the most daring night-raids on those boutiques, beauty shops and stores which stocked cosmetics notoriously tested out on animals. This was because Caro-Otter was, or rather had been, a model. But Otter (like her mother) was cunning; she had not advertised her strong views on the protection of animals to her agent, beyond declining gracefully to model fur coats (and that was by now a not uncommon stance among top models). Instead she had seized every opportunity to garner information as to which products were actually "guilty."

Then by night with Pussy she had poured superglue into locks, and sprayed walls with the red Innoright logo with its huge pathetic animals' eyes gazing out of the letter O. Otter and Pussy had a particular taste for paint-stripping the cars of the smart young (male) managing directors of cosmetic firms who dated Otter following a photographic session on behalf of their products. However mother and daughter were also careful to paint-strip women's cars as well; the fact that it was not so emotionally satisfying was, they agreed, no reason to avoid such a necessary task.

But Otter was dead, dead in a car crash, the car driven by one of those smart young executives who was dating Otter and had dined rather too well in the process. (The man himself had survived.) She would have been twenty-two this month—the same age as Princess Amy, something which Pussy occasionally bore in mind when looking at newspaper photographs of nubile Amy, Amy smiling fetchingly into the camera, 5′ 3″, plump and privileged Amy who was alive while 5' 10" attenuated willowy Otter lay in her grave.

Pussy had become quite ruthless since Otter's death, and her single-handed attack on butchers' shops (including the savaging of an Alsatian which guarded one shop at night) had caused some disquiet among the Innoright Overground Group who had not been consulted.

"Even if Alsatians are incurable meat-eaters, as you know we regard that as human failure," began the Chairman. "Besides which, the whole subject of canine re-education towards vegetarianism is in its infancy, and Innoright Overground policy—"

"That Alsatian tore a cat to pieces last week," said Pussy coldly.

"Yes, but surely using a *knitting-needle*—"

Monkey thought of that conversation now as he gazed at Pussy's broad slightly flushed face. He had been given a free hand to choose his own team by the Innoright Overground, and had thus not mentioned to them that he had chosen the woman who was known as Pussy. He had believed at the time that he could handle her, use her dedication, her madness springing from heartbreak, for the good of the cause. As with Beagle in the National Portrait Gallery, Monkey hoped he had not made a mistake.

Monkey put down the paper again. As though none of the preceding conversation had taken place, Monkey and the others had a series of quick, efficient, half-muttered exchanges on the subject of weaponry and the Lair. Whatever their dissensions, progress was being made. Fox was short and to the point. He announced that he had followed up those mysterious contacts to which he had referred at an earlier meeting, and expected to be able to provide the desired weapons—"purely symbolic of course," as he put it—at the appropriate moment.

Monkey, who knew about Fox's background, was not surprised; the others, if they were impressed, tried to hide it.

It was Tom who drew the meeting to a close with a sudden surprising announcement.

"Going to the Press Conference, aren't I, darling? Who's a clever boy, then? The Royal Press Conference, yes, not Number Ten and the Pri-jolly Minister. The Royal Press Conference."

Beagle smiled sardonically and said nothing. Pussy, Chicken and Fox stared. Lamb shivered. The train was drawing into a station. The doors began to open.

Tom swung on the strap above Monkey's head and was halfway out of the doors before anyone dared react.

Tom darted back to pick up a packet he had left—presumably deliberately—on his seat. Impudently he blew a kiss: was it in *my* direction, thought Lamb guiltily.

"Tell you more next week; look for me on telly in the meantime; creating a disturbance, Oxblood paint and all. No, Monko, that's a joke."

"Circle Line between Paddington and Moorgate," was all Monkey had time to say before Tom was gone. The stiffness of his tone reminded the others that according to the Underground Plan it was Monkey's right to leave the train first.

# FIVE

## Sex and Security

"Surely we can't ask her *that*." Jemima Shore leant over Rick Vancy's shoulder and gazed at the list of questions, neatly typed out under the heading of "TUS: From the Desk of Richard Vancy."

"Oh, I guess we can. Kind of late on, when she's relaxed." Rick Vancy spoke most agreeably. It was his habitual tone, Jemima had noticed. Since his arrival in England, Rick had not lost his temper or raised his voice on a single occasion; indeed, his voice actually got yet more agreeable when times were trying. His appearance was agreeable too: he might even have been English with his fair hair, high narrow bony forehead; an English intellectual, or rather film star playing an English intellectual since, come to think of it, English intellectuals did not actually look like the late and much lamented Leslie Howard in real life.

But Rick Vancy was not English, in spite of vague rumours that his mother had been English and equally vague counterrumours that it was actually Rick Vancy's first wife who had been English, or that Rick Vancy's first wife, herself American, was now married to an Englishman. There was even a suggestion that Rick Vancy had been to Cambridge—the University; but this rumour, coming as it did from an Oxford man in the shape of Jamie Grand, Jemima put down to his characteristic sense of mischief; the editor of *Literature* was wont to discover alumni of Cambridge University in the most extraordinary places. The real truth, thought Jemima, was that the English were simply unable to accept that anyone could look as "English" as Rick Vancy undoubtedly did and not have some ancestral connection with the country. It was either a rather touching form of possessiveness or less touching snobbishness.

The fact that Rick Vancy did show a certain degree of Anglicization as time wore on, Jemima attributed to an admirable ability to study his surroundings rather than to youthful experiences or genetic inheritance. His clothes for example: when Jemima first met Rick (at his suggestion, for a drink in the Palm Court of the Ritz) most of his garments seemed to have been bought in St. James's including, improbably, a waistcoat. Rick eyed Jemima's Katherine Hamnett total look speculatively; the next time they met, all traces of St. James's were gone and Rick Vancy was wearing something like the masculine equivalent of Jemima's radical chic. The result was that he no longer looked like an American aping an Englishman, but quite as English as anyone else at the Groucho Club (Jemima's suggestion); that is to say, aiming to look American.

"Surely we can't ask her that?" The question to which Jemima was pointing read: "Your Royal Highness, if you will pardon me saying so, you are a very beautiful young woman. How do you feel about the other very beautiful women with whom your fiancé has been linked in the past?"

Rick furrowed his clear forehead and re-read the question. "Yeah, I get you. You mean it's sexist," he said after a pause. "Have to phrase it round another way."

"No, you dummy, this is England, not so much sexist as impossible. Bang goes our exclusive interview. We'll be lucky if we get to talk to her dogs if you ask something like that." For a moment, Jemima looked puzzled. "Besides, I thought all the questions had to be handed in to the Palace. Rick, for God's sake, you don't mean you put this down on the list. No, I see you didn't. It was going to be a little surprise—"

"I thought this was going to be a fun programme," groaned Rick, taking out a gold pencil and scoring through the offending question. (Earlier when he had lent the pencil to Jemima, she had noted it had been presented to him for "exceptional broadcasting services" during the most recent Hostage Crisis.) "That's what they promised me back in the States. 'Richard, have yourself some fun.' they said to me, 'after Iran, Beirut, the Libya problem, Syria and all the rest of it, you deserve to have yourself some fun.' So out goes the sex angle, is that it? Can you be serious? I see you are. So what's left? Security, that's what's left. Out goes sex, in comes security. Not nearly so much fun. Now sex *and* security, that would have been great."

"I am sure you can have a great deal of fun with the security angle," suggested Jemima in what she intended to be a tone of gentle mockery.

But Rick responded quite seriously: "Yeah, that's right. I think I can. If we play it up: the fairy story that turned into a nightmare; correction, for the time being, the fairy story that *may* turn into a nightmare, and then when it does—well, the possibilities are awesome, aren't they?" He leant back and gave an appreciative sigh.

"Mmm. Opium, isn't it? No, not for the people, though I suppose Royalty is the new religion with you guys. Your perfume I meant. Mmm. Listen, I don't anticipate any problems on this one. Happily, I was able to question the Ayatollah Khomeini on security, compared to which Buckingham Palace, or whichever palace is involved, should present no problem at all." Rick Vancy, eyes closed, was by now leaning so far back that he was almost touching Jemima.

Privately, Jemima thought that the Palace could probably hold its own with the Ayatollah in its silence over security matters, but that would be for Rick Vancy to find out for himself. She also thought that if Rick Vancy was into perfume-guessing, he might find more problems in that direction too than he anticipated.

Aloud she said: "Miss Dior actually. The perfume. Opium comes on rather too strong for me."

"Then I'm going to get you a huge bottle of Opium; to see if I can make you change your mind." But Rick Vancy leant gracefully forward again as he spoke.

Rick and Jemima attended the Royal Wedding Press Conference attended by two historical researchers hired by TUS; one was English, one was American, both brandishing enormous folders full of genealogical details concerning the happy couple. Rick explained this was because "we don't want to look cheap-skates compared to CBS, NBC, ABC and co. Somebody had the bright idea of hiring a couple of royal biographers, titled ladies, I think, there's a whole crowd of them in your country, they do a family act on this kind of show, but anyhow the supply had run out by the time we got to think of it."

The conference itself was being held in the large modern Republican Hotel in Plantagenet Square, Mayfair (Rick Vancy thought the combination of names awesome: it took Jemima some time to see why). Cumberland Palace was deemed too small to handle the ravening hordes of Press expected to attend; hence the exclusive nature of Jemima's projected interview with the happy couple at a later date. (Something, she had learned, whose genesis lay in the bridegroom's business interest in the States . . . but no one was being too precise about that.) This would, she had been promised, take place in the Palace drawing-room, the Palace garden or whatever area the demands of the English summer dictated.

There was a security check at a large modern desk in the hotel foyer—rather a British check, Jemima felt. Passes were scrutinized and checked against a list, but no serious attempt was made to match passes to faces. After that, the arrangements irresistibly reminded her of some huge children's party, with journalists as clamouring already-spoilt children while sets of presents were handed out. The "presents" were contained in zipped-up plastic folders stamped in gold with a variety of symbols including coats of arms, bells, flowers and horseshoes, the formality of the heraldry contrasting rather oddly with the rest. Their colour, Jemima noted, was not quite Amy Blue, although the unusual searing turquoise of the plastic indicated that a gallant attempt had been made to match it.

Were these folders actually being presented by Cumberland Palace? Had Royalty really gone down

into the marketplace this time, Jemima wondered.
The answer, she discovered, was both yes and no:
yes if you considered such *objets d'art* inherently
vulgar and demeaning, even to a Press Conference;
no if you accepted that a large sum had been paid to
the Princess's favourite charity for the honour of
manufacturing and distributing them. In short, the
folders and their contents were the gift of a rival
television station. Since the name of the television
station was writ small, and that of the charity writ
large, Jemima supposed that the answer to her original question must be no. . . . She started to leaf
through her own folder.

Inside each folder were two thick dossiers on the
ancestry of the bride and bridegroom, which looked
imposing as well as substantial until a quick glance
inside revealed that there was not much here that any
quick-witted journalist could not have found out
from *Debrett's Peerage* or *Burke's*. TUS's English researcher was a girl in her twenties called Susanna
Blanding; her figure was quite plump although the
features in the makeup-less face beneath the mass
of untidy dark curly hair were in contrast delicate
and rather pretty. She was smoking, however, as
she entered the room and looked distraught at
being asked to stop. Clearly historical research was a
nerve-wracking profession.

Jemima watched Susanna as she opened the
embossed blue cover; her expression was first appre-
hensive, then relieved, finally indignant.

"I've covered all of this," she hissed at the American researcher who was reading the document quite
happily. "In here." She tapped her own voluminous
genealogical documentation.

"Is that so?" The American, a laid-back youth

called simply Curt (what on earth were his credentials? Jemima wondered) went on reading.

"There are at least two mistakes on the first page," went on Susanna Blanding in a louder voice. "I wouldn't take it all that seriously as a work of reference, if I were you. You might feed in wrong information."

"Is that so?" repeated Curt; he was almost as gentle in his tone as Rick Vancy. "Listen to this: the Prince's grandmother was a Russian Grandduchess who danced with Rasputin and bequeathed jewellery worth four million pounds. The so-called unlucky Rasputin sapphires alone were worth—"

"Great-grandmother," put in Susanna sharply without any attempt to moderate her tone. "And the Rasputin story is poppycock! What were they supposed to dance? Cossack war dances? As for the unlucky sapphires, in here I point out—"

"Anything you say," said Curt pacifically, continuing to read. Once or twice he was heard to murmur, "quite amazing," which incurred sharp looks from Susanna Blanding.

The other "presents" were less controversial if more childish: a huge unfolding family tree showing Princess Amy's place in the British Royal Family. Susanna glowered at it although she could not immediately spot an error beyond an irritated aside: "That's the *sovereign*'s coat of arms at the top; now you do realize, Curt, that Princess Amy herself has no right—" But by this time a plethora of objects, including a paper-knife with the royal cipher, pencils and biros with more gold symbols stamped on them and even AMY MEANS I LOVE YOU buttons were pouring out of the turquoise plastic. Susanna stuffed them in the pockets of her baggy velvet jacket, worn over a

man's striped shirt belted at the waist and a short
tight—too tight—dark-grey skirt. That left her free to
vet the sheaf of large glossy photographs provided
including one of the bridal coach.

"Would you say that was the Scottish State
Coach?" she asked anxiously, enmity temporarily
forgotten, "because if not—" Curt was however busy
pinning on his AMY MEANS I LOVE YOU button—special
blue and gold version, with a photograph of the
Princess, smiling rather shyly, taken several years
back, crowning the message. He evidently had no
views on this important question, and Susanna sank
back again in renewed disgust.

At the Press Conference itself, it was the topic of
sex which reared its ugly head first before that
of security. A French reporter, interrupting details of
arrangements for the Great Day itself with great po-
liteness, enquired of the Palace spokesman whether
Mademoiselle Mirabella Prey would be at the wedding breakfast. Major Pat Smylie-Porter, as opening
royal bat, was however more than equal to this query.
(Jemima suspected that the Major might prove a cool
customer when she noticed that he sported an AMY
MEANS I LOVE YOU button in the lapel of his dark-grey
suit instead of the expected carnation.) He bent on
the questioner—a small dark man in neat denims
with a large handbag over his shoulder—a benevo-
lent gaze. Jemima was reminded of a wartime story in
which an English officer put in charge of a platoon of
Jewish refugee intellectuals, anxious to fight for their
adopted country, announced that he anticipated no
problems "since he was used to native troops."

"A very private affair, the wedding breakfast,"
beamed the Major. "So private I haven't even seen

the list m'self. No idea who's on it, no idea at all. But I can tell you what they're going to eat—" He shuffled through a sheaf of papers. "Princess Chicken, is that right?" The Major chuckled. "Sounds a bit odd, I must admit. Now where are we? Here we are. *Poulet à la Princesse!* Sounds better in French, doesn't it. Even my French. Now you're going to ask me for the recipe, and I'm afraid I can't tell you that either." So the Major bumbled purposefully on, as though pinpointing possible trouble spots, darting little glances the while from beneath bushy eyebrows, which were very black compared to his silvered hair. In this way he was possibly more prepared than the rest of the restlessly heterogeneous assembly for the sudden irruption of a loud and strident voice talking very fast.

There was a general stir. Susanna Blanding turned and glared: she looked quite shocked at this apparent affront to majesty. Even Curt sat up a little straighter in his chair. A few moments later, Susanna, handing her clipboard to Jemima, left, as though such a distressing intervention had made a quick puff at a cigarette absolutely essential. On return, she certainly reeked of smoke.

"Talking of Princess Chicken," shouted the questioner from somewhere on the far side of the large room. "What about the Animal Rights demo outside Cumberland Palace the other day? Have there been any further threats from Innoright or any other Animal Rights group? Aren't you worried about security? What happens if—"

The heckler—for that was the impression these rapid questions gave—was cut short by something, or else the other journalists simply took the opportunity to join in. Jemima had a brief glimpse of him:

darkish, possibly Arab she thought. Then a host of questions merged into a babble, in which the words "security," "incident," "precautions" could be discerned. Jemima was just wondering wryly how the imperturbable Major would deal with this one—riot of native troops?—when his voice boomed out extremely loudly across the tumult. He had used the simple expedient of turning his microphone to its ultimate pitch.

"Gentlemen, I beg your pardon, ladies, ladies, gentlemen, one question at a time please. Now the gentleman there, would you wait for the microphone please, and repeat the question?"

A young woman, nicely but plainly dressed, crossed the platform and whispered in the Major's ear. She looked rather strained, but the Major merely beamed again; the expression of sheer good humour on his face made it difficult to believe the irruption had ever taken place.

"Good news," he said. "Their Royal Highnesses are on their way from the Palace. So we won't have time for very many more unprepared questions. I'm sure you'd all far rather talk to them than an old buffer like me." He chuckled again and then pointed to where a movable microphone was now installed. This time Jemima had a better view of the questioner: no, not an Arab; in fact his face was vaguely familiar and she wondered if she had seen him recently on television, or had she interviewed him for her programme on child brides? He had the kind of face which was familiar without being memorable.

"Jean-Pierre Schwarz-Albert," stated the questioner giving the name of a foreign news agency and now speaking quite slowly in a voice without a trace of an accent. "In view of the animal rights slogan painted on the walls of Cumberland Palace by Innoright," he emphasized the word, then repeated it, "Innoright, I wondered what arrangements the Palace was making if there was some form of incident or demonstration on the route?"

"Now I'm sure you won't expect me to give you the full security arrangements made by our excellent police," replied the Major; he glanced at a piece of paper handed to him by the neatly dressed girl. "As to the painting, that was an isolated incident of which there will be no repetition. Security has been stepped up at the Palace. Next question—"

As the next questioner—"Judith Spandau, Michigan TV"—began to speak, also on the subject of security, Jemima continued to gaze curiously at Jean-Pierre Schwarz-Albert. He in turn was gazing fixedly at the stage; there was something rather frightening about the intensity of his expression. Jemima shivered. Then she realized that Rick Vancy was nudging her.

"Hey listen, what we want to know is when do they tell us?" he whispered, "will they bring it to us live? If not, exactly when do we get the news?"

"What news?" Jemima whispered back.

"An assassination attempt or whatever. Will we get full coverage?"

Jemima realized that it was her duty to her transatlantic employers to ask some form of question on this subject. She for one definitely did not expect there to be an assassination attempt, or any other kind of violence shown towards the bridal couple— this was Britain for God's sake, and Princess Amy was scarcely in the position of an American President—but she could see that her conviction was not shared by the rest of her colleagues. Question after question referred to "live pictures" of something euphemistically described as "an unexpected incident." What was actually being asked of course was whether live pictures would be shown of dead people. . . .

"Ask him whether Prince Ferdinand will wear a bullet-proof waistcoat in the open landau," hissed Rick Vancy.

"What about poor little Amy?" countered Jemima. "Is she going to be left out? Surely I should ask first whether she's going to wear a bullet-proof bra?"

Rick Vancy frowned. "I guess that's rather tacky, isn't it?"

"I hear they're going to video any kind of rough stuff and show it later when the high-ups have okayed it," commented Rick's neighbour, a fellow American.

"That could be the next month or *year*, where this bunch is concerned," groaned Rick.

Jemima stood up. She caught the eye of the neatly dressed girl who had just returned to the platform and realized from her briefing that this was the Princess's lady-in-waiting, Ione Quentin, to whom she had spoken on the telephone about her interview. She had not recognized her. Susanna Blanding and Ione Quentin, both equally English looking, represented two opposing but eternal types of English womanhood: the one inconspicuous through elegance, the other conspicuous through lack of it. Yet in features they were not dissimilar. Ione Quentin for her part looked relieved at seeing a face she recognized, an *English* face, the face of a person guaranteed not to ask awkward questions; she directed the Major's attention in the direction of Jemima.

"Jemima Shore, Television United States—" she

began. But it was too late. A further emissary, this time male, equally neatly dressed, had joined the couple on the platform and was in his turn whispering in the Major's ear.

"I am so sorry Miss Shore, I am so sorry ladies and gentlemen," exclaimed the Major, giving Jemima a special beam as he picked up his sheaf of notes, "but their Royal Highnesses are actually here two minutes early. That's what really efficient security does for you, it whizzes you through our dreadful London traffic. I am sure under the circumstances—"

Jemima, privately rather relieved (after all she had an exclusive interview coming), sat down.

There was a general stir as the royal couple were introduced on to the platform, preceded by a couple of security men solemnly carrying two velvet chairs upholstered in Princess Amy blue. All present stood up, or in the case of cameramen snapped furiously away, jockeying furiously for position at one and the same time. In the hubbub a disturbance on the far side of the room passed quite unnoticed.

No one, naturally, paid much attention to the one journalist who wanted to leave the room just as the royal couple were entering it. Such a bizarre course of behaviour—to attend the Major's briefing and then miss the conference proper—was hardly believable. The cliché, "all eyes were fixed on the bride," was once fully justified, as the world's Press goggled happily at Princess Amy in her—thank Heaven—turquoise-blue dress, and scribbled away with equal delight at the sight of the enormous glittering ring displayed on the small plump white hand which rested on her fiancé's discreetly dark-blue sleeve. So that afterwards it was remarkably difficult to piece together when it was that the man who called himself

Jean-Pierre Schwarz-Albert had left the conference
hall.

Had he taken the opportunity of the royal couple's
entrance to elbow his way through the throng? Or
had it been slightly later? When Princess Amy was
answering questions? (In that attractively modest
manner, head drooping slightly, which made her
actual voice, clear, upper class, even slightly bossy in
timbre, always come as a slight surprise.) His neighbour at the briefing spoke of a note being handed to
him, a note which presumably caused him to leave;
but in the excitement of the royal occasion, could not
be precise as to when the note had been received.
Afterwards, when the exact moment became of some
import, those who had to trace Schwarz-Albert's
movements wearily found that it was like questioning
people about an incident which had occurred at the
same time as the winning goal in the World Cup.
Even if someone was prepared to come up with an
answer, you could never be quite sure it was reliable.

"You'd think they were doing it on purpose,"
moaned Detective Superintendent Portsmouth of
Central Squad, otherwise known as Pompey of the
Yard, petulantly, to his youthful-looking assistant
Detective Sergeant Vaillant. But Vaillant, knowing
better than to speak when his superior was in this
kind of mood, merely nodded his head sympathetically and looked as sage as he judged permissible
under the circumstances.

# SIX

# Frightening
# People

The death of Jean-Pierre Schwarz-Albert, journalist, although a subject of much interest to Detective Superintendent Portsmouth, received curiously little immediate attention in the Press and was not even mentioned on the television news. Perhaps there was something odd about this; or perhaps on the other hand the lack of interest, like the general indifference at the time, was simply due to the enormous attention lavished on the Press Conference given by Prince Ferdinand and Princess Amy.

Certainly the latter event was generally rated—by the media at least—a resounding success. The headline in the *Daily Exclusive* the next morning summed it up very fairly: AMY MEANS WE ALL LOVE YOU. Or as Rick Vancy confided happily to Jemima over a late lunch at Le Caprice: "She's a real star, that girl. How do they get to train them?"

"The Royals? I don't think they do. It's the luck of the draw. Some of them are just much better at it than others. I agree with you that little Amy is quite brilliant. Ferdy's performance was a bit lacklustre, I thought. Do you notice the way he always looks as if he'd had a very late night?"

Rick considered the point. "No, I went for that. Same as I liked the bags under his eyes; pointed up her performance. She the fresh young lamb; he the world-weary old wolf. Maybe they planned it that way."

"Maybe they did," agreed Jemima cautiously, sipping the champagne with which Rick had declared that they should launch their official collaboration.

About the same time, in Cumberland Palace, however, the fresh young lamb was enquiring the whereabouts of the world-weary old wolf with more than a little petulance; Rick Vancy might have been surprised at the abrasiveness with which Princess Amy was questioning Ione Quentin about the Prince's message.

Princess Amy was drinking Malvern water (unlike Jemima Shore and Rick Vancy, she had no taste for champagne or indeed any form of alcohol). Ione Quentin, looking exhausted in comparison to her employer whose cheeks continued to bloom pinkly despite—or perhaps because of—her recent ordeal, nursed the sherry for which she had been compelled, slightly embarrassedly, to ask: "Ma'am, do you think I might—"

Amy stared at her with the huge almost circular blue eyes which made her photograph so well. "Don't be ridiculous, Ione. Have whatever you like. Make yourself a Bloody Mary if you like, the way Ferdel does. And talking of Ferdel—" The famous pout was much in evidence.

Ione Quentin began all over again: "An old friend from abroad, Ma'am, a last-minute arrangement. He wasn't able to speak to you personally because of the Press Conference. Mr. Taplow came and picked him up, I believe, in the Prince's aunt's car. No, I don't know where they're having lunch, Ma'am. At the flat, possibly?"

Even to Ione Quentin the Prince's story sounded pretty thin and she frankly could not imagine—would in fact very much like to have known—why he had suddenly abandoned his fiancée at the last minute, leaving the faithful Ione, as usual, to placate. Out loud, however, Ione Quentin continued to deliver the message in her usual pleasantly neutral voice. "You remember Mr. Taplow, Ma'am," she added, as though hoping to distract. "He was the Duke's chauffeur in the country for absolutely ages. Rather creepy. You used to play with his little girl, funny little thing. No, it was a *boy* with long hair and sort of girl's clothes. Princess Sophie told me she used to tease him—"

"Oh, really?" It was clear that Princess Amy was not the slightest bit interested in the Taplows.

"Boys as girls. It's all wrong," pursued Ione, "as your nephew Jamie would say. He's making such a fuss about his page's suit, isn't he? When it's so divinely pretty—"

Suddenly to Ione's surprise Princess Amy burst out laughing in a way that made her look much younger than her twenty-two years; she had a ringing schoolgirl's laugh (something which the Press seldom heard). "I say Ione, you don't suppose this old friend from abroad is seven foot tall with long black hair like a witch and sports a puma in her luggage and talks like zeez? I read in the *Clueless* that *she'd* arrived." Ione breathed a sigh of silent relief; Amy in this mood helped to make up for the other less enchanting mood which had preceded it.

"What cheek, eh you old doggie?" went on Amy, patting one of the ancient spaniels. It was snuffling at the high-heeled white sandal which Amy had discarded now that there was no need for her to try to level up against her tall fiancé. "Standing me up like that, his dewy bride."

"You *did* look dewy, Ma'am," responded Ione quite sincerely. "It went terribly well, didn't it? Everybody thought you were wonderful. My cousin Susanna Blanding—she was there—rang up Lydia last night and told her you were wonderful."

"Susanna Blanding? What was *she* doing there?"

"Oh, she's with one of those amazing American TV stations. She's awfully bright, especially about history, always has been. She wrote that book about young princesses down the ages, don't you remember? *Dear and Royal Sister*. She sent it to you. It sold awfully well. And she's always on those quizzes on telly, the brainy ones. Now she's making a fortune out of the wedding."

"Making a fortune out of *one*?" But Princess Amy sounded very pleased. Susanna Blanding was evidently a far better note to strike than the Taplows and their son. Then she added in a different voice: "Lydia—how is Lydia?"

"Going on very well, thank you, Ma'am," said Ione quickly, a shade too quickly. "But as I was saying, the way you dealt with that dreadful American who kept going on about your self-image—"

"What on earth was all that about?" Amy pointed her neat little stockinged foot—she had the shapely legs and pretty ankles of some plump women; in fact her whole appearance was an intriguing mixture of things which were notably large (her eyes, her bosom) and things which were notably small like her hands and feet and ankles. "Was she going on about my lack of A levels? So drear. What does Ferdel care

about my A levels? He's never even *heard* of A
levels."

"I think she was going on about your attitude to
feminism, Ma'am."

"*Feminism!*" cried Amy in a voice of outrage.
"Whatever will they ask one about next? And I wish
they wouldn't keep going on about animals and
hunting and all that. Those people are just crazy. I
don't hunt, far too terrifying, took the opportunity to
give it up when Daddy died. Quel relief! Giving up
hunting I mean. Not poor old Daddy. So what's it all
to do with me?"

"There's a lot of it about at the moment," said Ione
diplomatically. "Animal Rights is flavour of the
month where demos are concerned. Hence the questions. The Cumberland Palace incident didn't help,
and I suppose there *might* just be further demonstra-
tions before the wedding. Coming to which, Ma'am,
there is just one thing I ought to tell you—"

As Princess Amy fished for her white sandal with
one toe (the spaniel Happy—or was it Boobie?—
thought it was a game), Ione Quentin broke the news
of the death of Jean-Pierre Schwarz-Albert. Like the
rest of the public, Princess Amy did not find the
death—having never known of the life—of a French
journalist profoundly interesting.

"How sad," she remarked rather absently, at the
end of her lady-in-waiting's recitation. "Does one
have to do anything about it? Write to anyone? I
mean, was he fearfully brave or anything? Do we
watch him on telly all the time?"

"Oh no, Ma'am, he was French," replied Ione, in a
tone that made it clear that the answer to all these
questions was in the negative. Amy kicked her shoes
aside again. She yawned. She was still yawning and

contemplating the short unpainted nails on her small hand, weighed down by its huge aquamarine ring set in diamonds (true Amy blue) when Ione spoke again.

"Yes, Ione? Oh God, why won't my boring nails grow. Look at yours—positive talons. It's not fair—sorry, yes?"

"Just one more thing, Ma'am."

Amy groaned. "More unpleasantness. I know it. You always say 'Just one more thing' when it's unpleasant. This is the second 'one more thing' in five minutes."

"The French journalist had a number of Animal Rights stickers in his pocket," continued Ione rather coldly; then her eyes fell on her own nails, not particularly long, but neatly painted a delicate pink; her expression lightened. Princess Amy on the other hand gave a little pout.

"How drear! Actually at our Press Conference? *Very* drear. How on earth did he get in? I hope he doesn't do it again."

"He's dead, Ma'am," said Ione patiently.

"Well I jolly well hope there aren't any more like him, frightening Animal Rights people, I mean, among the journalists. They're bad enough as they are, them and their questions." Princess Amy's pout deepened and for an instant she bore a strong resemblance to the late Duke of Cumberland when some household arrangement had gone awry. "Now Ione, let's forget about the drear journalists. I'm not marrying *them*. What did Ferdel say exactly . . . ?"

A few miles away Princess Amy's royal disregard for the subject of dead French journalists was not shared by Detective Superintendent Portsmouth (although he might have been more sympathetic to her views on the Press generally).

"Dead!" cried Detective Superintendent Portsmouth, and then, after pausing as though searching for the *mot juste*, added impressively: "As a doornail."

"To coin a phrase," remarked Detective Sergeant Vaillant smartly, and gave another of those sage nods which had caused Pompey of the Yard to mark him down as a bright lad.

Young Vaillant had however misjudged his moment. Pompey was in an irritable mood, suffering from what he mentally termed royal sciatica since his first bad attack had been at the time of the wedding of the Prince of Wales. On that occasion Mrs. Portsmouth had caused him to plant out rows of loyal red and white begonias, interspersed with blue lobelias, in their garden before the season or, for that matter, Pompey was ready. Prince Andrew's wedding had called for backbreaking work with tri-coloured geraniums, more sciatica. Currently Mrs. Portsmouth was massing petunias, crimson streaked with white, by the back door for the attack and wishing out loud that nature had created something properly red, white and blue.

Nothing, as Vaillant well knew, put his superior in a worse mood than being the brawn for Mrs. Portsmouth's brains where gardening was concerned; indeed, had he noticed the tiny trace of earth under Pompey's normally immaculate fingernails, he would not have risked his smart remark or anything like it but would have confined himself to the nod.

"Given the state of the city, I'm inclined to think that it was done on purpose to annoy us," went on Pompey, giving Vaillant a malevolent look. "To coin a phrase as you would put it. Certainly someone did something on purpose. To put it another way, a good many people did a good many things on purpose, leaving us poor critters to figure out who did which to what."

Vaillant knew better this time and merely nodded.

"For example the late Mr. Schwarz-Albert did a good many things on purpose. Including painting Cumberland Palace red."

"We're sure of that, are we, sir?" enquired Vaillant in his most sympathetic manner. Pompey ignored him.

"So what was he doing stone dead with a souvenir paper knife in his back in the corner of the lounge of the Republican Hotel?"

Pompey spoke in a tone remarkably close to a groan, something that Vaillant ascribed to his physical condition rather than to any faintheartedness over the case. "Answer me that one. Was he about to transfigure the lounge with violent red pleas for animal rights when he was struck down by someone with an even more violent dislike for Animal Rights activists? He was struck down—" as Vaillant leant even more sympathetically forward—"and with one of these. Sharp little buggers."

Pompey reached in a drawer and drew out a paper knife similar to those presented to the avid Royalty-observers at the Press Conference. At the time the knife, surmounted by Princess Amy's cipher in blue, had seemed yet another example of royal journalistic kitsch; now, looking at it, Vaillant felt that the strong slender blade had assumed an altogether more sinister aspect.

"Here's one of them. Masses of them about, of course. A thousand manufactured. Quite a job tracing them. At the same time, shouldn't be allowed, should it, giving something as sharp as this to a lot of journalists."

"They're not children—" murmured Vaillant. Pompey merely cocked an eyebrow.

"At least we know the murder weapon. Although we've kept quiet about the weapon for the time being to the Press. The hotel cooperated: *they* didn't want any bad publicity. We'll release that titbit when it suits us, not before. We also know the approximate time. But who and why: that, my boy, is what we are here to find out. At the moment it's strictly person unknown."

"What do we know about him, sir? Beyond the fact that he had a valid Press pass to the conference?"

"Give me that bit of paper." Pompey stretched forward. The movement made him wince. He stopped. "Go on then, read it out, boy."

"Jean-Pierre Schwarz-Albert, journalist. A.k.a. Animal Rights activist. Known to have joined several Animal Rights movements, most recently Innoright—Innoright? Reason to believe he was part of the Innoright cell that made the red-paint raid on Cumberland Palace last—" Vaillant stopped.

"Reason to believe, sir?" he enquired delicately. "Information received? You don't mean—we've got a source around that neck of the woods?"

Pompey grunted. "Something of the sort. As you know, we've all been scared silly about these Animal Rights loonies ever since the Westminster Square incident. Yes, loonies. I said loonies and I meant loonies. They're insane in other words. Terrorists and insane. You can't begin to predict what they'll do. Far be it from me to call for the return of your wandering Irish terrorist, let alone your friendly neighbourhood Arab—" Pompey grunted again and then coughed to show it was one of his jokes.

Vaillant, alerted, gave a discreet smile.

"But these fellows," went on Pompey, "men and women, the women being among the worst by the way, you've no idea what they'll think of next. So many amateurs getting into the game, too, none of them on our books already. Not playing the game by the rules, because they don't know what the rules are."

Perceiving this was not a joke, Vaillant asked: "Has terrorism got rules, sir?"

"The only rule in terrorism is that things will always be different from the last time. You know that. But terrorists, like any other professionals, have patterns of behaviour, and, even more to the point, professional links. They're not in the main criminals, but they do become criminals. In short, somewhere along the way, generally quite soon along the way, your idealistic terrorist meets up with the criminal fraternity. And that's where we come in."

"Because we meet up with the criminal fraternity quite soon along the way too. In the line of work," added Vaillant hastily.

"Exactly so. Of course we've got our links with the criminal fraternity—how would we get on without them? How would they get on without them? And that leads us to the terrorists; or in certain cases leads them to us. But these amateurs"—Pompey exclaimed with disgust—"many of them have never done anything wrong before in their life." He stopped and then added in a sombre voice: "But when they do plunge in—just think of Westminster Square again. The most frightful wilful destruction I can remember. And I've been a policeman all my life."

"Frightening people, sir."

"Frightening indeed. So that's when we decided to infiltrate them. Take them seriously, especially with

this wedding coming up. We've been lucky twice—
Charles and Andy. Got them home and dry, if you
get my meaning. And the young ladies too of
course," Pompey added hastily in case Vaillant had
what Pompey mentally termed "Views" on the subject of the opposite sex. "That still doesn't necessarily
mean that we'll be lucky the third time. Unless we
take all the proper precautions."

"No such thing as luck in our business," pronounced Vaillant sententiously. It was one of Pompey's own phrases. Vaillant was rewarded with an
approving glance.

"And this time," pursued Pompey, "we have a
royal young lady at the centre of it all. A born
princess and a born prince. What's more, a prince
who's a foreigner. He could attract all sorts—"

"He *has* attracted all sorts if you believe the *Sunday
Clueless*," began Vaillant recklessly and then stopped.
Pompey appeared not to have heard.

"What's more, a prince with an international sporting reputation. And by the way, my boy, when I say
sporting, I am not referring to the *Exclusive*'s intimate
revelations. Fancy reading that rubbish!"

Vaillant blushed: "It was in the line of duty, sir,
background material."

"Ah, just so. I must tell that to Mrs. Pompey. She
read it too, I believe, while I was pulling up the bulbs
in the garden, ready for her begonias. Could it have
been background material for her too, do you
suppose?"

But this time wild horses would not have dragged
a reply from Detective Sergeant Vaillant.

"Photographs of our Prince killing this, that and
the other plastered all over the Press. That could
bring the nasties right out of the woodwork. So, as I

was saying, we had a source inside it, a good chap too. Joined a lot of these organizations to get animal credibility as it were. Then concentrated on one of them: a small one. Innoright. Innocent Rights. Get it?

"He told us it was mainly full of nice innocent people who love Pussy and Rover and don't like the idea of any harm coming to them, let alone being cut up by nasty scientists. Hardly frightening people. Then there's the vegetarian brigade, nothing wrong with them either, I've got lots of sympathy for that, and as for these chicken factories, the calves—you should hear Mrs. Portsmouth on that subject. I sometimes worry about my steak and chips." Pompey laughed and after a moment Vaillant (who did as a matter of fact have vegetarian leanings, although no "Views" on women's rights) laughed too.

"Then our source got on to something more serious," continued Pompey. "Thought that Innoright might be up to something. Or *Inner* Innoright was up to something. By being all helpful about the place, and making friends, one particular friend, he stumbled on one or two clues."

"Clues?"

"People who were supposed to have formally resigned from Innoright in protest against this, that and the other. Putting it on record. Then still dealing with it secretly. Odd that. The last message he gave definitely implied there was something rather frightening going on. Connected in some way to the wedding."

"That was the last message. So what does he say now about all this?"

"He doesn't say anything. Because when last seen, he had a bright blue paper-knife stuck in him; which makes it difficult. Oh, didn't I make it clear?" Pompey gave Vaillant the full benefit of his most foxy smile. "Jean-Pierre Schwarz-Albert was our man inside Innoright."

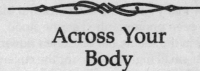

# SEVEN

# Across Your
# Body

A few miles away from both Pompey at Scotland Yard (shoes eased off) and Princess Amy at Cumberland Palace (shoes kicked off) yet another pair of shoes was lying loose. Ladies' shoes. However these ladies' shoes, except that they were also high-heeled, bore little similarity to those of Princess Amy. The shoes on the hearthrug in Eaton Square were in another sense of the world hardly ladylike. They were shiny black patent with inlets of glinting mirror glass and slashes of silver leather; the heels were extraordinarily spindly.

"Mirabella," said Prince Ferdinand, breathing heavily, "you are insane." For the woman who had stepped out of the shoes had also stepped out of her clothes, that is to say, a black crêpe dress ornamented with similar silver and glass motifs lay on the floor beside the shoes, the glass segments winking oddly as they caught the light; the impression was of fallen Christmas-tree ornaments.

Mirabella Prey raised her arms above her head in a graceful arc and pointed one toe in an equally graceful balletic position. The effect was not however of the ballet with its detachment and exquisite formality, but of something more primitive, a mating dance perhaps. Mirabella's naked body, sinuous (how many workouts, dance routines, exercises?) and brown (how many summers in Greece and Marbella?) could have been photographed as she stood, her face just slightly in the shade, her black hair flowing down between her small high breasts, for the cover of some Health and Beauty book.

As Ferdel, still breathing heavily, concentrated on this reflection to calm him, he realized that the thought was not a random one—Mirabella had appeared in just such a pose, with the sketchy addition of a highly cut-away black leotard, on the cover of her own best-selling book of exercises, every exercise based on the natural movements of the wild cat family or something of the sort. What had it been called? *Wild Woman, Good Life?* No, the other way round. *Wild Life, Good Woman.* That sounded even less plausible. He gave up, feeling calmer; all proceeds went towards the protection of wild life, of that he was quite certain. Exotic animals, naturally.

"*Alors, mon Prince, je te plais encore?*" Mirabella let her arms sink into some form of suppliant position; she managed nonetheless to continue to look uncommonly predatory.

"Mirabella, you are crazy," replied Ferdel carefully in English, taking a step back. Suppliant or not, he did not trust her. Mirabella stretched out one beautiful brown arm in his direction; the arm was not bare unlike the body from which it sprang, for on the arm glistened an enamel and diamond bracelet fastened with a puma's head. Ferdel recognized it because he had given it to Mirabella as—hopefully—a farewell present; he still remembered the fuss Mirabella had made about the anatomical details of the puma which the jeweler had stupidly confused with those of a leopard. Then he stepped forward again and picked up the glittering black crêpe heap on the floor.

"Cover yourself. At once."

"Oh Ferdel," purred Mirabella without moving. "You are squairre"—she extended the word. "The leetle princess, she does that to you so soon? *Merde, alors.*" Mirabella put her hand down as if to cover the noticeably large square black shadow on her brown body; the gesture could conceivably in another woman have been one of Eve-like modesty; in Mirabella however it was quite clearly one of Eve-like invitation.

"Darling, why don't we fuck?" she purred again, in an accent which was surely heavier than her usual one. "Just once, or maybe more than once. I like this room very much, *très homme*, it reminds me of you. It would be so amusing"—she perceived Ferdel's wince— "Darling, if you're tired . . ."

"Dress and get out. I have nothing more to say." Ferdel flung the clothes at her. He looked so intensely angry, his mouth a thin even line, that this time Mirabella herself took a pace back. The glittering clothes landed at her feet.

So she was still naked when the heavy polished doors opened abruptly and the butler Taplow, in shirt sleeves and an apron over his striped trousers, half fell, was half propelled into the room. Behind him, scarcely more appropriately dressed in jeans, anoraks, hoods and those creepy stocking masks which obliterate the features by substituting other less human ones, were two figures. One of them held an automatic pistol. Taplow was gabbling something like "Your Highness, I'm sorry."

Then the taller of the two men—they both seemed to be men although one could not be absolutely sure—pushed Taplow right down on to the floor and put his foot on the butler's white-shirted back. The pistol was now pointing unwaveringly in the direction of the Prince. All this time, Mirabella, although not directly threatened by any weapon, had stood still, holding her position of a lascivious Eve. Her clothes remained in the black and glittering heap at her feet. Ferdel made a movement, perhaps towards her clothes, perhaps towards the stationary and naked woman. Instantly the taller of the intruders, his foot remaining on Taplow's back, turned his weapon in the direction of the woman.

"Prince," he said in a muffled voice, more muffled than perhaps a mere stocking mask would explain, "you will now do what we say."

Ferdel made a gesture with his hands—long hands held high in the air, narrow lips curling slightly—which seemed to indicate both politely and disdainfully that in view of the threat to the woman he had little choice.

"Stand beside the lady." Ferdel hesitated an instant, noted the unaltered position of the gun, and walked slowly and coolly, sauntered as it were, in the direction of Mirabella.

"Take her hand."

This time there was a perceptible pause before the Prince did as he was commanded. After a moment the tall man in the stocking mask gave a small imperious wave of the pistol, still held on the woman.

"Take it. We mean what we say."

The Prince picked up Mirabella's hand with its many glittering rings in his. There was a tiny clink:

possibly one of her rings had clashed with his heavy gold signet ring. Then there was a sudden radiant flash as the diamond bracelet with the puma's head slid like a falling star along her naked arm. Ferdel's face was expressionless.

The short man than stepped forward and, raised on his toes, pulled at the Prince's dark-blue knitted silk tie. He succeeded in loosening it. Then he undid the top button of his shirt.

"Take off his jacket." The muffled voice of the man with the gun gave the order. At the same time the man with the gun edged his front foot forward, the other still planted on Taplow's back. Taplow however, was apparently so inert—was he conscious? his back was heaving in an odd way—that the pressure of the foot hardly seemed necessary.

As the short man struggled to remove Ferdel's dark-blue jacket, the Prince neither obstructed nor helped him; that in itself made it a difficult operation in view of the Prince's superior height. Eventually the jacket lay on the floor, joining the heap of Mirabella's clothes. Ferdel shrugged his shoulders as though to settle himself in his new garb and for a moment seemed about to put his hand up to his neck as though to assure himself that the shirt was properly set without the tie. It was obviously a characteristic gesture and as such not intended to be threatening. A look at the man with the gun however stayed his hand. Ferdel, who had not glanced directly at Mirabella throughout the episode, now stared ahead, her hand held stiffly in his.

The pair of them, the Prince in his dark formal trousers and white shirt, his black polished shoes, the woman naked, had the air of some corrupt painting.

"Do it." The tall man's muffled voice was now

louder as if he had gained confidence. "Do it
quickly." Then the short man produced from some
inner pocket a copy of the day's paper—it happened
to be the *Daily Exclusive*. Ferdel's expression changed
for a moment when he saw it and he glanced involuntarily in Mirabella's direction. The short man stuck
the *Daily Exclusive* into Mirabella's left hand. Her
instinctive gesture to hide herself with the paper was,
it seemed, what was wanted.

"Across your body."

Mirabella began to tremble slightly; the paper quiv-
ered. While it was still quivering, the short man
backed away from the pair of them, and producing
what was only too clearly a camera, began to snap
quickly, efficiently, fast, with a series of flashes. It
was almost over before it began; beyond a series of
blinks, Ferdel moved not at all. Mirabella continued
to tremble.

"Right. We quit." The tall man gestured to the little
photographer to precede him out of the door. The last
thing he did in the room itself was to scatter a series
of white and red papers like benisons behind him.
Taplow gave a kind of groan as the pressure on his
neck was released. Finally the tall man backed out
preparatory to shutting the heavy doors behind them
both. There was the sound of a key turning in the
lock.

The three of them, Taplow, Mirabella and the
Prince, were left in the grand room which Mirabella
had described only recently—but how long ago it
seemed—as "*très homme.*" Taplow was now audibly
groaning, almost sobbing.

Then Mirabella began to scream: the sound of her
screams echoed rather horribly in the high-ceilinged
room.

"It's all your fault, all your fault. You should 'ave loved me," she cried. "All you wanted was to . . ." A vivid scream of words, verbs, all meaning roughly the same thing, of which "screw" and "stuff" were the mildest, followed. Hysterically, without bothering to clothe herself, kicking aside a heap which included in fact the Prince's jacket, Mirabella began to pummel his chest with her fists.

Ferdel caught her hands in his. "Stop that," he said. "Put your clothes on at once. And this time I mean what I say."

"It was you," began Mirabella again. But the Prince merely transferred both her wrists to one hand and slapped her face hard. Now the noise of Mirabella's sobs joined the sucking and groaning noise of Taplow on the floor.

"Get up," said Ferdel curtly. The big man rose lumberingly to his knees, and then, panting, to his feet.

"Your Highness," he began, as Mirabella, crying more quietly, arranged herself in her clothes, long black hair tangling with the black glinting dress, sobs gradually diminishing.

"Where's that bloody detective?" Ferdel, having reassumed his jacket, was fastening his tie, stretching his neck as he gazed at himself in the huge gilt-framed Chippendale mirror over the fireplace. "What are these people for?" Ferdel's English was generally impeccable, the product of English schooldays; nevertheless his words suggested a European aristocrat speaking of peasants.

"Your Highness, we must ring the police—" began Taplow.

"First of all we must get out of here. Where is she? The woman. Your wife."

"She went out shopping. She said."

"And the detective?"

"He's coming back this evening. When you go to the Embassy dinner, sir."

"I shall speak to him. How did this happen? It's—it's monstrous. This Press of yours. How can the government let them do it?"

"I'm so sorry, Your Highness," wailed Taplow.

"It was not the Press," said Mirabella in a sulky voice. "Not how you mean it." She was standing parallel with Ferdel, but at a distance, sharing the wide mirror to repair her make-up. Like Ferdel adjusting his tie, she made her own series of little *moues* into the mirror as she patted her high cheekbones with a series of dark and light powders.

Ferdel swung round and looked at her.

"Ah. So they are friends of yours. These charming people. Your idea. I thought you were not capable of that. I was wrong."

"They lo-o-ve animals. That is nice." Mirabella's lip trembled.

"They love animals! They *are* animals." Ferdel started to stride up and down the room while Taplow, no longer shuddering, gaped at him. Suddenly the Prince stopped, whirled round and headed for Mirabella again. His expression was momentarily so fierce that the woman, wobbling slightly on her high heels, collapsed into one of the large leather chairs. From this lowly position, Mirabella's enormous eyes brimmed with tears. She looked a great deal more submissive than at any other point during her interview with the Prince.

"What happens now? What happens to the pictures? The filthy pictures? Do we see them in the filthy Press?"

"Oh Ferdel, you are so cross, it's ridiculous." Mirabella attempted a light laugh.

"And you are not cross? Than I shall give you something to be cross about." In response the Prince dived at her wrist and wrenched quite cruelly the jewelled bracelet fastened with the puma's head. He bent it violently; it snapped. He hurled it down into the fireplace where the pieces lay sadly glittering.

Mirabella gasped. After that she remained rigid. Taplow by now had resumed the impassive expression of the perfect butler, one whom nothing more could faze—not more naked female visitants, not more photographers, not more valuable jewellery broken and cast aside.

Ferdel turned back to Mirabella and eyed her speculatively. His gaze swept from her earrings, pendent and sparkling, to her many rings and the bracelets, less beautiful but possibly equally fragile, on her other arm.

"So. One more dead animal. Now you will tell me about this 'feelthy' plot. At once."

"It's to help the poor animals. It's not a plot. You will not see these photographs in the Press, not if you are sensible, they say. They are good people, not"—Mirabella cast around for the word—"not horrid blackmailers."

The Prince lifted an eyebrow; his face was hard in repose, and for a moment the skull of the older man he would become, lips too narrow, nose straight but long, deep incisions beside the narrow mouth, showed beneath the surface of the bonhomous man of pleasure, still in his prime.

"They wish you, they wish you and her—the leetle Princess—to speak to everybody. About animals.

That is all. It is a nice thing to do, Ferdel, not a nasty thing." Mirabella attempted a little winning smile. She fluttered her eyelashes. "And then they will give you back the boring photographs. And they will trouble you no more. *Je te promis.*"

"Unfortunately our Press Conference was yesterday," replied the Prince in a sombre voice.

"I know, but there is this woman, yes, you will speak to her? The woman with red hair, what is her name? You will speak to her, yes? You will speak to her on television. That is what they say. And with the leetle Princess, you will be very, very nice about the animals. Oh yes, my darling, you will." There was something artificial, almost automatic about Mirabella's wheedling voice; she was evidently still upset in some way by the recent episode, but whether by the Prince's anger, her own outburst, or even (despite her complicity) the photographic session itself, was hard to say.

"I shall do nothing—" began the Prince. Before he could say anything more, there was a noise of the key in the lock. Then the heavy doors opened and Mrs. Taplow, a strange expression which might have been anticipation or dread on her face, entered the room.

Whatever her expression betokened, she stopped abruptly at the scene before her, and stood in the doorway. It was noticeable that she did not look in the direction of her husband.

"Taplow," said the Prince sharply. "Leave the room. Take your wife. And no talk, nothing. I shall speak to you later. In the meantime no talk, no telephone calls, nothing. Both of you."

"Sir"—Taplow gave a little bow. Mrs. Taplow hesitated, then bobbed. The Taplows retreated from the room, shutting the door behind them. Once the door was shut, the Prince moved swiftly across the room, opened it again and removed the key from the lock outside. He then locked the door from the inside. Ferdel stood looking at Mirabella. Something had changed about his expression; no longer quite so hard, it was more speculative, even anticipatory.

"So, Mirabella, friend of the animals, we shall talk. We are quite alone here. I do not expect further interruptions—I hope I am right about that, my dear? I would not want the return of those other animals, or rather friends of the animals, your friends? Good. And by the way, you had better keep quiet about the fact you know them—knew them. Understood?" Mirabella nodded.

He walked towards her.

"Understood. So we are in agreement once more. I am glad. You see—what was it you suggested an hour ago? Let's fuck. Ah, you don't feel like it now? After what has happened, you don't think it would be amusing. A pity. You see I disagree. After what has happened, for the first time, I think it *would* be amusing. Very amusing."

He had reached her. The Prince stretched out his hand, the white shirt cuff protruding from the dark sleeve, in the direction of the tiny diamonded buttons which fastened her black crêpe bodice. He started, with a faint smile, to unbutton them.

Mirabella did not attempt to stop him. She was trembling slightly.

It was only much later when she said something low, like *"mon Prince,"* and he responded, equally low, *"Ach Gott,* Mirabella," that an observer might have supposed that the coupling carried out so violently on the carpet in front of the fireplace—the man first devouring the woman with his lips, then forcing her to take him in hers, finally subduing her harshly with his body—that action begun with violent possession had in fact ended in some kind of tenderness on both sides.

# EIGHT

# Royal Gossip

Lamb was lingering unhappily on the platform at Sloane Square station waiting for the Circle Line train; trains of the other lines came and went with what she felt was unfair rapidity. Lamb was unhappy first of all because she wondered whether, due to some vagary of the erratic Circle Line, she had missed the appropriate train. Life on the regularly flowing Central Line was infinitely simpler: there was always trouble when Monkey indicated the rendezvous was to be on the Circle or the District . . . Lamb always felt anxious. Lamb stopped herself. Lamb was not supposed to feel anxious.

The second cause for Lamb's unhappiness was, she decided, a legitimate one because it threatened the success of the Underground Plan. There were crowds of people, many of them foreign, standing on the platform, and not just because the Circle Line train was a long time in coming. London was filling up with tourists, some of them undoubtedly attracted by the coming spectacle of the Royal Wedding, others simply part of some slightly dazed routine which induced them to "do London." Then there were bodies, bodies of ordinary travellers. Goodness knows where they had been during the cold dull months of early spring; like bears they were out in the open now. Lamb allowed herself to worry about the question of security in these more crowded circumstances.

So far the Underground Plan, as devised by Monkey (and as suggested originally by Lamb, let her not forget, that was *Lamb's* idea), had surely been successful. No one could possibly have realized, could they, that the disparate group of travellers engaged in seemingly casual conversation in their series of moving venues, had in fact been engaged in conspiracy. Of course there had been other meetings where necessary, mainly in one particular private place, but the Underground had generally served to establish contact. And now?

The Circle Line train was signalled on the indicator, and almost immediately arrived. As Lamb had feared, there was a rush towards it. When she achieved the last carriage, as was the practice, the first person she saw was Monkey strap-hanging. Beagle was next to him, lounging upright in his characteristic stance, and being Beagle, disdaining to touch the strap; Lamb felt the familiar stab of fear, longing and, she had to face it, probably desire when she saw Beagle. Chicken was standing up, standing up and reading a paperback book called *Man and the Natural World*. Lamb recognized the book: Chicken had been reading it for some time. When Lamb had admired the cover, showing a variety of animals fleeing a forest fire, including a rather lovable if primitive lion, Chicken took the opportunity to explain that this famous painting, in a museum in Oxford, was not really so admirable since it depicted the classical myth whereby man discovered fire and in so doing succeeded in subordinating the animals to his sway.

Lamb nodded with apparent humility. She was good at appearing to look humble. Secretly she still thought the painting was rather lovely. Why not liberate it from the museum one day? As a symbol that animals were no longer subordinated. One day. The Underground Plan had to come first. All the same, it was an idea. Lamb pointed out to herself how she was absolutely full of ideas these days.

Unlike Chicken, Fox was sitting down—trust him. Lamb did not like Fox. Although he sometimes talked plaintively to Lamb (naming no names) about his unhappy childhood, a father who had never understood his artistic leanings—only Noel the dog really seemed to understand *them*—Lamb thought rather crossly that the main effect on Fox had been to make him extraordinarily self-centered . . . which was not the same thing at all as having artistic leanings.

Trust Pussy too to manage to get a seat when she arrived, which would be at the next stop, Sloane Square. With her mess of logoed plastic shopping bags about her, like sandbags surrounding her stout person, Pussy was not above demanding the right to sit down; she generally chose an inoffensive-looking young person, but on one occasion Pussy's black sense of humour (which oddly enough she did not lack) had led her to pick on Beagle. Lamb still remembered the look on Beagle's face when he refused.

"You must be joking," was all he said; it was the expression which was frightening, a kind of naked glee at the opportunity to wound, insult.

"Right in character, Puss," said Beagle later. "Catch the sort of person I am getting up for any old cow with her plastic shopping battering rams."

"I shall remember that, Beagle," replied Pussy

quite equably. "You see if I don't. I have my own character too, you know." And the incident apparently passed off. All the same Lamb wondered what Monkey thought of a complicated plan, involving watertight procedures, in which at least two of the characters involved cordially disliked each other—not to use a stronger word. Better far when they loved each other, like Beagle and Lamb. *Did* Beagle love her? He hated what he described her as standing for, he had always made that quite clear; but then so in a sense did Lamb herself. If something in Beagle's background made him peculiarly violent at times, frighteningly so, towards the notion of Lamb's upbringing, did she not share his distaste? Hence Innoright, hence her participation in the cell. Hence, so her doctor, the nice one, had said certain other things in Lamb's past. But Lamb loved too, she loved animals, the innocent, sometimes with a quite unbearable love. And she loved Beagle, whatever his past. Did he, then, love her?

Lamb could just imagine Beagle's reply if asked such a question; because she had worked towards it in the past: "This *is* love, my Lambkin," he had said upon one occasion, putting her hand firmly on his groin, with its large moulded lump inside the skinny jeans. "And this is for you." But now Pussy was getting into the carriage. That left Tom, due to arrive at Victoria.

Then Lamb noticed that Monkey was carrying an umbrella. How had she not noticed it before? No, Monkey must have somehow masked it with his body until five out of the six members of the Underground Plan cell were present; that still left Tom unaccounted for. Wait, Monkey had a blue handkerchief in his breast pocket where normally a white one was customary. Now *that* he had definitely put in place within the last few minutes; she couldn't have missed the blue handkerchief, which, coupled with the umbrella meant . . . Yes, meeting abandoned for the time being, same route to be tried again in four hours' time, same procedure. Any cell member unable to do that for personal reasons to tell the person closest to them in the carriage.

Perhaps Monkey like Lamb found the crowds oppressive. This was certainly no occasion for any kind of planning meeting. Four hours brought them well past the rush hour to another theoretically dead period, office workers vanished. The Underground Plan involved three possible times of day, the third (which would be used following an evening cancellation) being at ten thirty the next morning. But everyone found that time difficult, and it had so far only been used once.

"Good news," Beagle was saying in her ear. "We're really into something." Then he patted her bottom, felt it really, followed the shape of it with his hand. . . . Lamb gave Beagle a look of unforced indignation. "My place afterwards," he murmured. And was gone. Lamb left at the next station without further contact of any description with the rest of the cell.

Yes, she thought rather bitterly, seven o'clock was no problem to her. What did she have to do that was more important than Innoright? What did she have to *do*, come to think of it? But Lamb stopped that train of thought at once, that really was not the way to think, not in any way, not ever according to the instructions of the nice doctor. And although Lamb would never dream of telling the nice doctor what she was up to at Innoright, she still had a feeling that he, the doctor, would not totally disapprove. Lamb was after all thinking of others just as the doctor had told her to do, and at the same time valuing herself.

"Better to love others than hate yourself." Lamb was definitely loving others—the others being the animals. And Beagle.

Lamb picked up a taxi outside the Tube station and went home.

Lamb's sister looked up when Lamb entered the house; the front door of the little Chelsea house which they shared opened directly into the sitting-room. The first sight which should have met Lamb's eyes at this point was a large oil portrait—overlarge for the small room—which hung in a dominating fashion over the fireplace. It showed a man in military uniform; he had an incongruously fierce air amid the girlish chintzes with which the room was decorated. But Lamb took care not to look at the portrait and thus avoided the ferocious gaze which her father appeared to be bestowing upon the room's inhabitants. The nice young doctor had talked to her at length about "finding your own way of dealing with your father's memory." Lamb's own way was to refuse to look at the portrait altogether, otherwise she found rage, what was worse, helpless rage, welling up inside her.

It helped Lamb to inspect automatically instead the various photographs of her mother which stood in silver frames on the occasional tables, chintz-draped, scattered about the room. An observer would have noted the strong resemblance between Lamb and her mother, even down to the tense expression they shared; but between the girl now standing (unseeing) beneath the portrait and the portrait's subject, it was difficult to see any resemblance at all.

"Good day, darling?" enquired Lamb's sister as

Lamb entered. Her low-heeled court shoes had been kicked off and she was reading the evening paper. The tone was perhaps artificially bright, as though the conventional enquiry masked, for once, some real concern about the nature of Lamb's day.

"Mmm. Went to the Tate. Awfully crowded. And you?"

"Good day, bad day. You know how it goes. I've got the evening off. Am I going to make you some supper? Promise not a whisper of meat anywhere, or fish, no bouillon or naughty stock cubes, Chef gave me this wonderful recipe. I'm longing to try it."

"I'm afraid I have to go out," replied Lamb, "and don't frown."

"I'm not frowning," said her sister mildly. "I haven't said a word."

"Well, your look was worried. I can't bear that. You're not supposed to worry about me, I'm supposed to worry about me if anyone does. It's called taking responsibility for myself. I have to go out. Do you find that odd? As a matter of fact I said I'd go to a film with Janey. It's a long one. I might be quite late." Lamb was aware that she was speaking too rapidly.

"Sounds fun!"

"I don't know that it will be all that fun," began Lamb in a slightly childish voice. She stopped. "I may be late, that's all. Janey does go on a bit these days. Her parents' divorce. The whole thing."

"But that was ages ago. I mean, you told me she'd finally got over it the last time you saw her. You were so relieved. Anyway, darling, I don't think Janey really should burden you of all people with things like that—"

It was the turn of Lamb's sister to stop. Then:

"Darling Lydia," resumed Lamb's sister, Ione Quentin, in the same equable voice she was wont to use to Princess Amy in order to smooth over an awkward moment. "Why *not* go to a cinema indeed? I'll try the recipe another night. I'm whacked as it happens. P.A. *not* in a good mood because Ferdel failed to show. . . . Really that man, although I can't help fancying him when he's actually there. He looks a bit like Daddy, don't you think? Pictures of Daddy as a young man; not as you remember him. And of course P.A. fancies him like mad, so she gets all jealous." Ione Quentin stopped. "Am I boring you, darling? I'm sure you don't want to hear all this. Tell me what you saw at the Tate."

"No, no, go on," Lydia Quentin, known in some circles as Lamb, spoke with evident sincerity. "I love hearing about your life at CP. I like the little details. Go on about Ferdel. So what did he do? Go on about everything. What about all those awful wedding arrangements? You're so clever, Nonie, I really love hearing it."

The Quentin sisters settled down for a nice royal gossip until such time as Lydia Quentin had to leave again to keep her appointment at South Kensington station.

About this time, in other parts of the city, various other forms of what might also be termed royal gossip were taking place. For example, it would probably be legitimate to term the remarks made by a man leaning over some emerging photographic prints, as royal gossip; even if the remarks themselves were too scabrous to be printed in any actual gossip column.

As for Jemima Shore, sprawling on the white carpet of her Holland Park Mansions flat, with Midnight flumped down blackly beside her, she might be said at the very least to be studying royal gossip. All about her were notes, charts and newspaper cuttings, preparatory to her exclusive interview with the royal couple in the near future. When the telephone rang, she realized that it must be Rick Vancy making one of those checking calls from his car · telephone which somehow seemed to her to do little more than establish Rick Vancy's ability to drive and digress (on topics of the day) at one and the same time.

Jemima stretched out her hand without looking to where her own neat little telephone had been deposited on the carpet. In the course of the stretch, her hand encountered Midnight who moved out of the way with a small indignant cry.

"Hi," said Jemima. "How's the traffic?"—hoping he would not tell her.

There was a short silence. Then a voice—not Rick's—began speaking, and continued to do so at some length, carefully as from a prepared statement.

At one point Jemima did interrupt: *"What?"* The voice continued to speak. Then: "Who are you?"

A little later she said: "That's out of the question. Absolutely out of the question," she repeated firmly, "whoever you are. And whatever it is you say you've got."

# NINE

# A Dangerous Connection

It may have been successful, Beagle," Monkey was remarking in his (to Beagle) irritatingly lofty voice. "But it was extremely dangerous."

Monkey's suit was the habitual pin-stripe; with the handkerchief in the breast pocket once more white, the first impression was of the respectable city gentleman Monkey presented to the outside world. But Monkey was palpably disturbed by recent events; how could Beagle so blithely ignore *orders* when orders, correctly given, correctly carried out, were to be the secret of their success? Because of the emotion of this moment, Monkey's simian quality, conveyed by his long curbed hairless upper lip, the unduly splayed nostrils, was more in evidence than usual. Twirling his umbrella, Monkey today had, thought Lamb, the air of some heavy and slightly desolate primate.

"Careful planning, my old Monk, careful planning," replied Beagle easily. "Careful planning eliminates danger. Chicken here took the photographs. No sweat, no problem. No difficulty. No laughs. No tears. Well, maybe just a few. But I assure you it was totally non-violent. The pistol was a fake or rather it was a true-blue pistol, but unloaded. As used in some lethal drawing-room tragedy. Supplied by Foxy. All by agreement as you might say. A gentleman's agreement."

"Shouldn't we say a lady's agreement, Beagle?" Chicken as usual sounded earnest; but all the same there was a new ease about her, even an air of happiness. Pussy in contrast looked heavier than usual (like Monkey) and her expression as she gazed downwards at her single plastic shopping-bag was sombre.

"A lady's agreement, indeed, Chick. In more senses than one. So: no sweat, good photos, and now we use them."

"In fact," continued Beagle, "as you know, I've already set it up. Now don't panic, Monko—you agreed"—and as Monkey appeared to be about to speak—"don't give me a lot of shit about orders, orders correctly carried out and all that shit. I really don't give a fuck for orders, never have, my orders being of course different—" Beagle smiled: but it was demonstrably not a smile intended to rob his words of offence. "It just happened, right? Right and *Innoright*. There was I, photographing this lovely lady, clothes on, or most of them, and we get talking. Well, it was natural, wasn't it? We've got a lot in common, so we get friendly." Beagle winked with meaning, a parody of a lewd wink perhaps, but a lewd wink none the less.

In spite of herself, in spite of everything she had learned about self-esteem from the nice doctor, Lamb felt a violent lurch of jealousy, followed by the kind of spasm which just might turn to depression. . . . She would not, could not let it do so. Quickly, Lamb cast up counter-images on her mental screen to blot out the pictures already forming there of Beagle and Mirabella Prey, Mirabella's black hair, how very black, how very thick it must be everywhere, even where concealed by the *Daily Exclusive*, Mirabella and Beagle. . . . Instead, Lamb concentrated on other images, in themselves far more horrific but which actually served as mantras to calm her down, restore her to her sense of purpose.

The image of a pet cat called Snowdrop came first; the young white cat with a pink nose and occasional tabby patches which Lamb had loved as a child and which had vanished one day from a London street. Lamb imagined the cat with wires through her nose, and other wires applied strategically to parts of her body; Snowdrop's eyes gazed in silent terror and despair into Lamb's own, but in spite of her terror, Snowdrop had to remain mute because she no longer had a tongue or at any rate a tongue that she could use. . . . Lamb thought of the work of saving Snowdrop and all the other cats who vanished mysteriously in cities, from such a fate. She was already calmer and did not need to pass on to her next image, culled years ago from an Animal Rights handout, which involved a beagle, a cigarette, more wires, and the connection between smoking and human lung cancer. (A beagle! How odd! That Lamb had never been able to forget the expression in that dog's eyes had surely been an omen.)

Beagle was speaking again. "So I find out for her where the Prince is staying, that's not difficult, Fleet Street being what it is, and get a message to him to come home quick which as a matter of fact is not all that difficult either." Lamb closed her eyes and the wraith of poor Snowdrop floated away into the recesses of her mind for when it was next needed.

"It's easy, Monkey, so easy," Beagle was saying. "We're laughing. Just imagine them getting their knickers in a twist at Cumberland Palace. But there's nothing, bloody nothing, that they can do about it. 'Course no English paper will print them—you don't need to tell me that, I work for them, don't I? But abroad, that's quite another matter. I work for them too, don't I? And the date and all on the copy of the London *Clueless*. No way they can wriggle out of it."

"The date and the paper was my idea," put in Chicken. "I got it from the hostages, those American ones, or was it the Prime Minister of Italy? Both, I believe. They always photograph them with a daily paper to establish veracity. I fancy it was a professional touch."

"But the Underground Plan—" Monkey for once sounded irresolute.

"This is a development of the Underground Plan, a stage along the way. Can't you see that?" In contrast to Monkey's gloom Beagle was increasingly cheerful. "Just as we're no longer meeting in the Underground at this very moment, are we? Too dangerous at this stage. We've adjourned to my pad, as on previous occasions, have we not? And very nice too, I think you'll agree, if a little sparsely furnished. No prying landladies *here*."

Lamb looked around. Pussy was perched uncomfortably on a low curved white chair, her big knees held tightly together. That was because there were no other chairs visible, only the white cushions on the painted, shiny black floor. Monkey was standing, as was Beagle; some ridiculous prejudice had made Lamb avoid sitting on the bed—the familiar bed—

when she first came in, leaving Chicken and Fox to sit on it together. The slightly built man and the precise woman, adjoining but not touching, had the air of puppet monarchs.

The kingdom over which they ruled was literally an animal kingdom. Enormous blown-up photographs of animals covered the walls: animals without bodies, faces only, staring with huge bewildered eyes at the puny humans below them, faces of seals in particular (plenty of seals—Beagle might perhaps have chosen the code name Seal, given his preference for them). There was one mother seal, her coat slightly speckled in the photograph, who crouched protectively over her snow-white baby: that was Lamb's favourite. When Lamb first got to know Beagle, she had imagined rather vaguely that he was the sort of person who would turn out to live in a squat. Just as she had imagined him to be unemployed.

"A squat!" he had repeated disdainfully. "A squat brings you into contact with people—and I don't just mean the police. I have a perfectly good studio. And then I have this private place. As you can see, I'm for living privately with the animals." He had gestured towards the nearest seal's face: with its neat muzzle and wide-apart eyes it looked pretty and rather plaintive, like an attractive girl; where the average photographer might have covered his wall with the faces of glamorous models, big eyed and long eye-lashed, Beagle had his plaintive seals with long, appealing whiskers instead of eyelashes. Beagle's whole face changed and softened when he looked in their direction.

But then Beagle, thought Lamb, even if he was a photographer, was not an average one. And the room where he lived, although situated near newly fashionable Covent Garden, was not an average room. In many ways it was an ideal rendezvous for the cell— once the Underground had become too dangerous for detailed plotting—because it was situated over a deserted shop apparently awaiting conversion. There was a side door and a narrow staircase, and another door at the back of the staircase, leading out to a tiny mews yard. On the edge of the shining new Covent Garden development, yet not part of it, the dingy property was like something shipwrecked from another time.

"What about the owner of the shop?" Lamb had asked.

"The owner is sympathetic to our cause," was all that Beagle replied, leaving Lamb to wonder whether Beagle was not the owner of the shop. At least there was no inquisitive shopkeeper to monitor their arrivals and departures, the sort that Monkey feared. Was Beagle's flat suitable perhaps for the Lair? Was that the intention? But now Fox was speaking.

"I wish one could have introduced an animal, say a *dog*, into the picture! Otherwise, it could seem a little, well, *sensational*. . . ." Fox, who had the prints on his lap, sounded rather wistful; his voice trailed away as Beagle gave him a look of undisguised contempt.

"Do you introduce a dog into *your* work," he began and then broke off. "Oh, what's the use? Let's discuss the statement. Right, Monko? Right, Chick?" Lamb thought with a little stab of pain that Beagle seemed to be assuming some kind of inner command, now that he and Chicken had carried out this successful form of raid; then she laughed at herself. She could hardly be jealous of Chicken, now that would be ridiculous. Lamb, like the others, concentrated on the statement that Prince Ferdinand and Princess Amy

would be asked to make on television on the subject
of innocent rights. . . .

"Where's Tom?" asked Fox suddenly. He had been
silent during most of the discussion but Beagle's
brutal dismissal of the notion of an animal—possibly
a dog—lending the photographs some kind of symbolic dignity had evidently riled him; or maybe the
exchange had raised painful memories of Noel's
rejection at the main Innoright meetings.

There was silence. As a matter of fact Lamb had
been wondering for some time why Tom's absence
had not been explained; why Monkey for example
had given the signal to abandon the earlier rendezvous before Victoria where Tom was due to join the
train. There had been no explanation of that at the
time, but then things had happened fast once she had
glimpsed Monkey's blue handkerchief; Beagle, she
remembered, had been in a state of exhilaration—but
that was presumably explained by the successful
photographic raid on Prince Ferdinand.

"Where's Tom?" repeated Fox stubbornly. "Monkey, I think you should tell us. You're the leader."

Monkey cleared his throat and raised one eyebrow.
"I regret to tell you all—Tom is dead."

"Dead!" exclaimed Fox, petulance abandoned.
Lamb at the same time was experiencing a feeling of
overwhelming relief: now she would no longer worry
over Tom, lie awake at night worrying; above all she
would no longer have to keep her fear of Tom from
Beagle—his friend.

"How dreadful! He was so young!" That was
Chicken, as though talking of some former pupil.

"What does age have to do with it?" Pussy
sounded as if she was preparing to be difficult on

some minor point: she did not appear to be particularly surprised or even distressed.

"Well, wasn't it—a heart attack? Something like that?" Chicken again.

"Was it?" Pussy was increasingly captious.

"As a matter of fact it wasn't." This was Beagle. "As a matter of fact the police are treating Tom's death as murder. How about that, then?" He faced them, hands on his thin hips, smiling faintly. Like Pussy, he chose to express no regrets.

Lamb realized that she was the only one who hadn't said anything.

"How dreadful!" she exclaimed, echoing Chicken, whose sentiments, if banal, had been appropriate. She added piously: "It's even more dreadful if he was murdered, of course."

"How do you know all this, Beagle?"—Fox, high complaining voice.

"Can I tell them, Monkey?" Beagle was for once almost deferential. It occurred to Lamb that although Monkey knew that Tom was dead, he had not broken the news to them until pressed by Fox about Tom's whereabouts.

Monkey nodded.

"I was there," announced Beagle. "No, no, not literally there"—a shade of the old impatience returned. "I wasn't there when he was killed. No one was there when he was killed—except the killer that is. But I was at the Press Conference. Or rather I came late for the Press Conference, last job took longer than expected, but I did get there. Part of my work, isn't it? Photographing Royals—Royals of all sorts and in all sorts of positions."

Beagle pointed his trainer shoe in the direction of Prince Ferdinand and Mirabella, still lying on the floor beneath the sad soulful gaze of the seals.

"Tom was there too: he was a journalist. You didn't know that? Some of you knew that. He was a mate of mine, at least you all knew that. That's how we met, working together. That's how I knew he was a good bloke where animals were concerned. We cooked up something—but that's another story."

"He was killed *there*?" Fox was still incredulous. "At the Royal Press Conference, the one we saw on TV? But I watched that—"

"Not there. In the hotel lounge outside. Somebody went and stabbed him, cool as you please. The lounge had been full of people, was currently empty because of the conference, empty save for Tom—Tom and his murderer."

"Go on," said Monkey slowly. "They've a right to hear the rest of the story."

"Afterwards the police questioned everyone— everyone at the conference, I suppose. Must have taken a bit of time. Not the Prince and Princess, I dare say. Everyone else. Anyway they questioned me, because we were mates, as I told you."

"Who, who killed him?" began Lamb rather tremulously.

"*Why* was he killed?" exclaimed Chicken at the same time much more strongly, making Lamb realize that her question could be construed as being nothing more than inane, whereas Chicken as usual was able to make an intelligent case for her intervention. "When you know why, you know who, as they say in all the best detective stories."

"On that subject, Chick, you might feel like being in touch with the police," remarked Beagle, staring at Chicken. "If you're that interested. I'm sure they would be interested. To meet you."

Chicken stared back, but Lamb had the impression

that she was just slightly ruffled. Fox burst in, breaking the moment of tension: "I hope you won't dream of any such thing, Chicken. We don't want him connected to us now in any way. Now that he's safely dead."

"Safely dead," observed Pussy. "Now that's an odd way of putting it." Nobody seemed to pay her any attention.

"It could be dangerous, well, dangerous for the Plan," pursued Fox. "A dangerous connection."

"He is connected to us. He was connected to us when he was alive and he's connected to us now he's dead." Beagle's smile had faded. He sounded quite savage.

"What are you trying to say?" demanded Fox.

Beagle looked at Monkey. Monkey nodded once more.

"I am trying to say that Tom was a spy, a nark, an informer." Beagle spoke with increasing passion. "I'm glad he's dead in a manner of speaking because he would probably have ended by betraying the whole fucking Plan. In another way, I'm furious he's dead because it's brought all of us, and the Plan, into danger. From this, chaps, you may gather definitively that I did not kill him. In case you're getting any funny ideas."

Monkey lifted an eyebrow, preparatory to making one of his more sonorous statements. "From what Beagle tells me, we may have to change the Underground Plan. Tom knew far too much—well, he knew a great deal, if not everything. We'll have to rethink."

"At least let's be positive!" cried Chicken encouragingly. "The photographic coup, now that's going to help our cause a great deal. It'll be quite exciting watching the interview, won't it, and seeing them making the first really strong statement on behalf of the innocent that this Royal family has ever made. I honestly don't count Prince Charles and the under-privileged, I mean a man who goes hunting . . ."

"Can they now refuse?" enquired Lamb. Her voice to her own ears was anxious; but then anxiety on this particular subject was comprehensible.

"We've made them an offer they can't refuse, in the words of the movie," replied Monkey. "This is the text." He pointed to it. "And the presenter, Jemima Whats-it, is ready to receive it."

"So easy," murmured Fox. "If we can do this with mere photographs, what can't we do with our little Royal Madam herself."

Pussy smiled ruminatively, as though at some image in her mind, not necessarily a pleasant one.

"You know the new Underground Plan," began Lamb slowly. Tom was dead. She knew that she must now eliminate all the familiar feelings of anxiety, it was vital to proceed calmly, this was how she was justifying her whole existence, wasn't it?

"I have an idea," went on Lamb. "A new idea which might work. . . ." She explained, her confidence growing as she spoke.

"I could help on that," said Beagle. "Fox, you could help me."

"I could help you both," contributed Chicken firmly. "It's my special interest, you see."

So they plotted, as the seals continued to gaze mutely down on the various and varied faces of the people who had constituted themselves their human saviours.

# TEN

# Speaking Up For Animals

The terrible screaming which filled Cumberland Palace would, thought Ione Quentin, remain in her ears long after many sounds more generally associated with royal life (the noise of the bands, the noise of the crowds laughing and murmuring and clapping, the noise of the ceremonial horses clattering in the early morning) were forgotten.

"Ma'am, it'll be all right. They'll take care of it."

Princess Amy gave another scream which sounded something like: "They won't, they won't, they won't," though the connection was not clear. One word, "animals," could be discerned, and then the words became incomprehensible and finally turned into sobs. When the sobs were diminishing, Ione risked another gentle touch to the royal shoulder. Princess Amy raised herself on one elbow and gazed at her lady-in-waiting. Tears—aided by screams—had washed away most of her make-up: but the long eyelashes surrounding the enormous eyes which were her best feature were spiky-black with a mixture of tears and mascara. The full pouting mouth for once made Princess Amy look more like an injured child than a sulky young woman.

113

Unbidden, and irreverent thoughts came to Ione Quentin's mind: one of these unbidden thoughts concerned Prince Ferdinand. Ione thought it was a pity the Prince could not glimpse his fiancée now. Ione, whose language, at least to herself, could be surprisingly robust, thought: for once P.A. looks positively fuckable. If P.F. saw her now, he might not waste quite so much energy in other directions. . . .

Ione Quentin hurriedly pulled herself up and concentrated on the matter in hand. She put her arms round Amy's shoulders and Amy turned and buried her face in Ione's neat cream-coloured silk shirt, the shirt she wore so often (or something identical) that it was like a uniform. The feeling of Amy snuffling into the shirt, wet and still gasping or sobbing mildly, reminded Ione briefly of a pug puppy they had had as a child. Was that the pug Lydia had adored, the baby pug with a hernia who had to be put down? Another profitless line of thought. The sobs had turned to mere shudders of the frame held against hers. The worst was over.

Wait, thought Ione, what am I saying? The worst is only just beginning.

If the worst was just beginning, nevertheless Ione Quentin's arm round the weeping Princess Amy represented the last link in a long chain of shock, horror and disbelief since Innoright—or its representative—had rung Jemima Shore and requested certain public statements from the royal couple. Otherwise certain photographs would be released to the continental and American Press, and shown at least to the British Press.

"As if they'd dream of printing such filth!" one important person at another even more important palace had exclaimed, apprised of the emergency.

"Oh, I don't know," murmured Major Pat Smylie-Porter, taking another long look at Mirabella's sinuous naked frame. "Things ain't what they used to be where the Press is concerned, we all know that. Her without him perhaps. A Page Two picture."

"Don't you mean Page Three?" rapped back the important person irritably. "And anyway the wretched woman is hardly built for that kind of thing, our own horse would be—" He stopped to find Major Pat gazing blandly back at him.

On the other hand there was nothing bland about Rick Vancy, his usual clam tinged with manifest disgust at the idea of TUS's sacrosanct exclusive interview being tampered with by some "unfocused friends of the animal kingdom," as he termed Innoright. To Jemima Shore, he remarked over lunch at Le Caprice: "They have to find these gross people and they have to find them fast. Or find the photographs, and the negatives, *all* the negatives. We have to deaccessify them, correction, your police have to deaccessify them. What are your police doing?"

"Maybe we should send for the CIA," suggested Jemima Shore sweetly.

"For Chrissake, those bunglers," began Rick Vancy, before realizing that he had once again failed to identify a British joke; he really had to work on the whole subject of British jokes, thought Rick Vancy wearily, once this crazy business was over. A fun programme indeed! Even the animals were getting in on the act, it appeared, and that was not turning out to be much fun either.

From long experience, Rick Vancy knew himself to be a man of naturally liberal stance on every issue, without being so wildly liberal that TUS became greatly alarmed: it was good for them to be just a little alarmed, at least from time to time. For example, Rick Vancy was critical of the U.S. government on Nicaragua ("a revolution with *no* right to survive?") and stern towards the British government on Northern Ireland ("a colony with *any* right to survive?"). In a seemingly relaxed fashion, Rick Vancy, with his moral eyes half shut, could sense the public mood at its most liberal and push his own position just a little bit further in order to adopt that hard-hitting stance upon which his admirers counted.

But animals! The ecology was one thing: that could be political to put it mildly and generally was, but animal rights pure and simple! Animal rights when there was nuclear energy for or against, chemical warfare for or against, on another level Afghanistan for or against the Russian presence, Cambodia for or against the Vietnamese presence, or just the Middle East for or against, if you could put it like that, and after many years of sage reporting, Rick Vancy thought that you almost could. Either you cared or you didn't care, but you went there and reported anyway, with luck returning. And as a matter of fact, Rick Vancy did care.

With all this to be considered, Rick Vancy felt he might pass a lifetime of activity without getting around to animal rights for or against. . . . Not that Rick himself wasn't an animal lover; two English sheepdogs had graced the first Vancy marriage to a Norwegian (the one that was sometimes supposed to have involved an Englishwoman, maybe on the strength of the dogs). Another live-in relationship sans marriage which *had* involved an Englishwoman had also encompassed a relationship with a rat. Yes, a rat, Goddammit, a tame or tame-ish domestic rat, the marks of whose bites were still with him long after the scars left by crazy English Tammy, herself a bit of a biter, had faded. And Goddammit once more, Rick had been fond of that rat! He shared memories with that rat.

Some of this Rick thought of expressing to Jemima, irked, he had to admit, that their relationship remained friendly and nothing more. Frankly, this was not what he had been led to expect in New York. Lunch at Le Caprice was all very well: in fact it was very agreeable. And Rick Vancy had noted with quiet satisfaction the moment when the corner table had become his table and stopped being inevitably Jemima's. So that Jemima, giving a last-minute lunch to her old friend Jamie Grand, the powerful presenter of the new arts programme *Literature Now!* had had to bow ruefully in Rick's direction, seeing him already installed there.

On the other hand, thought Rick, however socially gratifying, this had probably not helped his cause with Jemima. Rick had a sudden inspiration. Would an account of some of Tammy's odder practices, with or without the rat, turn Jemima on? Maybe all Englishwomen of roughly Tammy's age and background shared the same odd predilection for domestic rats in intimate situations. Maybe the rat was the key. . . .

"Hey, did you ever know a woman who owned a rat, called Tammy?" he began. "The woman I mean, not the rat." Since Jemima continued to look politely blank, he added: "The woman was called Tammy. No, forget it. Listen, these people are sick. Isn't that right? All the causes in the world, all the dying babies in Ethiopia, all the dying babies in the Sudan— "

"All the dying *girl* babies," put in Jemima who suddenly remembered she had completed a programme on female infanticide (tentative title: "Death is a Chauvinist") shortly before leaving Megalith, and wondered what on earth had happened to it.

"Exactly. All the damn babies. And these guys go for animal rights. To me that's crazy. It's either crazy or it's sick. And given what they're asking us to do, it's sick. Come on, Jemima, give. These are your Brits for Chrissake. Do they just hate society? Is that it? Or just hate us humble humans without getting as far as a dangerously complicated concept like society?"

"I'm not sure about this lot," said Jemima honestly, bringing her mind reluctantly back from the fate of "Death is a Chauvinist" (a private call to Cherry perhaps?). "There are some very obviously violent ones around, animal liberationists, you read about them in the newspapers, horrifying manifestoes, threatening to burn, wreck, kill, whatever. Up till recently they tended to threaten but on the whole not perform. Or not perform particularly drastically. Then there was that incident in Westminster Square. You must have read about that. Ghastly! Carnage, that's the only word. The word everybody used and for once the right word. The fact that only, repeat only, horses were actually killed made it worse somehow."

Rick looked at her quizzically. "Better to have we horrid or humble humans knocked off than horses?"

"Does one have to choose?" countered Jemima. "No, no, I mean that it's surely specially frightful that people would kill or rather in most cases hideously maim—so they had to be destroyed—the very species they were allegedly trying to help."

"The old terrorist situation. The innocent tend to suffer along with the guilty. And I guess you have to locate these guys somewhere in the terrorist pantheon."

"Innoright itself hasn't so far committed an act of terrorism as such," Jemima pointed out. "And I should add that according to my pal Pompey—the policeman—Innoright doesn't exactly have a *violent* reputation. More crazy than sick, to accept your distinction."

"Oddballs?"

"What they're asking is not all that odd. If you believe what they believe. Not that we're going to give it to them," added Jemima hastily, in case Rick Vancy's suspicions about the general British softness on the subject of the fate of animals as opposed to the fate of the human race in general should be confirmed. "It's the principle of speaking up for animals. They feel no one does it, or no one of sufficient importance in the public mind. The Prince and Princess will do it, put it on the map for good. That's all."

She was eating fish as usual, having politely described herself as "almost a vegetarian" when she first met Rick (today: *salade tiède à lotte*). Rick on the other hand as he invariably did was eating chopped steak. And now that he knew Jemima better, he had slipped into drinking what she privately termed the Puritan champagne—Perrier water. I may be "almost a vegetarian" thought Jemima, but he's "almost a teetotaller" without liking to admit it. She herself was drinking white wine. To be frank, had it not been for Rick's sneaky abstemiousness, she would normally have diluted it with some of the Puritan champagne; as it was, she felt she must stand up for the rights of Sancerre to be drunk unadulterated.

"That's all!" echoed Rick. He pushed aside the steak (he always ate exactly two-thirds of it, as though he had measured it in advance, Jemima noticed) and began to tick off the Innoright demands: "No more animal laboratory experiments of any sort, even in the cause of medicine, experiments on human beings if necessary instead."

"Experiments on the human beings who benefit from the results," corrected Jemima. "That's what it said. Not the actual sick of course, just members of the human as opposed to the animal species."

"Okay, okay." He went on: "In no particular order: no more fur coats or fur garments or trimmings. Leather not mentioned, I note. They're soft on leather. So-called Fur Law to be introduced. All existing fur coats to be sold abroad, proceeds to go to the rehabilitation of animals rescued from scientific laboratories, factory farms etc. Any woman seen wearing a fur coat in the street"—Rick broke off. "Do you know something? This is fundamentalist rubbish. That clause about women wearing fur coats in the streets and the right of citizen's arrest, it reminds me of Iran, women without the veil, Pakistan, women with makeup— "

"Is it a fundamental liberty to wear a fur coat?" began Jemima. She stopped. "Listen Rick, I'm not trying to argue the toss. If I were to be honest, I suppose like most people here, and doubtless a good many people in the States, I have to face the fact that I simply shudder away from the subject of animal experiments. Just imagine if anyone were to lay a finger on Midnight!"

"Cats not rats," thought Rick irrelevantly. "No wonder she didn't relate to Tammy and her rat."

"On the other hand," went on Jemima, "leukaemia in children, for example, animals who suffer to save children from leukaemia, animals versus children—I just don't want to think about it. And I'm supposed to be an investigator!"

"You've never gotten around to making a programme about it."

Jemima smiled. "Now that's an idea. Instead of our exclusive interview with P.A. and P.F., I make a programme about Innoright. I show the famous photographs. I interview Mirabella Prey. The only problem being: where are the people behind all this? How do I lure them on to the silver screen? Any ideas?"

"This is the point, sweetheart. Where are they? And what are the police doing about finding them?"

"I may as well tell you one more thing, Rick. Now this is not crazy, this is serious. Far from killing, one of them was recently actually killed. A journalist who was a member of Innoright. One of them, one of the Innoright members died recently, was killed at a conference. Treated by the police as murder. Not much publicity, not exactly covered up, just not stressed when all attention was on the royal couple."

"Jesus!" Rick took a quick restorative swig of the Puritan champagne. "Murder! And what are the police doing about that?"

On the subject of what the police were doing about that—that being the unaccidental death of Jean-Pierre Schwarz-Albert—more voices than the plaintive voice of Rick Vancy were being raised. For example, Detective Superintendent John Portsmouth found his murder hunt suddenly interrupted by a series of interested enquiries concerning Animal Rights activists in general, Innoright in particular.

"Everybody keeps telling me in their panicky way that there has to be a connection," observed Pompey stolidly to Detective Sergeant Vaillant as they sat alone, at the end of the day, in the incident room set up for the murder of Schwarz-Albert a.k.a. Tom, a member of the Innoright cell. "And then they ask me will I please inform them what the connection is? The man dies. The photographs are taken. The threats are made: unless HRH speaks up— "

"Unless HRH and HH speak up—" corrected Vaillant.

"Unless they both speak up. But it's her they're after—cousin of the Monarch, member of the British Royal Family and all that. Could be seen by the ignorant—and a good many of *them* around—as some form of royal proclamation. A balance to all that hunting by You-know-who and all that shooting by You-know-who-else. Back to the connection. What I say is: if there is a connection, will those who know what it is, please inform me?"

Pompey gazed at Vaillant.

"So far as you know we've drawn a series of blanks. And not for want of trying. The photographer has an alibi, lots of witnesses that he came late, including the place of his other assignment which kept him. Still, we shan't forget him. Not us. We're having another look at him over the photographs of course. So are Special Branch. The film star—what's her name? Do you realize I know her figure better than I know her name?" Since Vaillant looked shocked, Pompey proceeded: "She swears she can't identify him. Swears she has no idea who knew she was going there to confront the wretched bridegroom. Well, that's what she says." He paused. "But he allowed us to search his studio, positively offered it, so that must be clean. Then there are the two women," Pompey added.

"The witnesses?"

Pompey pursued his train of thought. "Odd that

*two* women who made statements, apparently quite unconnected with each other—but we'll have to check that—should prove to be members of Innoright."

"There's a lot of it about," put in Vaillant helpfully.

"Ordinary rank and file members. All the same it's an odd coincidence. And—"

"In this office we don't believe in coincidences," finished Vaillant.

"Charity Wadham, a teacher if I remember rightly. Meeting a friend for tea in the Republican lounge, unaware it had been blocked off for the Royal Press Conference. Friend went happily to the other lounge, Mrs. Wadham strays into the wrong lounge and sees our man apparently sleeping. Friend confirms story. But Mrs. Charity Wadham is a member of Innoright, a founder member, what's more. The other woman— what is her name? something foreign, Muscovite . . ."

"Moscowitz."

"Big woman," went on Pompey. "Rather gloomy. Appears to be Polish. Doesn't sound it, but looks it. Ordinary member of Innoright. She finally admitted that she popped into the Republican merely to go to the ladies for free—felt hot and tired after prolonged shopping in nearby Marks and Sparks. Subsequently rested in the empty Republican lounge. Except it wasn't empty. It contained the dead body of our friend. She didn't notice. And didn't notice Wadham's appearance either. Doesn't know Wadham anyway."

"Plausible?"

"Why not? Innoright is a biggish organization, the outer layer of it, in some ways not unlike Greenpeace, with lots of different causes, all aspects of innocence abused is how they put it. Or some such phrase. Security all the while was concentrated on the actual conference inside the big double doors. The murderer certainly hit on a convenient moment to do it. No other clues." Pompey sighed. "With this interview business on top of it all, Special Branch not being very cooperative as usual, it beats me. Except I am not paid to be beaten. And nor, young fellow-me-lad, are you."

"A message came from on high," Vaillant spoke delicately, "while you were talking to Mrs. Pompey about—whatever it was you were talking about."

"Sutton's seed catalogue!" exclaimed Pompey bitterly. "She thinks I've hidden it on purpose. Go on."

"The Palace has said no."

"That's the message?"

"That's the drift of it," murmured Vaillant.

"So the interview goes ahead? And no statement? No speaking up for the poor little animals from our young couple!"

"Not a dog's bark if you'll pardon the expression," concluded Vaillant.

Pompey presumably did pardon the expression since he did not refer to it.

"Very interesting. Very interesting indeed," was all he said. "Have a look in the drawer will you and see if that damn catalogue is lurking. Do you suppose I ought to be grateful that Mrs. Portsmouth is into flowers not animals?"

But Vaillant knew better than to answer that one.

# ELEVEN

# Courtiers

"I guess I'm intrigued about *her*. I mean, how do you treat a guy when you find out he's been cheating on you? If you're a princess, that is?" added Rick Vancy.

"Just the same as any other girl?" suggested Jemima. "Unless you choose to stab him with the sharp end of your tiara."

"But how is that?" persisted Rick. "We have to know this." He sounded worried. "Susanna, do you have anything on this?"

Susanna Blanding, researcher royal to TUS, her lap piled high with the memos, documents, notes, and the various thick red books emblazoned with gold without which she seemed unable to move, was crouched in the back seat of Rick Vancy's car behind Jemima. Curt, her American colleague, whose whole role as TUS researcher had become no more precise over the last few days, was asleep beside her. They were all four on their way to Cumberland Palace. Rick was speaking in a lull between the many telephone calls both incoming and outgoing which were deemed necessary during the comparatively short journey from Jemima's flat to the Palace.

Susanna Blanding did not answer.

"Soo-zee, I'm talk-ing to you," sang Rick in his

melodious baritone voice, the voice which was as much part of his image as his English-film-star looks. "Do you have anything on the kind of emotions which could be coming into play here? And Soo-zee, would you extinguish that cigarette?"

"Emotions, Rick?" panted Susanna, stubbing out the cigarette across Curt's recumbent body. Jemima wondered into what delightful reverie of eighteenth-century royal descent she had been plunged.

"Do you have anything relevant on Amy's emotional makeup? In confidence, maybe. Psychological reports? Doctors? Anything like that? Something to help us build up the correct picture of the way this young woman will respond to the unique pressures currently being imposed upon her. I guess I'm talking about strain here, Susanna. Strain and Amy's emotional stability."

"I could research you some nice mad royal ancestors if you like." Susanna Blanding spoke cautiously, feeling her way. "For example the old Russian Princess, Amy's grandmother, was always said to be absolutely bonkers. Ended up thinking she was an Alpine goat: always wore a little bell round her neck and loved climbing stairs."

Jemima took a quick look at Rick's face and decided to intervene speedily in the interests of Anglo-American accord.

"We don't exactly know he's been cheating on her," she pointed out. "After all, he did have his clothes on."

"C'mon sweetheart—where clothes are concerned—" But perhaps fortunately Rick's rejoinder was cut off by the high loud bleeping of another incoming telephone call.

As they were slowing down for the small black

police post at the entrance to the Palace drive, a slight young man in horn-rim glasses walking a dog could be seen parallel to them on the pavement. The dog, which had a vaguely bulldoggish aspect, lurched silently into the centre of the road, causing Rick to brake violently. Susanna Blanding bumped her nose and lost her papers. Curt woke up.

"Noel, Noel!" came the high well-modulated voice of the dog's owner. The young man patted his cowering animal and glared at the inhabitants of the car as if dogs not cars traditionally occupied the tarmac thoroughfare.

"Dogs should be banned from urban conurbations!" exclaimed Rick; Jemima thought his unusual irritability was probably due to the ordeal ahead, something outside his usual experience of war-stained statesmen. "Do you know the figures on city-centre animal-related disease in children?"

"Daddy won't let Sabrina—that's my sister—bring Emma—that's her dog—to London," contributed Susanna, anxious to restore herself to Rick Vancy's favour.

Cumberland Palace had a placid air of early Georgian elegance. Its low wall abutting Regent's Park (on which Tom and Beagle had once plastered the words AMY MEANS TROUBLE) was now free from any such excrescence. In its graceful sylvan setting, green lawns surrounding, the plash of oars on a lake heard nearby, this might have been a mansion in a country park; as it was its look of *rus in urbe* made the outer serenity especially delightful to behold.

The inner serenity of the Palace, in so far as it had ever existed, was however at this moment markedly disturbed.

Over the heads of the royal couple, Ione Quentin's

eyes met those of Major Pat Smylie-Porter. The Major gazed steadily back at her without visible sign of either worry or exasperation, both of which would have been amply justified by the distressing circumstances in which the urbane Major Pat currently found himself. Nevertheless the steady look that passed between the two courtiers indicated that they understood each other perfectly; the situation, in a favourite cliché passed round Cumberland Palace in recent days, was desperate but not serious. As veterans of many similar situations—if never admittedly *quite* so serious—the two of them found themselves experiencing a certain not unpleasant quickening of the pulse at the challenge to their powers thus presented.

Although neither the Major nor Ione would have dreamt of phrasing it like that, certainly not to each other, they were aware of being needed. Never more than at the present time. And Ione Quentin, unmarried at thirty-one, highly competent and professional at her job, which despite its old-fashioned title of "lady-in-waiting" often called for executive qualities, as though she was in fact the manager of a popular star—Amy being the star—the efficient self-controlled Ione Quentin liked to be needed. She knew that about herself.

Major Pat, looking at her one more moment before dropping his eyes and fixing his tie, thought involuntarily what a thoroughly good girl—woman really—Ione was. In Major Pat's opinion, Ione was very much Colonel Q's daughter beneath that ladylike exterior; although thank God she didn't look like the terrifying old boy (Major Pat's former commanding officer). Nor did she collect guns: Major Pat still remembered certain evenings in the Mess centring round Colonel Q's collection with an admiring shudder. . . . All the same, Ione had something of Colonel Q's celebrated resourcefulness.

To put it another way, in the present crisis, thank God he had Ione aboard. Somewhere at the back of Major Pat's mind was another unspoken thought that he would probably end by marrying Ione one day, the Major being a widower with two increasingly recalcitrant teenage children. Ione would be good with them, God knew, given what she had been through with that pathetic drop-out sister of hers. Now *she* took after the late and disastrous Mrs. Quentin. Lydia. Christ, would *she* have to live with them? . . .

Oddly enough in the same frozen moment, Ione's own thoughts had veered briefly, as they often did, to Lydia Quentin, a.k.a. Lamb. Lydia was staying out very late these days, nor had Ione, no fool, believed for one instant in the endless stories of cinemas with Janey, Melissa, Gaby and so on. Sadly, Ione knew too much about her sister. Something more would have to be done about Lydia. . . .

The moment passed. Both the Major and Ione devoted themselves once more to the issue in hand.

Although the cameras had already been set up in the large Vienna Drawing-Room (so-called for its relics of the Congress, imported by some Austrian ancestress) the couple were still seated in Amy's delicately furnished blue sitting-room.

"I want to see them," Princess Amy was saying mutinously, "I want to see the photographs. Otherwise I won't talk to the Press. Not to these Americans, not to anyone. I don't care." She stuck out her lower lip. Recent events had thinned her somewhat. She looked very pretty indeed in an Amy-blue dress with an enormous white sailor collar, the picture marred only by the expression on her pouting face, somewhere between adult fury and girlish sulks.

Prince Ferdinand rolled his eyes.

"Please darling, be reasonable," he began. Then he burst out: "You're being utterly childish."

"I'm being childish, am I?" Amy's voice rose. "And you're grown up, I suppose. And that ghastly woman, is she grown up too? Is that the point? Go on, say it."

A footman entered, dressed in the discreet dark-green semi-uniform of the Palace, adapted long ago by the Duke from his regimental dress. He bowed his neck in the same discreet traditional fashion. "Your Royal Highness, Mr. Richard Vancy and Miss Jemima Shore have arrived and are in the Vienna Drawing-Room."

"Ma'am, do you not think it would be a good idea to join them?" suggested Ione in her agreeable, low voice.

Princess Amy looked at her, her expression was at its most Hanoverian, once again recalling her late father. Suddenly she stood up and gave a wide, ravishing smile. The sulky face was transformed, the pout totally vanished.

"Let's go then," she said. "On your heads be it."

"And what is that supposed to mean, my love?" enquired the Prince in a voice of barely suppressed *ennui* as he rose to his feet. Major Pat thought that the Prince's sudden passionate wish to find himself a million miles away from this wayward girl, instead of being committed to marry her within weeks, was only too apparent.

"I was thinking of the threats made by those Animal Rights people," replied Princess Amy, giving him a special smile, which was almost seraphic in its sweetness. "That's all. Come along, darling."

The Princess undoubtedly looked wonderful as she swayed out of the room on Ferdel's arm, although her high white heels hardly brought her up to her fiancé's shoulder. At the same time, Ione, seeing that particular expression, that glint in the royal blue eyes, feared something, without knowing quite what it might be.

The royal couple entered the Vienna Drawing-Room, dominated by the huge early nineteenth-century portrait of dancers at some grand ball held at the Congress, just as Jemima had finished explaining patiently to Rick Vancy: "I curtsey modestly off camera because I'm British, and you don't bow on or off camera." She wanted to add: "Because you're a genuine American republican democrat quite uninterested in the doings of British Royalty—which only leaves unclear what your television station is doing here in the first place." Instead she added: "I'll begin with 'Your Royal Highnesses' leaving you to continue the interview with 'Prince Ferdinand' or 'Princess Amy.' None of this makes you—or me for that matter—a courtier."

"The picture I have is that we're all courtiers here," Rick responded with something less than his usual urbanity.

"Trust me," murmured the (American) producer of the show yearningly, as she had indeed been murmuring yearningly at intervals since the project of the interview was first discussed.

Then Rick visibly cheered up at the sight of Princess Amy whose enchanting friendly smile, no less than her nubile figure, filled him with sudden hopes of achieving the first really *truly* informal interview with British Royalty. . . . Fergie was not a precedent. Remember after all that the Duchess of York, another lady with a nubile figure and an enchanting friendly smile, was not exactly Royalty to the palace born, having been actually born a commoner, a term which Susanna Blanding had recently dinned into his head. Unhesitatingly Rick Vancy dismissed from his mind all the many other really truly informal royal interviews: this and only this would be the one where the British Royals would be speaking as you have never heard them before, to coin the phrase that TUS would undoubtedly be using to promote it. After all no royal couple that he'd ever heard of (not Prince Charles and Princess Diana—another 'commoner' in Susanna's phrase; not Prince Andrew and Fergie, well, not exactly) had been threatened with recent scandalous pictures of him and her, her in this case being a naked film star. . . . Under the circumstances Princess Amy *had* to show herself yet more informal than anyone in the history of royal informality. As for Prince Ferdinand . . .

As the Prince and Princess entered, Rick stood up. Jemima Shore gave her discreet curtsey and Susanna Blanding a curtsey which was both deeper and less graceful. To his discomfiture, Rick Vancy found himself instinctively starting to bend a knee with them: he compromised by giving a bow which was at least less ludicrous (and anyway the whole thing was off camera).

It was not until late on in the interview that the incident took place. By this time indeed the American producer was congratulating herself that the material would in fact need remarkably little editing before transmission, scheduled to be networked later that day in the States, making it an evening show in England.

Princess Amy gave vent to a series of unexceptional views on such matters as the family ("I love children, little children, I love my sisters' children, they're going to be our bridesmaids, I'm sure I'll love my children"—laughter—blush—"our children"), and the man's position ("I love the idea of the man being the head of the family like they always have been, haven't they? It's traditional, isn't it? Although I'm also very very modern, aren't I, Ferdel?" Laughter, blush and even perhaps a slight pout). On being questioned about her new life in her fiancé's country, however, she declared more positively: "I'm not just going to stick in the country and be a cabbage, that would be utterly drear." (Sweet sidelong look at Ferdel, but a hint of steel here, too, thought Jemima: it was the first indication she had had that there might be more to Princess Amy than this pretty piglet in her pretty blue dress with its ruffled white collar.) Prince Ferdinand for his part declared himself, equally impeccably, as looking forward to introducing Amy to her new country. "And you will make a very pretty cabbage, darling—ouch—" So Amy followed what was presumably a royal pinch with a royal kiss on the cheek. At the same time Ferdel also stressed his English ancestry, his English schooldays, his English tastes—"This shirt is English," he told Rick Vancy, having observed that Rick was wearing a shirt from the same shirtmaker in St. James's. "Except for the coronet. That is not English."

Ferdel even remembered, as an afterthought and tribute to the programme's origins, to point out his many links with the United States, including a year at an American university. Currently there were what he pleasantly described as "sporting and business links"; but neither Rick on behalf of TUS nor the Prince himself, on his own behalf, saw any reason to give further prominence to what these links might be; even if in some publicly unacknowledged way, they had been responsible for the exclusive interview in the first place. Amy, he felt, would certainly enjoy the States with its friendly people. . . .

It was left to Amy, extracting what was seen to be a sweet revenge for the cabbage episode, to exclaim: "How fabulous! I'm *so* looking forward to seeing America! Now you've promised to take me, in front of all these cameras." The cameras (in fact only two of them) recorded and the American producer passed Jemima a white card: I.D. WHEN AND WHERE VISIT. But this the Prince smilingly declined to do.

Because matters had really gone so swimmingly, if not exactly excitingly, neither Rick, Jemima, the producer, nor, least of all Prince Ferdinand was prepared for Amy's sudden departure from the not-exactly-scripted, but not-exactly-not-scripted either, shape of the interview. Only Ione Quentin might perhaps have warned them that something was afoot. But Ione, seated at the back of the drawing-room with Susanna Blanding, had retreated to that ladylike obscurity which her office guaranteed for her on these occasions.

"Oh, but I do have lots of views of my own," exclaimed Amy airily as Jemima was questioning her concerning her wardrobe.

"Princess Amy, would you say that you are highly clothes-conscious? Or do you more or less leave it to the designers?"

"For example I feel very strongly about animals, and things like that," continued Princess Amy, leaning forward slightly; she sounded a little more breathless perhaps than previously, and her blue eyes were wide open, otherwise there was nothing to indicate the totally unexpected nature of her response. "And where clothes are concerned, I hate fur coats, don't you? I hate things like that. I think there ought to be a Fur Law, now how about that? People jolly well shouldn't be allowed to wear fur coats. And then there's experimenting on animals and horrid things like that, it shouldn't be allowed, should it? Now what about a law about that too? I mean, it's us who take all the pills and medicines and things like that, not the poor animals, so why not experiment on us instead of—" Princess Amy's eyes roved round and in a moment of inspiration, fell upon Happy and Boobie, lying slumbering magnificently on the Savonnerie carpet in front of the fireplace. "Instead of those poor old doggies." Out of excitement or pity, Amy's voice broke. "Too, too cruel," she concluded.

About the same moment, another white card from the producer had reached Jemima's side of the table, with something similar in front of Rick. KEEP GOING read Jemima's card, continuing optimistically THIS MUST BE PLANNED. Rick's card read: ASK RE PALACE BLOOD DEMO.

"Your Royal Highness," began Rick excitedly, democracy thrown to the winds in the new and invigorating atmosphere of a scoop: "Now regarding your very warm and human feelings concerning animal rights, there was, was there not, a demonstration not so long ago—"

But by this time, Prince Ferdinand, leaning forward, had picked up his fiancée's small white hand with its gleaming aquamarine ring, and was gving it a distinctly continental kiss: "I love you for your

compassion for all wild things," said the Prince
seriously. "You will love your new country where
there is so much work to be done in this direction."
His eyes met hers, a shot which subsequently fascinated all those who pored over it at TUS later. Was it
a look of princely command to which she responded?
Was the whole thing set up to avoid the tiresome
nuisance of those banned photographs marring the
wedding? How had Prince Ferdel persuaded Princess
Amy to do, in effect, his dirty work for him? Since the
photographs involved him not her. All these questions remained unanswered at TUS.

But that was later. At the time the TUS team
allowed themselves to be dismissed courteously,
more or less as arranged, with a few final platitudes
about "wishing you both every happiness," a few
final curtseys from Jemima and Susanna Blanding,
and a final bow from Rick (he reckoned they'd earned
it). Only Curt and the American producer remaining
sternly unbowed and uncurtseyed; but then since
Curt had taken no active part whatsoever in the
entire proceedings, his lack of gesture at least was not
necessarily to be interpreted in any positive fashion.

Nevertheless the unvoiced tension, at least on the
part of Rick and Jemima, as they drove away from
the Palace, was considerable. As was the surprise and
the excitement.

"There's that man with the funny-looking dog
again, the one that nearly got itself killed," remarked
Jemima by the way of light relief.

It was true: Fox and Noel, who had in fact been
circling the Palace anxiously during the duration of
the interview, had come to rest once more at their
previous observation post by the Palace drive. Noel
was manifestly exhausted: to tell the truth, the dog,

unlike his master, was not a great walker and would in dog terms probably have agreed with Rick Vancy's irritable remarks that dogs should be banned from urban conurbations, since that meant master-led long city walks instead of more leisurely solitary country rambles. But Fox's excitement at the prospect of the revolutionary programme which was being enunciated within the white walls of the Palace, had meant he had been unable to keep himself—and Noel—away.

Somewhere in the distance the bark of sea-lions from the Zoo caused Jemima to think of Louis Mac-Neice and murmur poetically: "Smell of French bread in Charlotte Square." This in turn caused Susanna Blanding to say: "I'm terribly hungry. That, or I must have a cigarette," and Rick to suggest that they talked the whole thing through at Le Caprice. (Curt, with his enviable capacity for relaxation, had fallen asleep again.)

"Isn't that dynamite we have there with all that animals lib talk from *her*?" he remarked as he dialled the Caprice number on the car phone. "Connections to the French lady only too easy to establish. Say, maybe *he* gets turned on by animals—"

"Maybe so, but it bothers me," confessed Jemima. "Why did the Palace—predictably—say no statement from them along the Innoright lines, we don't give in to blackmail etc. etc.? And then she made it. Whose plot was it, his, theirs—or hers?"

"Or those courtiers," suggested Rick, "those background figures, royal anchors, I guess."

"Not Ione Quentin!" exclaimed Susanna in a shocked voice from the back seat. "She's an absolute *pillar*. So's Major Pat. Still, you never know with the Palace. They can be awfully wily."

"If it was her idea," pursued Jemima. "Why? That's what I want to know. Why do it?"

A few hours later when the programme "Prince and Princess of Hearts" was being shown nationwide on British television, members of the Innoright cell who were watching it together, would echo the words of Jemima Shore more or less exactly.

"Why?" cried Lamb. "When they said they wouldn't."

"She said it—well, more or less," Fox sounded bemused.

"She did not," that was Pussy, four square.

The rest of the country turned their sets off with contented clicks.

"Listen to that, Kenneth," said Mrs. Taplow to her husband as they sat in their Eaton Square kitchen. "HRH has turned out very nicely after all, I couldn't have put it better myself about loving animals."

"Couldn't you, Lizzie? Are you sure?"

Mrs. Taplow gave him a sharp look, then addressed herself once more to polishing the Prince's already exquisitely shiny leather shoes.

"You'd better get on with that, Kenneth," she said after a moment; she spoke equably enough. "Otherwise it will never be ready." She pointed to some embroidery on the table: a royal crest was in the process of being created from silk and beads; it had the air of an intended wedding present. Taplow sighed but he obeyed her and picked up the embroidery; once he was immersed in its intricate design, however, his expression relaxed.

The Innoright members had no soothing tasks to which to turn.

"What do we do now?" Chicken turned to Monkey

who was still gazing stolidly at the blank television screen.

"We go on with the Underground Plan," replied Monkey sombrely. "We don't release the photographs but we go on with the Plan. Mark Two. That wasn't the statement we asked for, the reasoned statement, that was just an outburst from an hysterical girl."

"Grab her," said Beagle with a laugh. "Grab her all the same. She deserves it." He laughed again. "I deserve it."

Lamb, who tended to feel cold since her illness, experienced a special chill within her.

# TWELVE

# St. Francis

"You're not really expecting anything to happen?" enquired Jemima of Pompey over their respective "jars" (white wine and whisky) in Jemima's secluded top-floor flat overlooking Holland Park. He had dropped in for an early drink on the way back from work to Mrs. Pompey: his pretext being that Jemima needed a little off-the-record background briefing on security arrangements for the wedding.

"From our point of view something *has* happened," pointed out Pompey: but his relaxed tone was not one that Detective Sergeant Vaillant, for example, would have recognized. "A man was killed and we're not much nearer solving the case," he added. "One or two things have come up of course: there's a man with a dog. At the Republican, *with* the bloody dog that afternoon except they wouldn't let him in without a fuss. Said he was a humble fan of Princess Amy, always tried to follow her public appearances from *The Times*, nothing wrong with that, was there?"

"And was there? A good many people are like that."

"True. But this man had once been a member of Innoright, resigned when there was some fuss about the very same unwelcome dog. We had some leads

141

on him; small, of restricted growth I should say, works on and off for Leaviss"—he mentioned the name of one of the leading theatrical costumiers— "non-violent, or so we believe, but loves to distribute anti-vivisection posters in the most awkward places. Could well have been intending to do so at the Republican if the dog hadn't scuppered his plan."

"The dagger—paper knife—is odd, Pompey. It didn't *have* to be someone at the Press Conference, did it? Quite a few of them of course."

"Quite a few paperknives, too. And anyone could have helped themselves to the kit, including paper knife, after the conference began. Knives and kits not picked up remained at the checking-in desk. By then empty. Your Americans must all have had knives."

"I'm currently using mine. Useful for dealing with royal memoranda from our industrious English researcher." Jemima picked it up from the table in front of her and felt the point. "Yes, bit of a mistake in manufacture, that. Very sharp indeed. Rick has presented his to the aforesaid industrious researcher, who claims to have buried hers somewhere in her historical files. Curt, the silent American, uses his to pick his teeth; when he's awake, that is."

Jemima, discussing the new details of the case, thought how she had developed an excellent if unacknowledged working relationship with Pompey since their first association (over a television appeal for a missing child).

Jemima was tacitly allowed to give vent to her natural inquisitiveness by discussing those details of a case that Pompey found it discreet to reveal over a "jar" (as a matter of fact not a few). Pompey on the other hand was a man on whom life with the hardworking albeit whimsical Vaillant sometimes palled.

Besides, as he put it, the necessarily hothouse atmosphere of the incident room could also produce "a wood for the trees" situation. In these moods he welcomed Jemima's proffered "jars"; including contact with her aforesaid inquisitiveness.

It was true that Jemima's famous "woman's instinct" was the subject of many traditional jokes between them in which Pompey gave way to heavy gallantry while defending the superior role of patient relentless investigation in the solution of a murder case. Jemima for her part generously allowed Pompey to term it a "woman's instinct" from long usage (furthermore it did not do to argue overmuch with a contact). Nevertheless she contended strongly that the famous instinct was in fact no more than the thought process of a reasonable human being—not necessarily female.

"What about his own private life? Nothing there? Although I agree it's odd that whoever killed him should choose such a bizarre occasion as a Royal Press Conference if there was no connection. Odd or cunning."

"Lamentably respectable," replied Pompey. "Unmarried. Not gay but no regular girlfriend. Several he took out confirm that."

"That's *too* respectable," said Jemima firmly.

"He took out that woman who's working for you once or twice, the writer who goes on history quizzes on the telly; Mrs. Pompey likes her. Nothing in it, however." In case Pompey should have seemed to imply that Mrs. Pompey's taste had corrupted his official judgement, he added quickly: "We checked it out. Talked to her."

"She didn't tell *me*," thought Jemima. "But then, why should she? Besides, Susanna Blanding's attention at present is equally divided between the Cumberland family tree and Rick Vancy."

"Then the woman Moscowitz—remember I told you about her? Going to sleep in the lounge with dead-as-a-doornail Schwarz-Albert lying there all along? We've checked her out, naturally. Seems her daughter was a well-known model who died in a rather hideous car crash. Caro Moss. Very beautiful, rather weird. Decapitated."

"Ugh. I remember the case." Jemima also remembered Caro Moss from the famous advertisements for health foods: an exquisite giraffe-like girl gazing up at a real-life giraffe munching leaves from a tree: "Since I can't reach a tree," ran the wistful faintly accented voice-over.

"Mother made a scene at the inquest, and again when the male driver was not sentenced to prison, only a fine."

"One can hardly blame her," Jemima reflected. "No chance that Schwarz-Albert was the driver of the car and Mrs. M the lurking figure of vengeance from the past, as in an Agatha Christie?"

"No chance at all", replied Pompey coldly, who, unlike Jemima, did not retain a strong worship of Agatha Christie. "Naturally we checked that out. Caro Moss's slaughterer—manslaughterer—is alive and well elsewhere." He added with a return to joviality: "So what does your woman's instinct say?"

"My perfectly good *reasoning* powers," riposted Jemima, "suggest that it isn't a coincidence your chap was killed at the Republican and at the conference. Someone took a risk—because it was a risk worth taking. Or because they didn't have another good opportunity. Yes, that must be it."

Seeing that Pompey's brows were still drawn together at the mention of Agatha Christie, Jemima decided to return to the subject of the Royal Wedding. "My question meant: are you—or they— expecting something to happen at the wedding itself?"

Since Pompey did not choose to answer, Jemima pressed on: "Did you see the story in the *Exclusive*?: A CITY PREPARES. Plus a lot of stuff about offices along the route being secretly commandeered. Either for some secret hidden marksmen. Or to prevent terrorists getting there first, it wasn't quite clear which. Some maps and photographs of likely angles. Explanations of how specially vulnerable this route is because it isn't the usual one from Clarence House or Buckingham Palace. The bride has to come from Regent's Park and they both go to the Palace for the wedding breakfast. Then Westminster Cathedral is bang in the middle of Victoria Street. A busy place. Lots of offices. Not cut off at the end like Westminster Abbey."

"A CITY PREPARES indeed! It certainly loses nothing in the telling," was Pompey's comment. "That sort of thing only encourages the buggers of course: gives them some bright ideas about the weak links along the route, I always think. But what can you expect? In spite of their reputation Special Branch adore publicity. Always sneakily talking to the Press . . ."

Pompey seemed fortunately unaware just with whom he was sitting at the time of this less than generous comment concerning his colleagues.

"Am I naive in assuming the IRA are not interested since this is a Catholic wedding?" queried Jemima.

"It seems that Royal Weddings in general leave them cold," grunted Pompey. Was he showing signs of sharing the feelings of the IRA on this issue if no other?

"I seem to remember that they made a statement to that effect at the time of Prince Andrew's bash. Unlike the rest of the world who get keener and keener. Has Mrs. Pompey—"

"She has, God bless her. Red, white, and blue begonias. I planted them out at eleven o'clock last night. Ouch." He winced.

"I went along the route today on a recce. And to the Cathedral with my American pals. Saw some very fine begonias on the way." But Pompey only winced again as if in sympathy with fellow planters throughout London.

"A CITY PREPARES. More than one way of preparing," was all he said.

Jemima had been well aware that it was necessary for her to follow the royal route if she was to be able to provide U.S. audiences, sleepily awakening to this archaic British ceremony, with enough entrancing anecdotes to make it worth their while. TUS had provided a cheerful English driver named Harry but Jemima chose to sit in the back seat with Susanna Blanding. The latter sat with her head bowed over a clipboard, occasionally looking out of the window in order to reconcile passing buildings with her notes. Rick sat in the front seat (there was no sign of Curt, whose absence Rick explained rather vaguely along the lines of, "I guess the guy slept late").

Unfortunately the comments of cheerful Harry— with which he had been enlightening tourists for years, so he told them—were somewhat at variance with those of Susanna. Nor did she accept the variance tamely. Rick had asked her not to smoke in the car, a prohibition which she had accepted but which undoubtedly increased her professional irritability.

"Queen Elizabeth II was *not* born at Number One London," she explained indignantly at one point. "Number One London is Apsley House, home of the Duke of Wellington as I would have thought absolutely anyone knew." Susanna scowled at the driver's back.

"You win some, you lose some," was all Harry said in reply, infuriatingly jovial. "Any of you ladies like to know the origin of the Wellington Boot?"

Rick in the front seat moved restlessly: there was no telephone in the car, an administrative error he was determined should not be repeated.

"A lot of flat roofs round here," he said suddenly. "Susy sweetheart," Rick turned round and gazed tenderly into her earnest face. "Could you hold on that historical stuff for the time being? We have a security situation here that I'd like to talk through with Jemima."

"Of course, Rick." Susanna subsided. This confirmed Jemima's fear that Rick's handsome face and agreeable tones were making Susanna's heart beat significantly faster; it was noticeable that Susanna pardoned in Rick an almost total lack of interest in British history which she would have found unforgivable in anyone else.

"For instance, do you have some good assassination stuff there?" Since he was still looking at Susanna, it was she who answered, albeit hesitantly.

"Do you want historical assassinations? I can do you William the Silent. The Duke of Guise. That sort of thing. I'm afraid they do tend to be men, by the way. Unfortunately women weren't often assassinated in those underprivileged days." As Jemima wryly noticed the principles of sexual equality being applied even in this unlikely area, Susanna continued more brightly: "There was the Empress Elizabeth of Austria, of course—now she was assassinated. That was a good one. And it so happens that Prince Ferdinand himself is descended—"

"No, Susy, no." The melodious tenderness was in danger of wearing thin.

"I take it you want the Roman Catholic Cathedral," interrupted Harry, not necessarily out of any sense of diplomacy. "See the spire if you duck and crane your head. Its exact height is—"

Rick Vancy found his fingers itching for a telephone to transport him to a wider world.

Just as Harry swung the large dark-blue car into the road leading to the Cathedral's piazza, Susanna gave a little squeak.

"Look! The Guards! Dressed up for rehearsal! Their history is absolutely fascinating—" She looked nervously at Rick's back. But even Rick was murmuring approvingly: "Great pageantry."

Suddenly to Jemima the scarlet-coated guards, their heavy cuirasses and plumed helmets gleaming in the sun, the jangling bridles and sweating flanks of the huge black horses, spoke not of pageantry—nor of history—but of violence and threat. Once upon a time men dressed like this or something like this, had ridden to battle to ride down other men dressed similarly. Now their role was apparently merely ceremonial: the visible guarding of the monarchy on occassions of official pageantry. Plus various clanking trots applauded by tourist London. Yet not so long ago men like this had died in London itself in an outbreak of terrorist bombing. Someone took the ceremonial sufficiently seriously to blow them to bits.

Horses like this had suffered an even worse fate if you took the line that the horses had not voluntarily enlisted in the service of the State. . . . And if the horses and guards were worth sacrificing, what price the equally ceremonial figures that they guarded?

As Rick observed in a most melodious voice: "Where pageantry is concerned, the rest of the world is over the hill compared to you Brits." Jemima shivered.

The lofty twilight interior of the great Byzantine-style cathedral, with its glinting mosaics and towering bands of green and rose marble, came as a relief. Jemima's morbid thoughts vanished as she observed with interest the considerable quantity of people—worshippers, tourists?—moving at some speed through the various aisles. It was four o'clock on a weekday afternoon. It was not just the advancing priests in their traditional long black vestments or the busy nuns (whose short skirts and briefly veiled, mainly uncovered hair would have been witnessed with horror by Jemima's old headmistress Mother Ancilla). There were quite as many lay people bustling about and the judicious development of the Catholic Church since Jemima's schooldays (a Protestant, she had attended a Catholic school) was attested by a large exhibition of photographs concerning relief in the third world.

"Good heavens, there's my cousin Lydia Quentin," exclaimed Susanna. "I didn't know she was a Catholic these days. Still I wouldn't put it past her. I wouldn't put anything past Lydia. Poor Ione, that's Princess Amy's lady-in-waiting, you know her, the ever calm one, she's had a ghastly time with Lydia. Ever since her father died, the famous Colonel Q, you've probably heard of him, *terrifying*! But rather marvellous. Then the house and everything had to be sold. What with that and her mother, Lydia picks up with the most terrible people—Moonies, Trots, people like that. Then Ione has to come and rescue her." Susanna had on her important voice with which she generally imparted historical information. "Now I suppose it's subversive nuns."

Jemima gazed at a distinctly thin and rather pale girl. There was some resemblance to Ione Quentin, not only because both had dark hair; but where Ione radiated quiet strength, one would scarcely suppose that this frail creature possessed any strength at all. Cousin Susanna, with her sturdy frame, was a third version of the same model.

In one of the side chapels, behind a silver grille with its gates open, Lydia Quentin was kneeling as though in prayer in front of a large mosaic picture. Banks of little yellow candles twinkled on a stand outside. There was no nun, subversive or otherwise, to be seen. In fact Lydia Quentin was kneeling in a row with several other people and there were further people bent in prayer behind her. It struck Jemima that this was an especially popular shrine. The next door chapels were empty. Given the fact that their lips were moving in prayer, it occurred to her that this little group, if it was a group, might be taking part in some communal novena. Which said, the afternoon was an odd time for it to take place.

Jemima knew she should really be concentrating on the interior of the cathedral. This was her opportunity since TUS like all other foreign stations would not be allowed to have a camera inside the cathedral on the day itself. TUS would be obliged to take the BBC coverage with their own commentary superimposed as necessary. The TUS team would thus be installed in a specially built studio overlooking the piazza. All the same, curiosity—or perhaps even the famous instinct to which Pompey sometimes gallantly alluded—drove Jemima to investigate this popular or populated chapel further. The mosaic showed a man in monk's clothing, his hands outstretched, a group of birds perched upon them.

This must be the chapel of St. Francis. White marble lettering surrounded by an acanthus border confirmed the fact. A rather less elegant wooden box nearby had a slit for donations and for candles (there was a large heap of candles in another box on the floor). Jemima wondered why she persisted in feeling the kneeling people were united in some common cause. The empty chapel next door was dedicated to St. Paul; perhaps St. Francis was more in keeping with the spirit of the times than St. Paul. But then, further down, the chapel of St. Patrick was empty too and it could certainly be argued that St. Patrick had kept up with the times. For a moment she had even thought they were talking to each other instead of praying—which was absurd.

Lydia Quentin for example was kneeling next to a young man in a T-shirt with some conventionally protesting slogan on it. She was now gazing intensely in front of her. The young man turned his head and briefly his eyes met those of Jemima. There was no recognition in them although Jemima, with her distinctive colouring, apart from anything else, was used to the surprised flicker which the public sometimes accorded her, springing from the true late twentieth-century familiarity of television. Oddly enough, in this case it was Jemima who felt she might have seen the man somewhere before . . . some-

where recently . . . the wedding . . . what was
it . . . the memory nagged at her and vanished.

It was fortunate that the man known to his fellow
worshippers as Beagle was a sufficiently common
type for there to be no certainty.

"Nosy bitch," said Beagle in a low voice. "If you'll
pardon my language in this house of prayer. Jemima
Shore Investigator as ever is. Not satisfied with that
interview and all that royal rubbish."

"Do you know her?" asked Chicken, kneeling on
the other side of Beagle.

"I sat next to her at the Press Conference. I came in
late. She won't remember. And even if she does—
what's *she* doing here I want to know?"

"Same as us, I dare say," murmured Chicken drily.

"Not *quite* the same as us, I hope, dear." Pussy
shifted the parcel at her feet and plunged her face
once more into her hands.

Of the members of the Innoright cell, only Monkey
was a practising Catholic. It was Monkey, with his
usual sense of planning suffused with irony, who had
suggested the cathedral for a meeting place, and the
statue of St. Francis, patron saint of animals, for the
rendezvous.

"The Church. Another place where anyone sits
next to anyone, as you put it, my dear Miss Lamb.
Like the Underground."

Fox, however, if not actually a Catholic (he had
never been officially converted) was a man of romantic temperament who, in his single life with Noel,
often dropped into Soho churches. He was not exactly seeking God, more enjoying the incense and
music and above all admiring the vestments—a bus-
man's holiday from his own work. When had he not
loved costumes, dressing-up? It was a passion rooted

deep in his unhappy childhood. Fox however had not turned his head at Jemima's approach. He took the opportunity of the respite to pray, a frequent prayer that he would somehow die with Noel; Noel who had been parked, panting, outside many churches and was in fact waiting panting outside the cathedral now.

Chicken, raised as an Anglican, had long ago abandoned that wishy-washy religion as she saw it, for a single-minded adherence to her campaign for the rights of the innocent. She felt marginally uncomfortable in her present Catholic situation but as a disciplined person, she was used to putting up with such things in the cause of Innoright. Pussy on the other hand, although she literally detested the Catholic Church for daring to state that animals unlike slaughtering, meat-gorging humans, had no souls, had been raised by a Polish Catholic mother. She thus slumped down easily in her pew, crossed herself quite naturally and in general looked much like all the other middle-aged women with shopping bags scattered round the cathedral.

Jemima Shore wandered away to rejoin Susanna and Rick. Monkey was the last person to catch her eye: this was because this prosperous-looking person, conventionally dressed, appeared to be praying aloud.

"So, ladies and gentlemen of Innoright, fellow animals—" began Monkey again. Even a simulated prayer, Monkey's voice was sonorous.

It was some hours after this that Jemima, pouring another whisky for Pompey as she described her recce, remembered where she had seen Beagle. The recollection, including the group of disparate worshippers at the shrine of St. Francis—St. Francis, patron saint of animals, animal love, interesting that, there seemed to be a lot of it about, even within the cathedral's precincts—the recollection did not then seem important enough to relate. But it did seem important enough to file away in her memory, like one small piece of the mosaic on the cathedral walls. She thought of saying to Pompey: "What was the photographer called? The one who was a friend of the murdered man? The one with the alibi?" That too would wait, if not for ever.

Thus it was part of her general thought process on the subject of the Princess, her security, and the past threat posed by Innoright, that she observed aloud to Pompey: "They're at the opera tonight. I shall have to throw you out in order to get ready for Covent Garden. Royal Gala!"

"You to your garden and I to mine," observed Pompey wistfully.

"Still, they'll be safe enough at the opera," said Jemima.

# THIRTEEN

# Evening in
# a Good Cause

Against the red velvet frame of the box, Monkey looked both substantial and dignified in his white tie and tails. Moreover the crackling white waistcoat stretched smoothly over his broad chest unlike those of some of his contemporaries, sorted out from disuse for the occasion of the Royal Gala. But Monkey was used to white-tied City dinners; he was also used to benefits in aid of good causes of which the present Royal Gala might seem to be just one more example. Monkey even sported on his chest a minor medal incurred for philanthropic work and donations—in another life before Innoright.

For Monkey, however, it was not just one more evening in a good cause. Or not in the sense that the world generally would understand the phrase. The presence of Lamb beside him, thin shoulders peering out of a plain pale-pink satin dress with shoestring straps, signified that. Lamb herself was as appropriately dressed as Monkey. If her dress was slightly dowdy, an unusual lotus pattern diamond circlet sat upon her dark head. Ione Quentin, who had lent the dress (as a lady-in-waiting, she had numbers of such inconspicuous long dresses available, this one being cut sufficiently straight to accommodate Lamb's much slimmer figure) had also insisted on Lamb wearing the tiara.

"Mum's tiara," said Lamb doubtfully, weighing it in her hand. The box in which the circlet had been housed was ancient battered red morocco, and the red velvet interior, unlike that of the Covent Garden box, distinctly shabby. But the diamonds shone in all their yellowish eighteenth-century lustre. "I thought you usually wore it at this kind of bash."

"P.A. won't mind. P.A. won't *notice*." Ione, as so often with her sister, was determinedly cheerful. "She's the veritable star of the show this evening. No other Royals going. Well, one or two royal-ish ones. The younger lot. But P.A. outranks them all. The Duchess, who frankly loathes the opera, has got one of her frequent convenient illnesses. P.A. loves that, of course; after all the Gala is for her—him too, naturally. Even if it was all rather last minute, slotted into the schedule. I told you."

"Yes, you told me." Lamb continued to weigh the tiara as though it represented a subject she was weighing up in her mind.

"Go on, Leelee, put it on." Ione used the name from their childhood as she seldom did nowadays; it seemed to upset Lydia, reminding her of their mother who had never called her anything else. "Besides it will help me to keep an eye on you. Also, I want to see what's his name. What *is* his name? The dirty old man who's taking you."

"He's not a dirty old man." Suddenly Lamb wore her intense look, the one that made Ione's heart sink, and Ione cursed herself. "He's a very fine person who does a lot of good in the world, unlike all your lot with their show-off jewels. Princess Amy should meet *him* instead of that awful Gala committee. Do you know how much suffering—"

"But darling, it was a joke. I'm sure P.A. would *love* to meet him. You *said* he was a DOM, do you remember?" Ione hastily retrieved the tiara from Lamb's agitated hands and replaced it in the shabby box. "And anyway I looked him up and saw that he married a sister of Mum's friend, Penelope, my godmother; wife deceased; no children; never remarried. So I said he must be looking for a young wife and you said, no, that's not what he's looking for, a wife, he's a Dirty Old Man. It was a joke," concluded Ione patiently.

In the end Lamb wore the tiara. Ever since her illness she often did what people wanted in small things in order to save her energies for resistance when it really mattered. Lamb smiled to herself as she allowed Ione to fasten it on. She thought she might sell the tiara and give the money to Innoright. After everything was over. Then what would clever Nonie do? The tiara had after all been left to them jointly. Ione saw the smile on her sister's sad little face and was not reassured.

It would undoubtedly have surprised Lamb to learn that Ione's supposition concerning Mr. Edward James Arthur Monck MBE's intentions were not really so wide of the mark. Or perhaps fantasies would be a better word than intentions. As Major Pat Smylie-Porter sometimes confidently dreamt of the day when he would marry Ione Quentin, Edward Monck also secretly dreamt from time to time of taking her sister as a second wife. He would review the years without his beloved Cynthia, she who had been so very different (not only physically) from

Lamb and whose pointless death of an embolism during a minor operation had driven him on his first steps down the path of obsession. First making money—what else was there to do?—then giving it away—what else was there to do with it? Cynthia had left no children—finally Innoright, his own protest against a cruel world, and the Underground Plan, its supreme expression.

His mission accomplished, the Underground Plan accomplished, might he not allow himself at last the indulgence of a second bride, a child wife, one who would combine in those two things, two attributes so long missing from his life?

Tonight was not the night for such dreams. Edward Monck a.k.a. Monkey, took one more quick look at Lamb's pale skin glimpsed above the smooth satin which virtually matched it and pointed his thoughts back sternly to the matter in hand.

At that moment there was a hush then a rustle in the audience. The starched white waistcoats crackled as their inhabitants struggled to their feet. Long skirts were retrieved uncomfortably from beneath the next-door seat. Like animals feeding together, who turn their heads in unison at a sudden noise, the whole audience now craned in one direction.

Princess Amy, a tiny shining figure, appeared in the Royal Box, in the centre of the right-hand tier of boxes facing the stage, followed by Prince Ferdinand, darkly handsome with the green sash of some appropriately Ruritanian order across his chest. While flunkeys in the flamboyant Opera House uniform were visibly hovering around them, the more discreet figures of Ione Quentin and Major Pat Smylie-Porter, the latter with several medals of a genuinely military nature on his chest as well as others gained in the royal service, could be discerned behind them.

Unlike Monkey and Lamb in their box on the opposite side, framed in red velvet alone, Princess Amy and Prince Ferdinand stood in a bower of blue flowers, swags cascading from the rim of the box itself, and great pilasters of blue surrounding them on either side. Was the blue a delicate tribute to Amy herself? But then speculation about such a comparatively minor matter as the flowers faded in favour of universally admiring exclamations concerning the Princess herself. Or rather almost universally admiring: an exception to the general chorus of admiration would have to be made in the case of Chicken and Pussy, sharing a second-tier box.

"Little Madam," said Pussy to Chicken, putting down her impressive-looking binoculars. Lately she had taken to using Fox's phrase for Amy, rolling it succulently on her tongue, in preference to her own "spoilt brat." "I believe that was a fur stole that was being stowed away at the back. And after what she said on television! They're all the same. Hypocrites. I'd like to give her one."

"You may soon have an opportunity," murmured Chicken drily. But her words, as she intended, were drowned by the sound of the National Anthem. Chicken, believing herself to be potentially far more ruthless than Pussy—in a good cause and at the right moment—disapproved of the latter's habit of indulging in such blatantly vicious talk. Chicken rustled the score which as an opera lover (if mainly on Radio 3) she had brought in order to calm her nerves. With her usual forethought Chicken had taken care to remove all personal marks from the score; nevertheless she was aware that if anyone cared to look closely with their own binoculars into what was in effect a corner balcony box, next to the stage itself, they might be surprised to see an Indian woman sedulously following the musical score.

For some at least of Pussy's ill temper and Chicken's irritation was caused by the unaccustomed style of dress in which both women were attired: Indian and bejewelled would be the best way of describing it. As a matter of fact, Chicken and Pussy, with the connivance and advice of Fox, looked surprisingly convincing. It was true that neither of them would be taken for the kind of lissom Maharani of popular imagination (or the *Heat and Dust* style of film). But Pussy's dour build and basically dark complexion had needed very little adaptation to give her the characteristic phlegmatic look of an Eastern female; Chicken presented at first sight more of a problem. But: "Nothing we can't overcome," Fox insisted; his enthusiasm making him suddenly seem stronger, more forceful—or perhaps he merely displayed something more of his real character. So Pussy in voluminous turquoise, Chicken in neater red, inhabited their eyrie and gazed—across, to the right and downwards—at Princess Amy in the Royal Box. An observer might also have noticed that there were only two people in a box meant for four; although of course the restricted balcony view made this a practical measure. But who looked into a balcony box on the night of a gala?

These dissentient voices apart, it was generally agreed at the time—not only afterwards when such a retrospective judgement became perhaps inevitable—that "little Amy" had never looked more beautiful. Expert analysis would indeed be needed to realize that what actually glittered at Amy's round white neck, at her little white ears, at the not inconsiderable cleft between her plump white breasts, and filleting her elaborately ringleted blonde hair, were the famous Russian sapphires belonging to Ferdel's great-grandmother (she who had or had not danced with Rasputin but had certainly known how to amass a wearable fortune in jewellery). Probably only Susanna Blanding, opera glasses trained, immediately recognized them for what they were. "The so-called 'Rasputin sapphires.' Unlucky?" she murmured to Curt, without expecting an answer from this normally comatose source.

At the time it was Amy herself, eyes shining in palpable triumph at the applause her appearance evoked, rather than the provenance of her *parure*, which aroused the happily startled gasps of admiration.

She raised her plump little white hand—no ring but the engagement one—in a gracious royal wave and said something to Prince Ferdinand.

Once again it would need expert analysis—from lip-readers—to reveal what Princess Amy actually said. Fortunately there were none present, despite the increasing employment of them at such events as royal weddings so that the avid public might share the last-minute thoughts—or even, daring hope, last-minute *second* thoughts of the latest bride.

It was fortunate there was no lip-reader present because what Amy actually said to Ferdel as she smiled and waved was: "You never told me that bitch was going to be here."

There had indeed been a moment of more than usual awkwardness—or a moment of highly enjoyable drama, depending on your point of view—when Mirabella Prey's large limousine, of hearse-like length in the American style, had swung in to the pavement in front of the Royal Opera House just as the royal car was expected. There was no doubt in the minds of the numerous cameramen present, both for the newspapers and television, that enjoyable drama was the way to look at it; these representatives of television including Rick Vancy and Jemima Shore for TUS (looking for some footage for their Wedding Special).

As their driver, jovial Harry, he of the TUS London tour, would exclaim appreciatively later to his mates: "Did you see her? Did you *see* her? Cor." He shook his curly head under its blue cap, leaving no doubt that what he—along with millions watching the TV news—had seen was a ringside view of Mirabella's magnificent body.

Surely even that body had never been seen to greater advantage—certainly not in Beagle's infinitely cruder nude photographs. Tonight Mirabella's spangled white crêpe dress paid no more than a graceful tribute to the idea of concealing her small high breasts. In other places the dress was stretched so tight that the two slits on either side of the skirt revealed not only those celebrated long legs but also delicious brown thighs: the slits at least could be justified by the need to manoeuvre out of the car, which would otherwise have been quite impossible.

More was to come. As on-lookers—and cameras—found themselves transfixed by Mirabella's *pièce de résistance*, something which looked like a jewelled tiger's head in her exposed navel, the royal chauffeur for the night, Taplow, could be seen approaching at the wheel. Amy, unaware of what had happened, did however catch a glimpse of Mirabella's sinuous back just ahead of her as she stepped up the red carpet. She thought the presence of another individual so close vaguely odd: but by this time the Chairman of Covent Garden, having hissed: "Get that woman out of here and into her seat and fast," was already bowing over the Princess's hand. What Ferdel's thoughts might be was not clear: he looked impassive. Did he perhaps recognize the famous back more swiftly? He had had after all ample opportunity to study it both in the distant and more recent past.

The Chairman of Covent Garden, one who like the centurion in the Bible was accustomed to say, "Go, and he goeth," in his most recent command had reckoned without Mirabella Prey.

"I am c-c-crazy about this Gala," she was saying to the eager pressmen in her thrilling husky voice. She paused naturally enough on the red carpet in order to do so: incidentally providing an opportunity for yet more revealing shots. "You know I am doing so much work for this wonderful charity."

No one had the gall to ask Mirabella if she knew what the charity in question, for which the Gala had been hastily assembled, actually was. But the exchange had been enough to enable Princess Amy, herself also in white, several inches shorter, weight about the same (very differently distributed) to catch up with her. This time the Chairman waited for no man to do his bidding and literally shoved the vagrant film star off the royal route. It was an action much misunderstood by those avidly watching the whole episode on television at home: for surely the Chairman was being not so much dreadfully unchivalrous towards Mirabella—the line generally taken—as wonderfully and vainly chivalrous towards Princess Amy, in a way of which Sir Walter Raleigh himself would have approved.

As it was, the Chairman's precipitate action merely

enabled Mirabella, graceful to the last, to sweep a deep curtsey to the Prince and Princess as they passed. Ferdel looked straight ahead; Amy looked directly down, down Mirabella's cleavage as a matter of fact, or so the photographers made it appear.

IF LOOKS COULD KILL was one headline already planned for a morning newspaper. For once the headline was probably a pretty fair estimate of the Princess's feelings.

Now, safely installed in the Royal Box, Ferdel did not answer his fiancée's remark, hissed between her gritted teeth and smiling lips. Instead he lifted her white-gloved hand to his own lips and kissed it. It was a gesture which delighted one half of the audience (mainly female) and infuriated the other (predominantly male). "So romantic" and "Crafty foreign bugger" were the respective expressions most commonly used. No one in the audience was aware that as Ferdel lifted Amy's hand, he gave it a painful little nip, not in the least bit romantic, with his long brown fingers. If they had known, both halves of the audience would surely have been united in disapproval.

"What's the piece?" enquired Rick lazily of Jemima. "They didn't give me anything on that." Rick and Jemima were sitting in a box, with Curt and Susanna (the latter agreeably taking the fourth back seat on a high stool) which was directly opposite the royal one.

Because Princess Amy and Prince Ferdinand were the focus of everybody's attention—including Jemima's—it took some time for the latter to take in the existence of the box next door, although Jemima was actually sitting cheek-by-jowl with its inhabitants. She glanced to her left. She saw a thin young woman wearing whitish satin, cut rather too like a nightdress for Jemima's own taste, the diamond circlet on her head was however exquisite; it must be real. As Jemima recognized Susanna Blanding's cousin (and the lady-in-waiting's sister), Lydia Quentin, she realized that she had also seen her companion, a much older man, presumably her father, before. If he was her father he was a wealthy father, because he had installed two people only in a box meant for four. The same man had been with Lydia Quentin praying in Westminster Cathedral. But Susanna Blanding had said that the Quentins were horribly poor and their father, the celebrated Colonel Q, was dead. . . . An escort then, an older escort, a much older escort. Why would a much older escort pray with a young girl in the middle of the afternoon? For rejuvenation? Filing the puzzle away at the back of her mind, Jemima returned her attention to Rick Vancy.

Like Prince Ferdinand, Rick looked remarkably handsome if slightly actorish in his white tie: his resemblance to Leslie Howard was more pronounced than ever. Rick's gift for verisimilitude was once more demonstrated by the fact that he had actually secured a tail-coat which fitted him, unlike his sidekick Curt who had only got as far as a dinner-jacket—which manifestly did not.

"The 'piece' is *Otello*," said Jemima.

"As in Shakespeare?"

"Exactly. Arias instead of soliloquies."

"Isn't the particular story-line rather gross tonight?" Rick rolled one eye in the direction of the minor boxes opposite, where a couple of dignitaries in Arab dress could be seen (those in white ties might perhaps envy them their freedom of movement). Then he looked down at the elaborate Gala programme, magnificently inscribed, "In the gracious presence of Her Royal Highness Princess Amy of Cumberland and His Highness Prince Ferdinand of . . ." A long string of foreign names followed, one of them actually sounding rather like Ruritania.

"Since it's for Eastern Relief, you could argue that *Otello* was in fact peculiarly appropriate," suggested Jemima. "Eastern Relief" was in fact a tactful umbrella name for Middle Eastern War Relief, its hasty organization due to the latest unpleasant twist in the situation in that area, where an increasing amount of homeless and sick of one country declined to receive the refugees of another. "But I doubt whether anybody thought of the story of *Otello* at the time. More carried away by the unexpected presence of Ignazio Dorati in London due to a cancellation. He's behind Domingo and Pavarotti, but they, whoever 'they' are, say he's going to be even better. At least in this part. And goodness, he's handsome. Look out for squeals at the curtain. He's a terrific favourite here."

"So what do you know? Arabs at the opera." Rick leant back and closed his eyes as the house lights dimmed and the first stormy bars of the overture were heard. Jemima hoped that he was not going to emulate his compatriot Curt in publicly going to sleep.

Whatever the Arabs thought of *Otello*—at charity prices, they must have paid a fortune for that box next door to the royal one, once again two people only occupying a box for four—the rest of the audience thrilled to it. Moreover, since Ignazio Dorati, not for nothing nicknamed El Dorado, made such a handsome bronzed fellow of the Moor, no insult to the Arab race could surely be intended. As for Mirabella Prey, sitting gorgeously in the front of the stalls circle, her lovely eyes glowed as the unfamiliar—to her—plot unfolded.

"I love this story—yes," she exclaimed at one point to her escort. A Greek-looking person of heavy build, he wore gold jewellery which could be matched with that of many of the women in the audience. Mirabella's voice was however rather too loud for the regular opera-goers closer to her and there was some indignant shushing. Unabashed, Mirabella was later overheard comparing El Dorado to a puma, notoriously her favourite animal as her many admirers would testify. (The large puma bracelet flashing on her arm was either the broken one restored, or a re-creation.) Nor did the end of the opera dissatisfy her. Mirabella breathed an orgiastic sigh as the athletic Dorati straddled his plaintive but well-built Desdemona in order to strangle her.

"She's strong, that one." Mirabella nodded approvingly. "But he is stronger."

By the time the great finale of the opera was over, the evil figure of Iago breaking loose to escape his just deserts, the whole of the audience from Princess Amy, the "Rasputin" sapphires glittering at her throat, to a couple of obscure Indian women high up in a balcony box, with much humbler incrustations, seemed ready to erupt into applause. As the great red curtains fell, their clapping began to explode in rounds of wild energy like the sound of fireworks being released. First the whole company, then the company with the conductor, then the principals in ascending order of importance, appeared before the curtains, held back for them by flunkeys. So that when the call came for which a high proportion of the audience had been holding back their ultimate ferocity: El Dorado himself, alone on the apron of the stage, not so much fireworks as thunder was the impression given.

There he stood, bowing, smiling, his face still mildly darkened, looking indeed much like the puma to which Mirabella had compared him, but a pleasant, cheerful panting puma, relaxing after the kill.

"El Dorado! El Dorado!" Monstrous bouquets in huge ugly cellophane wrappings were being carried on by the flunkeys and other single flowers began to rain down from the upper galleries. The whole audience, including Princess Amy and Prince Ferdinand, rose to its feet in tribute. Jemima, clapping away at Rick's side, was highly surprised to note that the inhabitants of the next box—Lydia Quentin and her elderly escort—had already left. Then she turned back to Ignazio Dorati. By now the sound was sufficiently all-consuming for it to take some moments for anybody, even the Covent Garden officials, to realize that the fireworks and the thunder had in fact been joined by another noise: that of an explosion. A minor explosion it was true, just enough to set off what appeared to be a smoke bomb in one of the balcony boxes. Smoke began to billow outwards.

But it was only when an enormous white banner was draped down from the farthest box on the right-hand balcony side, that heads actually began to turn away from El Dorado, still bowing and smiling on the stage, in the direction of the smoke. The logo of an animal's face, enormous sad eyes, dominated it. But to most people the words were even more striking:

INNORIGHT it read. PROTECT THE INNOCENT. And then: THE TRUE GOOD CAUSE.

As the audience, now staring and murmuring, began to take in something of what had happened,

and Covent Garden officials scurried in the direction
of the banner—"Get the police," one of them was
heard to say, "there are enough of them outside"—
two middle-aged women of inconspicuous appearance, one fat, one thin, emerged from the ladies'
cloakroom on the upper level. Their dark dresses
giving the impression of having done service in some
office earlier in the day, the two women hastened
down the side staircase. Someone else was talking
about "those damn Asians."

"We must hurry, dear," said the fat one, clutching
her large plastic shopping bags to her. "Do come on.
We must make the last train home."

"Wasn't he wonderful?" sighed the thinner of the
two women. "What a relief to have the full opera. The
Zeffirelli film was definitely not for the purist." She
added: "Don't worry, dear, we've got plenty of time."

And Chicken was right. The timing worked out by
Monkey, and gone over many times by the rest of the
cell, had so far worked to perfection. The exactness of
the royal schedule—characteristically exact—was of
course a considerable help. As Ione Quentin often
observed to her sister on this particular subject:
"When we say 'Cars at 11:02,' we at CP do not mean
11:03."

So that Lamb entering the receiving room at the
back of the Royal Box knew to the instant the moment
at which the Prince and Princess were scheduled to
desert the applauding audience and retire to the back
room. Lamb smiled at Fitzgerald, the Princess's detective, whom she knew through Ione, and explained
that she had arranged to make a presentation to
Princess Amy; the detective nodded. The unscheduled confusion, caused by the Innoright banner, was
as a matter of fact also working almost perfectly to the

timetable they had planned. After that, several things happened at once, none of them expected within the royal receiving room, all of them planned by Monkey.

As Lamb said to Princess Amy, "Ma'am, Ione said I could come—" the Princess turned towards her with a faintly puzzled but still courteous air. After all, the evening had been full of the unexpected. It was Ione Quentin who cried: "Leelee—no," as two Arabs were revealed standing behind her.

Both men held automatic pistols. Both men were now masked beneath their Arab headdresses. To those outside, the loud plop of another smoke bomb, followed by more smoke billowing out, coming from a box adjacent to the royal one, created further pandemonium. But to those inside the box, there was the noise of a shot, a shot followed by a scream.

"Your Royal Highness," said a muffled voice. "You are to come with us."

Elsewhere in Covent Garden, the noise and confusion following the Innoright demo still held sway, as sturdy men attempted to haul back the banner, with its defiant red legend: PROTECT THE INNOCENT.

# FOURTEEN

# "Palace Mystery"

In spite of the late hour, Major Smylie-Porter's voice was extraordinarily urbane on the telephone: "Pat here . . . Dear boy, this is probably the ultimate favour we shall ever ask you. . . ." And, added Major Smylie-Porter to himself, the ultimate test of my ability to handle anything, but anything, however big, big being not quite a big enough word. To his surprise, he found that at the same time he was uttering a rough prayer (surely he hadn't prayed since he was a young man in Malaya and those bandits attacked). He also found, going still further back to childhood, that he was keeping his fingers crossed.

But then Major Pat was well aware that for him personally this was the make or break of a so far modestly successful professional career. The retrieval of a twenty-two-year-old missing princess, not only that but the retrieval *without* such immediate attendant publicity, newspaper headlines, clarion screams, blaring shrieks of anguish and excitement as to make the most impassive courtier blench, and as for the Monarch . . .

Here Major Pat checked his thoughts. Had he been a Catholic like Monkey (whom in some ways he resembled) Major Pat would have surely crossed himself at the thought of the Monarch to whom his devotion was both awed and total.

In short, the retrieval of Princess Amy *without pre-publicity* would place Major Pat in a strong position to be considered for yet higher office in a yet more august palace, when such a post should next become vacant.

First catch your hare, in the words of Mrs. Beeton. The twenty-two-year-old Princess had yet to be retrieved, and retrieved in one piece, what's more. Surely the police could be trusted to do that, he thought, almost irritably, his finger reaching towards the next highly private number of a Press magnate or an editor or some other person within the mysterious purlieus of the BBC or the IBA . . . or just one of those amazingly influential people who still, thank God—another sigh, the habit was catching—permeated English society. Many of them, thank God again, had been encountered at school or in the army or were even related to Major Pat, or possibly to his late wife, poor Louise.

Throughout the night he worked.

"Jumbo?" he began the next call, "Paddles here." The nicknames went back a long way; but there was nothing childish or frivolous about the total blanket which Major Pat, with the encouragement of the police and the agreement of certain august personages, was seeking to have imposed upon the news of Princess Amy's disappearance.

The price? The price would have to be paid. Like Rumpelstiltskin in the fairy story, the Press would be back for their due and promised payment. The full or at any rate fullish story of the hideous events which had led up to that disappearance, the mental anguish of the Princess (if nothing worse: only guessed at at the present time), the mental anguish of her *mother* (well, he did know all about that, the wretched Duchess having retreated into what in any other woman would have been described as an alcoholic stupor at the news, and for once the Major hardly blamed her). Newspapers and television from the BBC to the *Daily Exclusive*, would all have to receive the full or fullish story. When she was found.

That was the price of silence.

Ironically enough, it helped, it helped very much indeed, that most of the papers of the *Daily Clueless* calibre (long might that nickname remain apt) were happily obsessed with what they innocently took to be the main drama of the evening.

Pictures of Mirabella Prey, prettily outrageous in her white dress, wide questioning dark eyes fixed on Ferdel as he passed, were already being prepared for many a front page. As for Princess Amy's glance—a glance born in fact of sheer astonishment—that apparently icy expression, together with her jewels and upswept hair gave her quite a look of her ancestress Queen Victoria; at any rate the resemblance was sufficient for one newspaper, ignoring the rival claims of IF LOOKS COULD KILL, to try out the well-worn WE ARE NOT AMUSED.

Ione Quentin, lying in bed in a half-darkened room, gazed desperately at this particular paper, among those scattered on her white lace counterpane. Amused? To herself she said aloud: No, I should think not. Poor child, oh, poor child. Ione swung her legs over the edge of the bed and began slowly, methodically, as was her wont, to work out a plan of campaign.

Another helpful factor lay in the particular circumstances of Princess Amy's disappearance, or rather her *non*-appearance, at the front door of the Royal Opera House, immediately following the Gala. The bewildered Committee of the charity for whom the evening was being held, still in the ground-floor foyer to bid her farewell, assumed after a short while that the smoke bombs and the demo had caused the Princess to be smuggled out of a side entrance (which was, as a matter of fact, perfectly true). Outside, Bow Street, a narrow, crowded, two-way street at the best of times, was totally packed after the performance. A section of this crowd was stationary, and prepared to behave in quite an aggressive manner towards any force which might try to move it on.

These were the people, fervent monarchists or Amy-fanciers with I LOVE AMY buttons displayed, who waited by the royal car as, with Taplow at the wheel, it purred waiting for departure. But to be frank, at this hour of the night, the largest, most stationary— and most aggressive—portion of the crowd were milling round the Stage Door in adjacent Floral Street, or had somehow spilled over from the Stage Door crush on to the further pavements.

These were the expert fanciers of El Dorado, the would-be lovers, the aficionados, whom nothing, or nothing short of physical violence, seemed likely to budge from their stance. Not for a mild departure, deprived of their hero, had they raced down from the gallery and the amphitheatre; as they ran, they had either ignored such pathetic un-operatic distractions as the Innoright poster or assumed it to be yet another demonstration of adulation for Him. Even the first smoke bomb left such fanatics singularly unmoved, and by the time of the second one members of Innoright, impressed by the poster, might have been surprised at their disdain or sheer inattention. On the other hand a member of Innoright who was also an operagoer such as Chicken was well able to anticipate such a Gadarene rush at the end of the evening—had indeed anticipated it, nay counted upon it, during the planning meetings of the Innoright cell.

In Floral Street, therefore, ordinary red programmes were there to be signed and there were also some of the elaborate Gala programmes to be seen. El Dorado was known to be generous towards his fans in this respect, and they would expect him to sign a fair amount before the time came to commence that late night roistering with his comrades by which he normally relaxed. There were photographs also to be seen: the black eyes, white teeth and merry smile of the famous face, framed by a romantic white frilly shirt open at the neck (Rodolfo in *Luisa Miller* was another favourite role) flashed before the gaze, as fans respectfully harboured their copies in the crush. These El Dorado would normally sign as well, particularly after what was generally agreed to have been a superb performance.

When an unexpected and quite violent irruption of police, followed by the speedy cordoning off of Floral Street, occurred, El Dorado's single-minded fans were still quite unmoved. Subsequent events—in any case getting late for the first editions of the morning newspapers—were literally chaotic.

Princess Amy's followers at the front Bow Street entrance were left with two contrary impressions: the first was that the Princess had left by another entrance (true enough) in order to elude them (not true); the second impression given by the police was that they were determined to push the crowd around in order to prevent them witnessing the Princess's departure from *this* entrance.

The continued presence of the royal car at the front, Taplow looking obviously bewildered at the wheel, did seem to militate against the first impression, but after a while even the royal car moved. Someone—a policeman—said something to Taplow: the cordon was lifted and the car departed, rapidly.

As for El Dorado's fans, in time they were more courteously instructed to disband: "Mr. Dorati has left by another entrance." (This was indeed true, or about to be true, no one wanting to risk losing yet another star, in so far as anybody backstage had a glimmering of what had actually happened.) This instruction was however greeted by the Dorati fans not with apathy or resignation but with outright and vociferous protest.

In all this combined front-street and side-street drama, the noise of an ambulance which came to the side entrance, and to which a stretcher was rapidly and expertly carried, passed almost unnoticed. Stretchers and ambulances were not unknown at Covent Garden. Someone had fainted, a heart attack at worst—maybe the smoke was responsible—these things happened and were regrettable, none of this was particularly interesting to the populace at large since the person concerned was hardly likely to be Princess Amy or El Dorado. (Once again, true enough. The person concerned was the detective, Fitzgerald, shot in the chest in the line of duty, while trying vainly to protect his royal charges.)

Then Little Mary, she of the *Daily Exclusive* and *Jolly Joke*, decided to run her own special version of events. This involved Princess Amy deliberately leaving the Gala early without saying goodbye to the

Chairman, the Gala Committee (again, all too true) owing to her disgust at the presence of Mirabella Prey. As a matter of fact, informed by a stringer of the Princess's unscheduled private exit, Little Mary had no reason to believe this was the actual reason for it: but she was currently carrying on a vendetta with a member of the Gala Committee and this seemed a good way of suggesting that a successful evening had in fact ended in failure.

As for the smoke bombs and the Innoright demo, the mention of smoke bombs could have been amusing if Little Mary had known exactly at whom they had been directed; the subject of animal rights on the other hand was inclined to be a slight drag where her readers were concerned in Little Mary's knowledgeable opinion. Their way of life might be threatened by such tiresome shenanigans: besides, bitchery concerning a good friend (she of the Gala Committee) was so much more amusing to read first thing in the morning.

It was all the more ironic that for once Little Mary by featuring the Mirabella Prey story earned the heartfelt gratitude of Major Pat Smylie-Porter and other loyal parties interested in the great cover-up. It was not that the news could, finally, be held for very long, for all Major Pat's heroic efforts, particularly in view of the enormous, if undercover, police operation now underway. It was just that by coincidence Little Mary did provide that titillating, if inaccurate, explanation for Amy's disappearance which the situation demanded for the more sophisticated. (For the rest, the Innoright demo and the smoke bombs were explanation enough.)

PALACE MYSTERY ran the headline of Little Mary's column. What was more, Little Mary, ever game to display a knowledge of the arts, managed to re-tell the plot of *Otello* in a way that linked Princess Amy, Prince Ferdinand and Mirabella Prey most satisfyingly if it might have outraged Boito and Verdi, let alone Shakespeare.

"PALACE MYSTERY," repeated Major Pat, mopping his brow with his large white linen handkerchief. "If only they knew."

"PALACE MYSTERY," echoed Jemima to Rick Vancy, with whom she was having (somewhat reluctantly) a working breakfast. At least she was allowed to stage it in her own flat and did not have to attend Rick's hotel. "I do believe, Rick, that there was something odd about the way they went. Or does the demo explain it? I see the placard was awkward and not exactly conducive to the cause of Eastern Relief. Innoright strikes again! I must say that the smoke bomb or bombs were quite unpleasant: it says here there were at least two, and certainly we saw a second one in the Arabs' box, didn't we? After they'd left. But the *Guardian* only mentions one. It all happened so late: the Gala must have finished near to midnight."

"Arabs at the opera! I never did buy that one," was Rick's comment. "So they were animal freaks like the rest of the world." He shook his head as though the Middle East had let him down personally.

"PALACE MEES-TERY! So ridiculous. Why always this Palace, this Princess? The British are crazy about these things." The voice today was husky as ever, but for once the effect was more cross than thrilling. The morning was never the best time for Mirabella Prey, who was woken at eight a.m. in her hotel suite by the *Evening Exclusive* (sometimes lovingly known as the Evenmore Clueless), demanding her comment on the events of the previous night in general, and Little Mary's column in particular. Since Mirabella had recently taken much trouble to speak beguilingly to Little Mary, she was disconcerted to read a version of events in her column in which she featured most unflatteringly as Iago, not Desdemona; worse still she was omitted altogether from the headline. Then other members of the Press began to ring too.

"Dulling," purred Mirabella to one of her favorites. "How silly this paper is: to you I am telling the true story. It is Theodoros who is loving the opera—" Then Mirabella talked at length about her new Greek-ish friend.

It was earlier that same morning that Pompey and Vaillant at Central Squad, still doggedly pursuing the solution to their own Palace Mystery (Death at the Palace Press Conference might have been a suitable title for that) had received a new and important piece of evidence. Thus the headline in the morning paper's gossip column passed more or less unnoticed, except for a brief appreciative chuckle from Pompey; which Valliant thought it tactful to ignore.

"She was threatening him," said a new witness who had come forward in answer to repeated police appeals. "The foreign-looking chap, the one in your photograph. I was at this Underground station, I shall never forget it, I sat down on the bench with them, gave me quite a fright. Very intense she was; I would say she had burning eyes, to be exact." The witness, who was in fact a man who had been at the time on his way to a creative writing school in Oxford Street, paused expectantly as though in search of commendation. "Burning eyes and dark hair," repeated the witness more lamely, before continuing:

" 'I'll kill you,' she said. 'See if I don't. You think I

won't but I will. I'm quite capable of it whatever you think.' Or words to that effect."

"We'd like to get the exact words, sir, if possible," was Pompey's patient response. "And a more detailed physical description. You see, burning eyes might mean a number of different things to different people."

In the shocked Eaton Square household, or what was left of it, Prince Ferdinand having been removed to Cumberland Palace for safety, "burning eyes" might also have been a suitable description to apply to Mrs. Taplow's expression as she sat facing her husband. Taplow's head was bowed on his arms; the large man was weeping uncontrollably, without pretence. In part these were the tears of sheer exhaustion: Taplow's ordeal, begun so shockingly with the instructions given to him outside the Opera, had continued most of the night with the organization of the Prince's belongings, and other duties. It had started again very early in the morning when Taplow, red-eyed from lack of sleep, had decided to communicate certain facts to the police.

But there was a further hopelessness, beyond mere exhaustion, about Taplow, as he sat there weeping in front of his wife; her fiery gaze suggesting that she might pounce and devour him the moment he raised his head, like one of Mirabella Prey's favourite pumas. It was as though he wept not only for the frightful present but for decades of humiliating memories.

"I shall never forgive you for this, Kenneth, no matter what happens." Mrs. Taplow's voice was the more menacing for remaining low as though they might be overheard.

Taplow mumbled something.

"What's that, Kenneth?"

"Your *fault*, Lizzie," and then more strongly: "Your *fault*. All the dressing-up, encouraging him to be different. You dressed him up as a girl. That's where it started."

"Seeing as he didn't have a man for a father," his wife hissed back.

One way and another, neither Taplow had time to look at the morning paper. But a very senior policeman did, and exploded, as though in relief, to have something inanimate but actual to crush in his hand.

"PALACE MYSTERY indeed! Carefully planned from the beginning, the whole thing. So why was it a mystery to us? We knew about the threats to the wedding itself, so why didn't we know about all this?" He threw the paper aside and began ticking off on his fingers: "Terrific timing throughout. The demo at the exact moment that singer was taking his bow. One smoke bomb set off up there to cause the maximum trouble and direct all the attention to that upper level, as distant as possible from the Royal Box. The next one set off in the box next door timed for the precise moment of the grab, so that the getaway is covered by the second wave of chaos."

"Someone knew their opera form all right!" (Chicken would have been proud to hear him.) "Seats, no, boxes paid for in cash. The Indian women who unrolled the banner and set off the first smoke bomb must have been in the plot. If they *were* Indians, which we doubt. Easy to escape down the stairs from the balcony level and saris only too easily disposed of. There's a pretty unused Ladies right there behind the balcony boxes."

His expression darkened to one of ferocity as he continued to tick off: "And while we're on the subject of foreign dress, HRH bound, gagged, possibly drugged, we're not sure, and bundled into some Arab robe, yashmak, chador, whatever, face hidden, *nose* hidden in one of these sinister black jobs, and supported, carried rather, down the stairs and out of the Royal Box private entrance, deserted on the night of a Gala, out to a waiting car by two solicitous Arabs, supporting her! Important sheikhs," he almost shouted. "A car with a chauffeur, a chauffeur in cap, ready there waiting. Planned to the minute."

The very senior policeman looked round as though for something else to crush. "How's Fitzgerald?" he concluded, the anger draining from his voice.

It was only a short while later that his most trusted assistant returned and said: "The good news is: we think we know where they're holding her. The bad news is that we've received their demands. And this time, with Fitzgerald in mind, we know they're serious."

# FIFTEEN

# Violence

"I've lost one of my new Russian earrings, Ferdel will be so cross." For the first time since her abduction, Princess Amy's face crumpled and she began to cry. Dishevelled, the blonde ringlets now a wreck of the formal lacquered hair style, her face dirty, and still the Rasputin sapphires gleaming at her throat and weighing down her creased white dress at the breast, Princess Amy looked like Cinderella just after midnight struck. Already the finery was disintegrating; rags and ashes would soon follow.

"Don't worry, it will be found, people always find things like that. Besides, we are not interested in your jewels. Only in you." Through her brown nylon-stocking mask, Pussy's voice sounded muffled and horrible. The effect on Princess Amy was to stop her new-found tears abruptly: at the same moment involuntarily she wrinkled her nose in disgust. It was actually the strong smell of Pussy's lavender water which disgusted her, reminding her of a tormenting governess in childhood.

"You're supposed to make friends with your captors," thought Princess Amy. "I've read about it, and there was that cousin of Ferdel's in Italy, that boy, he did it and it worked. But I'll never be able to make friends with *you*. You're really cruel under that awful mask. I know it."

Amy, carried down the special stairs and out of the side entrance used for private visits to the Royal Box in Arab woman's clothing, had not been drugged, as the senior policeman suspected. She had been gagged, her disguise hiding the gag. Beagle, who did the gagging (as he also bound the other inhabitants of the box including the Royal Box Steward who had been serving the party) did it expertly. It was something he told the cell that he had learned from some kind of military anti-terrorist manual borrowed from a friend. Wherever he had learnt it, it seemed to work.

"She is sick," was Beagle's reply to a reaction of surprise from the attendant at the bottom of the stairs. "It is the smoke," he muttered, rather than spoke, in some vaguely foreign accent, his face stained, shrouded under his own Arab headdress, robes flowing. "We must go to the car."

Both Fox and Beagle were carrying loaded pistols: but only Fox knew that they were loaded since at meetings Fox had carefully promised a couple of *unloaded* 9 mm. Berettas, looking absolutely for real, via theatrical contacts for supplying such, made at Leaviss. He had already successfully supplied something similar to Beagle on the occasion of the photographic foray; but Beagle's pistol had had a solid barrel. For the climactic night of the abduction, however, Fox had obtained pistols used for firing blanks—and replaced the blanks.

Nevertheless Fox stoutly maintained that his decision to load them with real bullets was absolutely the right one. He also defended his shooting of the Princess's detective, who had flung himself forward as the "Arabs" produced their weapons, even in the face of Monkey's appalled reaction.

"That was violence, Fox. We agreed that simulated weapons should be taken: that it would be enough to frighten them."

Yet Fox was almost blithely impenitent. He merely pointed out that the detective's precipitate action would have in fact scuppered the whole plan if Fox's weapon had not been loaded. He seemed to think the detective had been quite unreasonable in his behaviour. Fox argued this on the grounds that it had been decided in advance that the sight of a Beretta pointed at the Princess's temple would immobilize him, as indeed it had immobilized the other occupants of the box—Prince Ferdinand, Major Smylie-Porter and the flunkey; Lamb had immobilized Ione Quentin by her own method of flinging herself into her arms and hugging her as if for protection.

Fox even regarded himself as a bit of a hero. Monkey on the other hand thought there was something positively frightening about the way that Fox, a young man apparently dedicated to a life of nonviolence, shrugged off what Monkey himself considered to be a serious crime against a fellow human being; Innoright was after all specific in *not* condemning the whole of humanity in favour of the animal kingdom.

At this point—in the car—they had no idea whether the man had lived or died; probably the latter, judging from what Beagle had told Monkey briefly in the getaway car.

Monkey, dark uniform cap hiding his high forehead and receding hairline, scarf round his neck to conceal the white tie, had been satisfied that he looked the image of some rich Arab's chauffeur, at the wheel of a large, dark-blue Mercedes with elegant darkened glass windows; leaving the opera discreetly early, Monkey had brought the car up from where Chicken had parked it earlier in the evening. This chauffeur waited ready just at the side entrance for a quick, a very quick departure; it was something Monkey, with his awareness of such procedures, had arranged in advance, knowing that the police presence would be concentrated on the front entrance from which the royal party was scheduled to leave.

Fox had hired the car from a company who leased out such things for films (although it was currently showing false number plates). In the meantime the whole operation of the getaway had needed and received immaculate timing, where possible rehearsed, where not, estimated, discussed and re-estimated.

Monkey thought fleetingly that where violence was concerned, you could never really judge a character in advance until the pressure came. Out of Beagle and Fox, two young men who had little in common but their age, he would have backed Beagle any day over Fox to pull the trigger. Was it Beagle who had killed Tom? Monkey had always secretly dreaded that it might prove to be so. Or was perhaps Beagle's vaunted air of violence a mere carapace for a softer nature? They would soon find out. (In any case there was a flaw in Monkey's reasoning about Beagle: it was Beagle who did not know that the guns were loaded whereas Fox, who had procured them, did.)

That had been Monkey's real mistake; underestimating not only Fox's steak of viciousness but also his independence. If only people would carry out orders! . . . Coolly—he prided himself on his driving—Monkey drew the Mercedes with its false number plates into the little yard at the back of Beagle's lair. The distance from the Opera House was so short that the whole journey had taken a matter of minutes even though Monkey had driven fast, but not too fast, to avoid giving the impression of escape.

Chicken and Pussy were waiting. As Fox and Beagle, Arab costumes discarded, carried the wrapped body of the Princess through the narrow back entrance (she was surprisingly heavy for such a small person, thought Fox, panting), Monkey moved over into the passenger seat of the car. Chicken got swiftly into the driver's seat. As well as long white gloves, she was now wearing a fake tiara and diamond earrings supplied, had they known it, by Leaviss; but the opulent fur jacket which she wore was real. It had belonged to Monkey's wife Cynthia and he had given it to her long before he appreciated the cruelty and violence involved in the fur trade. He liked to think that she too would have wanted to abandon it had she lived; as it was, this last ceremonial and sacrificial use of the jacket in the cause was to Monkey's way of thinking, absolutely appropriate.

Monkey removed his cap and scarf, to reveal his white tie and tail-coat once more. Pussy removed the false number plates. In a small street off the Law Courts, deserted at this hour, Monkey and Chicken abandoned the hired Mercedes (and the Arab robes in the boot) for Monkey's own car, an ancient but highly polished Rolls, which he had left there before the Gala. Monkey and Chicken together, he with his medals, she with her tiara, now conveyed (he felt) the perfect image of a prosperous operagoer and his wife; the latter driving as being the more sober of the two following the necessary refreshments in the interval

to make opera at least palatable to a tired businessman.

Only a short while after the Princess's body had
been taken from the Opera House, Monkey arrived
back at his flat in South Eaton Place. There Carmencita, his Spanish housekeeper, had laid out a cold
supper for two: she, like Monkey, entertained secret
sentimental hopes of the sweet little Miss Quentin
even if she was a bit young for her stately employer
(and needed fattening up—but then Carmencita
would do that). Composedly, Monkey sat down to
eat both portions of the cold supper. There was only
a slight tremble in his hands and that he cured by
draining a small glass of brandy more or less at a gulp
before he began to eat.

Chicken, dressed once more in her inconspicuous
clothes (Monkey would now dispose of the jacket and
tiara as Pussy had disposed of the saris en route),
walked to Victoria and hailed a taxi home. She left
Monkey to work his way through gazpacho and cold
Spanish pancakes: unlike Lamb, he needed no fattening up but Carmencita was such an excellent cook,
particularly now she had been trained to vegetarianism, that it seemed a pity to waste the food. He was
magisterially confident that he, the master planner,
knew where all the members of the cell were. It had
gone right and in the morning Innoright would
deliver their demands. At least, it had gone *almost*
right: but already under the influence of the brandy
and some excellent burgundy, Monkey was beginning to forget about the injuries to the detective.
Sooner or later, he would fit that into the scheme of
things, as he had fitted in the death of Tom: part of
the means which the noble end justified.

Momentarily however the trembling had returned:

Monkey drank some more burgundy—from the other glass, forgetting in his temporary agitation that Lamb never touched alcohol. Now he was restored. He put down his glass and raised one eyebrow: for a moment he looked purely simian, a very clever ape indeed.

But Monkey did not know where all the members of the cell were. He did not for example know where Lamb herself was. He imagined that when the hue and cry at the Opera House itself was over, the immediate horror of the abduction understood if not accepted, she would be taken together with that unnervingly correct sister (now she would be an obstacle to his romantic dreams) back to their Chelsea flat.

That was not the case.

"What the hell are you doing here?" asked Beagle, coldly furious. "You could have got yourself shot coming to the door like that. He's a bloody maniac, our Foxy." Beagle hesitated; in spite of his anger his voice remained low. He pointed to the ceiling. Lamb imagined masked Fox and masked Pussy, the former still armed, holding the Princess captive under the sad gaze of the wide-eyed seals in the blown-up photographs.

"Look at you," he went on, taking her thin bare arm in his fingers. "Wearing a fucking crown through the streets of London"—with his other hand he touched the tiara—"no coat. This is the English summer, okay? Not your favourite Port-oh-feeno." (Lamb had once unwisely revealed her predilection for the Italian resort.) "Dress which reveals your boobs, if you *had* any boobs."

Lamb's eyes were enormous in her pale face. "I wanted to be with you," she began, and then altered it to: "I wanted to be of help."

"Obey orders, my dear Miss Lamb, obey orders. That's the way to be of help." Beagle mimicked Monkey. Nevertheless the anger was fading and he relaxed his grip on her arm. "You're shivering. Better put on something else. I'll get you some jeans and a jersey from upstairs. Even though you'll swim in them. It's bad enough having our little Madam looking like something out of a bodice-ripping movie without you too."

"How is—she?" Lamb found her lips were too dry to pronounce Princess Amy's name and her heart was pittering very rapidly as she watched Beagle's reaction.

"The patient is as well as can be expected. Phew! Am I glad to leave my mask off." He made towards Lamb as if to pull the stocking down over her head. "Do you want to go up and have a look? I'll prepare you for the operating theatre."

Lamb shrank back. "No, no, I don't want to— besides it's far too dangerous."

"Dangerous!" Beagle gave a short low laugh. "That's rich. Do you realize what Foxy has gone and done? He's shot a fucking policeman. That little wimp, didn't know he had it in him, did I? In short, darling, that's torn it. We're for it. They'll never let us get away with that. Oh yes, darling, kidnapping a Princess to call attention to a good cause is one thing, particularly if we treat her nice; shooting a policeman is quite another. He hasn't even chucked his gun away: mine went down a fucking drain right away."

He whistled. "Oh, we're for it all right, the lot of us. Including that pompous bastard, Monkey—he's got his eye on you, by the way, hasn't he? The only question is, how we go—and who we take with us.

And what we do before we go. I've a few plans meself."

Pussy appeared silently at the door of the barred and shuttered ground-floor room, which had the outward appearance of a small grocer's shop in disrepair. In fact, it was not in disrepair but very well prepared. Behind the dusty tins lay fresh new ones, the deep freeze was working and stocked with supplies. . . . Lamb had a moment to think how specially gross Pussy looked in her mask (unconsciously echoing the earlier thoughts of Princess Amy) before Pussy took it off.

"Lamb!" she exclaimed, crossly.

"Leave her be, Puss." Lamb was relieved to find that Beagle now sounded protective. "She can't go upstairs but she can stand guard down here. When she's got some proper clothes on and got rid of all this tat." He touched the tiara again. "What happens to this, then?"

"I'm going to sell it and give the proceeds to Innoright," said Lamb, with a defiant look at Pussy.

"There's a good girl. Now Pussy, that lets you and Fox get on with the delivery of the demands: two heads being better than one. You've got to ring Monkey at the agreed time and the telephone here has been disconnected as you know. Why don't you take Fox to your flat? You've never been connected as a pair."

"He wants to be alone with her." The thought flashed unbidden: Princess Amy with her bodice ripped. . . .

Pussy frowned. Latterly her original dislike of Beagle had faded in favour of an irrational dislike of Lamb: it was irrational, for Lamb, unlike Beagle, had humbly sought to placate the sombre older woman.

Lamb was not to know that Pussy's unstable loves
and hates, all springing from her daughter's death,
had now veered round and focused on young upper-
class women who played with the cause, leaving
Caro-Otter to die for it. (For that was how Pussy had
now come to view Otter's death in the car crash.)
Young upper-class women such as Lamb.

Another thing that Lamb did not know about
Pussy was that, with the intuition of another obses-
sive character, she had easily caught a whiff of
Lamb's jealous fears concerning Beagle.

"Just as you say, dear," replied Pussy to Beagle
with something like a smile. (Pussy's smile, thought
Lamb, always had something unpleasant about it,
even at the best of times.) "You take over upstairs,
throw down the clothes for our little Lamb here, or
send them down with that naughty Mr. Fox. After
what happened, he probably shouldn't be here anyway, I'm sure I don't know what Monkey will say
about *him*. That'll leave the lovebirds together," she
added.

What lovebirds? asked the now awakened monster
in Lamb's breast. What lovebirds does she mean?
Pussy's smile was by now positively malevolent. "No
more violence, mind. Protect the innocent. Don't
forget."

When Fox came down bearing a pair of Beagle's
jeans and a khaki jersey, it came quite naturally to
Lamb to say to him: "Look, Fox, give me your gun.
You shouldn't be found carrying that thing. I'll look
after it."

"Careful how you handle it, it's still loaded. I'm not
sure how many I've fired." Fox still sounded almost
blithe on the subject.

"I'll get rid of it, I mean," said Lamb. "It's nice to
think that for once I can do something really helpful."

Once she was alone, Lamb sat with the pistol listening for the sounds which might come from the room upstairs, the room where Beagle and Princess Amy were now also alone—alone with each other.

"What are you going to do with me?" Then: "This won't work, you know. You won't get away with it." Finally: "I think you had just better let me go."

To her surprise, Princess Amy managed quite a creditably imperious tone: which was what she intended. The tears which the loss of the sapphire earring had temporarily evoked were gone. She had no intention of giving anyone the satisfaction of seeing her crying again—if she could help it. Was it acting pure and simple, or an imitation of her revered if notoriously tetchy father? Not acting: "I was never any good at acting at school," she thought, "and as for imitating Daddy, well, I can't even begin to imagine Daddy in this situation. He'd have *exploded* long ago." Even in her present dire situation, the idea of the late Duke of Cumberland captured by terrorists after an Opera Gala had a certain grim humour about it.

"I suppose I'm behaving like *their* idea of a Princess," thought Princess Amy. "I only hope I can keep it up. Goodness knows, I'm not being treated like one."

"I'm going to let you sleep." Beagle spoke in a voice which was both reasonable and distinct, so that unlike Pussy he did not sound, as well as look, menacing.

"Sleep! Where?"

Beagle pointed to the large low bed in the corner of the room.

"I assure you I have no intention of sleeping. Not with you in the room. As a matter of fact"—and as

Princess Amy spoke she decided it was true—"as a matter of fact, I'm hungry."

"You can have food. We have food. You can even have a drink if you like. Wine, and I believe there's some whisky. The vintage may not be what you're used to— "

"I never drink," interrupted Amy coldly. "My mouth hurts. I would like a drink of water."

Beagle went to the basin and poured out some water into a china mug with the Innoright logo on it. Princess Amy made a grimace.

"I assure you it's quite clean," he said.

"How do you expect me to drink it like this? Please undo my hands. I shan't try to escape. I'll give you—my parole, I think it's called."

Beagle considered. Amy's ankles were bound as were her hands: she was also bound to the white chair in which she sat, the single chair in the room. Shouting would get her nowhere above the deserted shop. It seemed safe enough to comply (despite Monkey's explicit instructions to the contrary); besides which, he had his own reasons for wishing to do so. He undid the ropes round Princess Amy's wrists and handed her the cup of water, which she gulped down.

"Will you try to sleep if I get you some food? It's better for you. You've got to wait till morning anyway."

"Wait for what? What do you want anyway? You're the same people who took those horrible photographs. You must be. Who are you?" Amy's glance wandered to the blown-up pictures of the seals on the walls. "Did you take these?" Beagle nodded.

"So it was probably you who photographed *them*—" she thought. No, she mustn't let herself dwell on that, not think about Ferdel. Oddly enough it was the thought of Ferdel—where was he? what was happening to him? would he try to rescue her? or was that only in fairy stories?—which had produced her sudden rush of tears earlier. "Who are you?" she repeated instead.

"Innoright." He turned the logo on the mug towards her. "And we are the same people who took the photographs. Innoright: protection of the innocent. That's what it's all about. Now how do you feel about that, Your Royal Highness?" The title sounded vaguely sarcastic on Beagle's lips.

"You know how I feel about it," replied Amy with spirit; she found that talking—rather than thinking—was reviving her. She just wished that this unknown young man (she assumed he was quite young from the style of his clothes) would take his mask off. All the masks, including his, were so creepy. "I said all those things on television, I *love* animals. Everyone knows I love animals. Besides, it's nothing to do with me. Talk about protecting the innocent! I *am* innocent," concluded Princess Amy firmly.

"You're a Royal, aren't you? Where the innocent are concerned you're a royal symbol of oppression."

"Are you sort of Communists?" ventured Princess Amy, her tone beginning to waver: this kind of language was both more familiar and more worrying. "I mean, as well as being terribly keen on animal rights," she added hurriedly.

"Personally, I'm a keen monarchist," replied Beagle. "And I'm specially keen on princesses. And out of princesses, I'm specially keen on you, Your Royal Highness. Or should I say My Royal Hostage?" Princess Amy guessed that he was smiling behind the mask; that thought did not reassure her either.

"Look, I'll show you something," he said suddenly. Beagle took a small key and unlocked the cupboard beneath the basin. He drew out further rolls of photographs and started to strew them round the floor, on the boards, on the white cushions, finally on the bed. These were not photographs of seals, or indeed of animals, wild or domestic. With increasing apprehension, Princess Amy recognized herself in a series of enormous images, some clearly cropped from bygone royal functions (at which she had in fact cut an extremely minor figure), some snatched as she entered the Cumberland Palace gates. One actually showed her leaning out of the first-floor window at Cumberland Palace, laughing. Laughing! What on earth had she been laughing *at*? Don't brood, *talk*, Amy told herself fiercely.

"So you see, Your Royal Highness, you're my little private passion," observed Beagle pleasantly. He stood over the photographs on the floor for a moment, gazed at Amy as though to compare them, and finally rolled them up again. "Now will you go to sleep? With or without food. I wouldn't let any harm come to you, would I? No violence. My little private passion."

# SIXTEEN

# In a Secret Place

"They're holding her. In a secret place," said Ione Quentin. "Now will you help me?"

Jemima Shore's first reaction was that Princess Amy's normally equable lady-in-waiting had taken leave of her senses; presumably under the strain of the wedding preparations. But wasn't that exactly what she was hired for? A talent for calm administration. Oh well, people went mad at all sorts of awkward moments and for all sorts of awkward reasons.

Ione Quentin's arrival at Jemima's Holland Park Mansions flat had several bizarre aspects to it. For one thing, her name on the intercom had not been immediately recognizable (Jemima tended to think of her merely as "the lady-in-waiting") so that Jemima took her at first to be some importunate fan; Megalith was not supposed to divulge her address, but there had been visits in the past and after all Megalith was no longer bound to protect her. Jemima did distinguish the word "help" and decided she was not in the mood for offering kindness to strangers.

It was Rick Vancy, lingering after the so-called

working breakfast (actually coffee and orange juice with bran muffins), who rolled his eyes and said: "Hey, that sounds interesting. I haven't seen you in your sleuth's role before. I'm kind of curious to watch how you operate." At which point Jemima decided that in order to get rid of Rick Vancy ("I'm afraid I never allow outsiders in on this kind of thing" she observed sweetly), she would pay the price of attending to a distraught member of the public.

Rick Vancy, thus dismissed, passed Ione Quentin coming up the stairs; he too did not recognize her, or not immediately. He did place her a minute after she had been admitted to the top-floor flat but by then it was too late—too late to satisfy his curiosity about the nature of her mission. He made a mental note to enquire what that was all about when he next talked to Jemima. (It would probably be gross to call her from the car, and the woman, Quentin, might still be there.) Is Jemima holding out on me over something, he wondered. Much later Rick Vancy would curse the rare impulse towards reticence which had possessed him at this precise moment.

In the meantime Jemima was staring at Ione. Both women remained standing. "Why are you telling me this? Surely the police—my God, what are *they* doing about it?" And the journalist in Jemima caused her to add in spite of herself: "Why hasn't anything appeared in the Press?"

Ione explained in a surprisingly steady voice just why nothing, so far, had emerged. Agitated at the beginning, or merely nervous, she had regained her poise, it seemed. "They want to get her back first. Naturally. A free hand to act. I suppose it always happens in kidnapping cases if one did but know:

they try to keep it all quiet. But they won't get her back. Not without your help. And my help."

Ione was looking straight at Jemima as though willing her to agree; there was something fierce, almost domineering about her gaze; suddenly she flinched. It was in fact the cat Midnight who had wandered insouciantly through the open balcony window and was now rubbing himself against Ione's leg. "Oh, a cat. I thought—" she managed a smile. "I'm not like Lydia, I'm not a terrific animal lover, I'm afraid. Humans very much first."

"Lydia?"

"My little sister, Lydia. That's the point. That's why I'm here. I'm afraid she's terribly involved in all this. I know she is. She led them into the box, the men who grabbed the Princess. She asked if she could present her host to Princess Amy—he's some kind of philanthropist. So I arranged it. That's how they got in, not the philanthropist but some Arabs, or men dressed as Arabs. And now she's vanished. She ran off, didn't come home with me. That's exactly why you've got to help me."

"Lydia Quentin!" exclaimed Jemima. The girl in the box next to her at the opera. The man in the box: that man who had also been at prayer in Westminster Cathedral. She had a vision of the intense face of her neighbour at Covent Garden, eyes staring ahead, staring indeed at the Royal Box. "Burning eyes." Where had she heard that phrase and heard it extremely recently? Pompey, who had called her only minutes ago about the new witness in his murder case. Was that Lydia Quentin? She felt she was on the edge of understanding. For the time being she turned back to Ione.

"Miss Quentin, what can *I* do?" But to tell the truth

Jemima was attending to Ione with only half her mind. The other half of her attention was focused on the fact that here she was, Jemima Shore Investigator, being presented with the scoop of her career, the scoop of anyone's career, and what on earth could she do about it, what on earth *should* she do about it?

Ione's voice cut across these thoughts.

"You see, Jemima, I know where they're holding her." The fact that Ione addressed her unasked by her Christian name was now the single sign of disturbance that she displayed. What an incredible woman! thought Jemima. She witnesses her mistress kidnapped, abducted, or whatever you like to call it, she has reason to think her own sister is involved and she's still as cool and collected as if she's wearing a hat and white gloves at Ascot.

"Then you *must* go to the police—"

"If I go to the police, something ghastly will happen. I know it. She might even kill herself."

"Oh surely not, Ione"—since they were friends— "I would imagine that's the last thing she would do! Not that I know her as you do of course. One interview and that's all. All the same I thought she came across as surprisingly spirited, for Royalty, if I may say so without offence. Not at all the suicidal type."

"Royalty?" Ione looked fleetingly puzzled. "Oh Royalty. No, Jemima, I'm not talking about Princess Amy. I'm talking about Lydia. My sister."

Jemima reflected that under the circumstances it was a fairly amazing thing to say but then the circumstances themselves were fairly amazing. And Ione Quentin was adding to them, minute by minute, in this tale she was unfolding.

"There's this man who got hold of her, I know he

did, got hold of her and made her do all sorts of things. She's so impressionable, Lydia, and she's been badly ill. She's really not responsible for what she does, you must see that. You made that programme, I watched it when Lydia was—well, in pretty terrible shape. "Look To The Weak." It helped me get through. I've done what I can since our mother killed herself, that's when it all started, really started. Lydia adored our mother. It was such a shock." Ione paused. "But she was always—fragile is the word I use. Or weak—your word. She had a little collapse once when a dog had to be put down when it bit someone, a grown-up who was teasing it. Our father as a matter of fact. Leelee said all sorts of wild things about putting down the grown-up instead— Daddy, that is. He was terribly strict—they didn't get on. She hated all his shooting and things like that. And he was so much older. She was easily upset, you see. Tender hearted. She loved animals, Jemima. She thought they were innocent! She's always felt so guilty herself. This photographer, the man who got hold of her, played on that."

"Animals and innocence. So this is Innoright. And a photographer—" The shape of the conspiracy was beginning to appear to Jemima: an intense girl, a middle-aged businessman, and a rangy-looking young photographer who had come late to the Republican Hotel and sat next to her. All of these, and perhaps some others, had been gathered in that chapel at Westminster Cathedral. Was she at the same time stumbling towards a solution of Pompey's murder? In the meantime Ione continued to pour out her confidences concerning her sister.

"Of course it's Innoright! I've tried so hard to save her from it all. I used to go through all her things but she got cunning. Then I took to following her; there were certain stories she always told me about cinemas with girlfriends, late nights listening to their troubles. Whenever she told me about listening to other people's troubles, I knew she was, well, in trouble herself. I was always wary then. Poor darling, it wasn't so difficult to follow her, thinking she was so clever with her changing Tubes and her codes and all that. In many ways Lydia is still a baby."

"This man, I gather, is not a baby."

"He has this place in Covent Gardens," continued Ione as if Jemima had not spoken. "I'm sure that's where they are. Horribly sordid. But that's not the point. If we went together we could talk to her. It could all be settled. Quietly. I'd take her away, take Leelee away. I do realize she'd have to go away—"

"Whether you're right or wrong, we *must* tell the police." Jemima displayed a firmness at least equal to Ione's. "These people are dangerous maniacs. No, not your sister. The others. As for your sister—" she stopped. She thought Ione Quentin had probably got enough to cope with at the present time. Besides it was important to keep her contentedly, or more or less contentedly, in line with what Jemima now proposed to do. For the time being, "dangerous maniacs," politely excluding Lydia Quentin with her burning eyes, was appropriate enough.

"Dangerous maniacs" was however the mildest of the terms currently being used at Scotland Yard where the Innoright demands had just been received. Chicken had delivered them: she had been chosen as the least conspicuous of the cell (of those not currently involved in other tasks such as the guarding of the Princess). Moreover she assumed a traffic warden's uniform to do so, courtesy of Leaviss, which in a true sense made her even less conspicuous. Shortly after Chicken delivered the flat envelope to Scotland Yard, Fox telephoned to advise of the demands' arrival.

Fox was deputed by Monkey to do so: Monkey did not trust his own rather plummy voice to be sufficiently concealed, besides which he had been seen publicly with Lamb. Fox made the call from Pussy's flat, taking care, he hoped, to deepen his own naturally rather high voice. (Fox, a frustrated actor-turned-costumier, was proud to perform the task.) Pussy's flat was arranged, he found, like some kind of chapel; but as Beagle's secret studio was dedicated to animals, Pussy's flat centred round huge photographs of a blonde girl with long hair. Fox vaguely recognized her: wasn't that some well-known model? But Fox was not interested in Pussy's private life: having telephoned as arranged, his chief concern was to get back to Noel.

"Would you be interested in meeting Noel? That's my dog," he could not resist asking in the temporary mood of exhilaration which seized him after he had made the call.

"A *pet*?" Pussy's voice, the voice of one referring to some truly barbaric practice, was icy; too late Fox remembered Pussy's views about pets and the story, the hideous story, about Pussy and the Alsatian. If she were to lay a finger on Noel! Pussy was dangerous. That sort of thing was the work of a maniac. . . .

"Dangerous maniacs!" The phrase, with others considerably less agreeable, continued to be bandied about Scotland Yard.

"Princess Anne held up in The Mall, attempted kidnapping, that man in Her Majesty's bedroom wanting to talk to her or so he said, and now this—at the opera of all places—where will it end?" intoned a senior policeman in a doleful litany.

"It's simple, now, isn't it?" said an even more senior policeman patiently. "Now we know where she is. We agree to them all, these demands, don't we? For the time being."

One of his colleagues began to list the demands in a kind of rising frenzy. "So where do you suggest we start?" he ended aggressively. "The free-zone for animals in Windsor Great Park, for example? Incorporating the animals in the Windsor Wild Life Park—I think I'm quoting correctly. The whole of Windsor Great Park to be running wild with sweet little wolves and tigers and seals and dolphins right up to the castle itself. Correction: seals and dolphins don't run.

"Shall we start there?" he went on. "Or the airlift to Africa and India perhaps, the airlift of all the animals in British zoos hailing from there? Shall we begin with the airlift perchance? Seeing as I note the Windsor Great Park scheme merely needs a public broadcast to inaugurate it. No problem, that.

"Or, let me see, Regent's Park, another free-zone, no, I beg its pardon, Innozones is what they will be called. Zones for innocents." His voice rose and he was almost screaming. "Isn't that lovely? Lions and tigers milling all about the American Ambassador's residence. That should take care of our security problems there nicely. No more guards necessary."

As the senior policeman remained impassive, his colleague looked at the paper again and made a visible effort to control himself. "As a matter of pure interest, if we do promise all this, what guarantee have they got, Innoright, these nutters, that the demands will be carried out? Once we've got her back."

"The idea is: it's pledged, it will be done."

"And you're talking about the *government*," he snorted. "Government pledges! Where have these people been living? Who on earth believes *government* pledges? Now I know they're seriously crazy."

The patience in the voice of the very senior policeman was by now about saint-like: "No, not the government. The Monarch. Not likely to break the royal word, given in public. That's the idea. In the meantime, shouldn't you be seeing about those snipers, there's a good chap. I must get back to the Home Secretary. Now why didn't they think of grabbing him?" The very senior policeman sounded quite wistful.

As a matter of fact, when Jemima Shore succeeded in getting through to the right quarters—"I have, or think I have, some information about a certain missing person"—the Home Secretary proved to be her chief problem too. That achievement of the right quarters was itself only performed with the help of Pompey—desperately sought and found at home on garden duty. It was illogical, Jemima realized, to be disappointed that the whereabouts of the "missing person" were already known; even if those whereabouts had not been known for very long. In another way she found she was relieved that Ione Quentin's story was not a total fantasy produced by an overworked brain; and that too was illogical.

"Acting on information received," was the only elucidation she received. "I am afraid we are not authorized to tell you any more at the present time." Information received: who? Clearly not Ione Quentin. But who? A traitor in the ranks—the ranks of Innoright?

It was when Jemima pressed the claims of Ione Quentin, accompanied by herself, as an intermediary, that she found the image of the Home Secretary conjured up against her, an image which was defeated by the unexpected aid of a psychiatrist. This expert on sieges suggested that the calming presence of Ione, as the Princess's lady-in-waiting, was in itself desirable. Cumberland Palace, in a situation where everything seemed wrong, could see nothing particularly wrong with that. It even gave Major Smylie-Porter a vague feeling of relief that Ione should be involved. The family were beyond thinking of matters in those terms. As the Duchess of Cumberland kept to her darkened room, Amy's sisters, the vivacious Princess Sophie and the melancholy Princess Harriet, inhabited the Vienna Drawing-Room with their amiably undistinguished husbands—Scots and French respectively. Were any of them safe? In their distracted state, the sisters took refuge, as it were, in fears for their own children. The Vienna Drawing-Room was made into a kind of redoubt, at least in their imagination.

Thus the great ballroom picture, in its ornate golden frame, which had only recently formed the background to Amy and Ferdel's interview, now looked down upon the golden heads of Amy's little nephews and nieces: Jamie and Jack and Alexander, Isabelle and Chantal and Béatrice. All six of them owed their presence in London to their appointment as pages and bridesmaids at the Royal Wedding.

The Princesses had not the heart to interrupt the excited games of the children as they raced in and out of the famous silk and gilded "Vienna" furniture.

Ferdel, smoking heavily—a habit which came as a surprise to his future sisters-in-law—hardly appeared to notice them, even when baby Béatrice, the smallest and blondest, clasped him round his dark-blue trouser leg.

"I love you," she cried, gazing up at him. Ferdel smiled rather vaguely in her direction as though she was some importunate dog—or rather puppy.

Little Jamie, sensing the abstraction of the grown-ups and seeking to turn it to his advantage, asked loudly: "Mum, why can't I wear my kilt at the wedding instead of that silly page's suit? It makes me look like a girl. I want to wear my kilt," he concluded in an even more stentorian voice.

"I think that is a skirt—" piped French Isabelle in her know-all way till she was shushed by Princess Harriet. But when Princess Sophie, normally a stern mother, responded by bursting into sobs, even Jamie was abashed. Putting his finger in his mouth, a gesture he was thought to have abandoned, he ran over to his father, who was sitting in the window (wondering in point of fact whether it would be bad taste to ask for a dram of whisky so early).

"Come on, old chap," said his father gently, disturbed from his reverie. He drew Jamie on to his lap. "Let's be specially nice today, shall we? Mum's having"—he paused—"a specially difficult time," he ended rather lamely.

All in all, the attendance of Jemima Shore upon Ione Quentin, at the latter's suggestion, passed almost unnoticed in the devastated community of Cumberland Palace. It was in this way that Jemima found herself travelling in a police car, beside Ione, through the bedecked streets of London—bedecked in a way that seemed particularly bizarre to Jemima, since the decorations were all for a wedding that seemed at the moment peculiarly unlikely to take place.

There were displays in the shop windows: brides in numerous guestimates of Princess Amy's wedding dress, ranging from the super-frilly to the super-sleek. Prince Ferdinand for the most part had to make do with Ruritanian-type uniforms: since no one was quite clear just what he could wear at the ceremony. The *cognoscenti* knew that a European Catholic wedding involved a white tie and tails; but a sombre baffled statement from Cumberland Palace had not made it quite clear whether this would be the case at Westminster Cathedral. Maybe, as more than one shop-window dresser decided, one could let the imagination roam? As a result, Jemima was whirled past various wax dummies of Prince Ferdinand, bending over the hand of his fiancée, and wearing a variety of white, green and even pale-blue uniforms, which would not have disgraced the male lead of an operetta.

"We're still in a kidnap situation," said the policeman who appeared to be in charge to Jemima; he spoke, in a seemingly offhand manner, from his position in the back seat between the two women. Ione Quentin's outward demeanour was impassive but Jemima noticed she had twisted a small white handkerchief so tightly round her wrist that it had the look of a tourniquet.

"A kidnap situation?" It was Jemima who asked the question; Ione did not—or could not—speak.

"A kidnap situation, not a siege. That is to say, we know where she is, but they don't know we know. We'd like to avoid a siege, if possible. Just get *her* out quietly"—a pause and then some emphasis—"All the same, we have marksmen in place." Another pause. "Naturally."

"Naturally," echoed Jemima. Ione still said nothing. Then she murmured something desperate, and Jemima, turning, saw that there were tears in her eyes. Jemima realized that what Ione had actually said was: "Marksmen." She added more distinctly: "She may be killed."

The policeman gave her a slightly cold glance. "Miss Quentin, it is our sincere aim that no one should be killed. Not even the killer."

"The killer?" repeated Jemima.

"Detective-Sergeant Fitzgerald, who was shot in the Royal Box whilst attempting to prevent the abduction, died in hospital shortly before you telephoned. The person or persons we have reason to believe are holding HRH . . ." still that pause, then ". . . are wanted on a charge of murder."

After that there was silence in the car and even when they arrived at the edge of the Covent Garden backwater, where operations were being directed from a hidden police command post, Jemima said very little.

Ione Quentin, twisting the tight white tourniquet, said nothing at all.

## SEVENTEEN

# End of
# a Fairy Tale

Princess Amy woke up first. It took only an instant for the horror to return: an instant in which she realized that the curious dark object next to her, lying on the pillow beside her, was a masked head. For a moment she thought—some battered but beloved toy of her childhood; then reality, terrible reality, flooded in.

"I must not cry." Sayings of the past came back. That governess, the cruel one: "Tears don't help." Her father, overheard saying gruffly to her mother: "Now Henriette, here's my handkerchief, you know I can't bear to see a woman cry." (What long-forgotten peccadillo had he committed to make her mother cry?) She braced herself. One of her wrists was tied to Beagle's and the other to the bed, but her ankles were not tied. She gave a tentative wriggle.

Beagle was awake immediately at that; her movement must have disturbed him. He had not in fact intended to fall asleep at all, not only for reasons of security (although Lamb was guarding the house downstairs) but also to have time to reflect, to savour . . .

211

"I want to see your face," said Princess Amy. She spoke softly but urgently as she struggled in vain to sit up until Beagle cooperated by sitting up with her. Then she had to lean awkwardly against the wall until he bent to release her other hand.

"No, not to identify you," she went on. "You know why. I want to *see* you." She had the impression it had been removed at some point in the long night—but then darkness had surrounded her, had surrounded them both.

There was a long pause while the other figure on the bed, still disfigured, appeared to consider her proposition. Then Beagle took off his mask. In the eerie morning light filtering through the heavy shutters, Princess Amy stared at him. Then she put up her newly freed hand and touched his cheek. It was in no way a tender gesture, more an enquiry or a gesture of exploration.

"Recognize me?" he asked. There was something almost pleading about Beagle's question. "Amy," he added. The Princess dropped her hand.

"How should I recognize you?" she asked coldly.

"We've met before. We played together. You once gave me a toy dog for Christmas, black and white spotted. Somewhere I've still got it."

Amy's expression showed quite clearly that she feared, apart from everything else, she now had to cope with madness.

"Oh don't worry, Your Royal Highness." This time Beagle spoke with something of his old familiar and sardonic tone. "I don't expect you to remember. You must have played with so many people. And given away cart-loads of spotted toy dogs. I'll end the dreadful suspense. I'm Josh Taplow these days, Jossie when you used to know me. Jossie Taplow the chauffeur's son. That's right, Taplow who used to work for you and now works for his Highness Prince Ferdinand, your oh-so-noble fiancé—"

"I *do* remember," said Amy slightly incredulously. "Jossie Taplow. Ione said something the other day. Didn't you have long hair? And you were dressed— " She stopped.

"Like a girl. But of course I'm not a girl. Explains a lot, no doubt. And I expect that toy dog explains a lot too, an early love of animals, even when stuffed." Beagle laughed. It was not a pleasant sound.

"So your *father's* involved—"

"Oh, don't blame him, Your Royal Highness. He's been blamed enough already. Principally by my mother. She *is* involved in a way: not that she knew everything. But she's always backed me up—unlike my father who at one point chose to term me the rotten apple. Charming! As a result I haven't spoken to him for years."

Princess Amy said nothing.

Beagle went on almost eagerly: "This place is actually in my mother's name, you know, so as to keep it *really* quiet. No links to me. And it is *really* quiet, isn't it, Your Royal Highness? As I was saying, I'm sure the shrinks will blame my mother for everything, including setting up this flat, if they ever get hold of me."

Since the Princess was still silent, Beagle turned her face towards him. "So what do you think of all that?" he asked.

"I think—I'm sorry for you," said Princess Amy slowly. It was not true. She was not in the slightest bit sorry for Beagle; all her energies in that direction were occupied in trying not to feel sorry for herself. But it occurred to her, if only she could keep calm and think *straight*, that there must be some kind of advantage to her in this weird conversation. Jossie Taplow! Princess Amy did not even remember him as clearly as she had pretended; that had been mere instinct, keep the man talking, don't give up, don't despair. But a recent casual remark by her lady-in-waiting about dressing little boys as girls had stuck in her mind because Ione had connected it to her nephew Jamie's repeated complaints about the girlish nature of his page's suit.

"Boys as girls! It's all wrong." All wrong indeed.

"Yes, I'm sorry for you," she repeated more strongly.

It was at that moment that Lamb, alone in her self-imposed vigil at the door, cramped, stiff, icy with a despair as acute in its own way as that which Princess Amy was trying to keep at bay, decided that death was the only answer.

She wondered how she would make out with the automatic pistol: was it easy to fire? With some confused idea of target practice, Lamb fired two shots rapidly into the door jamb.

When the sound of shots—and the instantaneous police reaction outside—reached Beagle upstairs, he recognized it to be disaster. He had been half expecting it of course. For one thing Beagle knew that he should not have taken off his mask and that some time in the remote past his mother (who liked such things) had read some silly fairy story to Jossie a.k.a. Beagle (who did not) in which a princess persuaded a prince fatally to unmask . . . everyone turned into an animal, no, a swan. Or was it only the prince? In this case the story was somewhat different: Beagle was already the animal and nothing could turn him back into a prince. Beagle, once Jossie, jerked himself into the present.

Ever since the wounding—or possible death—of the detective, Beagle had been seized with a feeling of doom. He knew the disaster to be irreversible. There would be no kingdom of the innocent now, he was aware of that. He was doomed. As he had told Lamb the night before, it was more a case of who or how many he took with him. And yet—it had been worth it, hadn't it? What he had planned, worked and waited for, in one way he had achieved it. Beagle, aware, since Lamb's unwise shots, of the strong police presence outside, felt none of the sick tension and fear which had possessed him throughout the Royal Gala, leading up to the climactic abduction from the box.

When the noise of the loud-hailer reached him, the strong voice of authority reverberating in the tiny mews, he knew that control had already passed from Innoright, in so far as they had ever had it. It was over, all over. Wasn't it? And no fucking fairy-tale ending either. Not for this prince. He was still, in a strange way, happy.

But it wasn't all over. Not for Lamb at any rate, crouching outside the studio door. She gripped the pistol in her hand. Lamb, intent on what now seemed to her the only possible solution as dictated by a mind already beginning to spin away, away from all it had once held dear, had not heard or not taken in the police reaction outside. Despite a childhood spent despising and protesting against such country pursuits as shooting, she was confident that in an atavistic way she now knew quite enough about the gun to use it—just as she had managed easily to fire it downstairs. Colonel Q's daughter. . . . Somewhere in her spiralling state, Lamb managed to be grimly grateful for that loathsome upbringing. That horrifying collection of guns, guns for killing *animals*, her father used to display to them in the library, making her feel utterly powerless and distraught. ("Just smile and say nothing, Leelee," Ione used to urge her. "Above all don't cry; Daddy hates tears.")

Lamb did hear the loud-hailer. She heard it without taking in the full import of the words, more taking the echoing sound as a kind of call to action—her predetermined action, the action which she had sometimes turned over in her mind in the past, during the long nights, caught as she was in the bondage of her jealousy, her lust—and her despair. The image of suffering Snowdrop, her calming mantra, had long ago vanished to be replaced by that of Colonel Q, the hunter.

To Beagle and Princess Amy, frozen the pair of them like the figures on a Grecian urn—*what mad pursuit? what maidens loth?*—the words declaimed by the loud-hailer were not only totally audible but immediately and totally understandable.

". . . We have you completely surrounded. Do not attempt to escape. You are surrounded. There are marksmen on the roof. Throw your weapons out of the window. . . . Do not attempt to escape." The loud-hailer continued to give its sonorous message. Then: "Do you hear us? Send out your prisoner. You may indicate with a white cloth or some other signal that you are sending out your prisoner. . . . We can see where you are holding your prisoner. Repeat. We see you. . . . We have you surrounded."

How could they see us? wondered Beagle. Those new X-ray spy cameras no doubt. Their range was extraordinary even if their use in surveillance circles,

British as well as Iron Curtain, was not advertised to the general public. Then he wondered how they had traced the lair. The possibility of confession by Mrs. Taplow, betrayal by his father, had not occurred to him, when another quite different voice, the unmistakably well-bred and surprisingly collected voice of Ione Quentin, was heard. Beagle immediately assumed Lamb to be in some way responsible for the betrayal.

Ione Quentin was addressing her sister: "Lydia, no harm will come to you if you surrender, Lydia. . . ."

"The bitch," he thought, "I should never have got tangled up with her. I have to admit that royal connection turned me on. And she was raving for it. But she's a loony. Never trust loonies. It should be a motto, Innoright's motto. Protect the innocent! Avoid the loonies. Just supposing there's a difference."

Princess Amy remained silent. She could not trust herself to speak, since the prospect of rescue had the effect of diminishing rather than increasing her reserves of courage. At Beagle's side she began trembling violently. The voice of the police—and wasn't that Ione?—by bringing reality into what had been a kind of hideous dream sequence, fundamentally unreal however horrible, actually terrified her.

Was he now finally going to kill her? But he didn't seem to have a gun. Would he let her go? She must try and assert control again, she must, she had been getting somewhere with him, hadn't she? They had even been in an odd way friendly this morning, they had talked about the past, he had talked about his mother, that was a good sign, wasn't it? Above all, she must stop trembling. She suddenly remembered his name, his childhood name. She would use it.

"What are you going to do with me, *Jossie*?" enquired Princess Amy in a small hoarse voice, the best she could manage.

Hearing her say "Jossie"—and aware perhaps of the effort it had cost her, otherwise how explain his ironic smile?—Beagle began to guide Princess Amy, still bonded to him at the wrist, in the direction of the shuttered window.

What had he intended to do? Was he going to open the window? And was he then going to show her, tattered but like the princess disguised as a goose-girl in another fairy story, still recognizably her Royal Highness Amy Antoinette Marguerite Caroline, Princess of Cumberland. . . . But the exact intentions of Jocelyn Taplow, photographer, a.k.a. Beagle, would never be known for certain and in so far as they subsequently became a matter for debate, it was an academic debate at best.

For it was at this point that Lamb, touched off finally herself to action by that whispered breathless "Jossie," pushed open the door of the room. The blown-up images of Princess Amy were still strewn about; Beagle had pinned some of them up to cover the huge photographs of the seals. Lamb thought confusedly that the seals who survived were gazing at her reproachfully as though at an act of betrayal; but that was wrong: it was Beagle who had been the betrayer. She tore down the photograph next to her with her left hand.

What happened then, unlike Beagle's intentions, did subsequently become the subject of quite hectic debate—none of it academic. Nevertheless, for all this debate, the exact course of these events, too, would never be known for sure, even if in this case some kind of official solution had to be proposed. Witnesses, as so often with a violent but unpremeditated crime, witnesses and their actual state of mind at the time of the crime were the problem.

Certainly Beagle shouted: "Don't shoot!" as Lamb lunged forward with her pistol and having lunged forward apparently recklessly, stood quite steadily with the pistol levelled in the direction of—but that was when the questions began. Was Lamb's pistol levelled in fact at Princess Amy or was it all along levelled at *him*, Beagle, Josh Taplow, the man with whom she had had some crazed and mixed-up sexual relationship?

Princess Amy cowered instinctively backwards, tried to put up both hands to cover her face, made it with the free hand, but the use of the bound wrist pulled Beagle closer to her.

"No! Don't shoot!" shouted Beagle and at least one person—Princess Amy—believed afterwards that he had actually been trying to save her from the shots fired at point-blank range by Lamb in rapid succession. Certainly his body fell heavily down across hers as if he were already curled around her. He had protected her, taken the fire and fallen. That was Princess Amy's version of events; and she herself was quite convinced that she had been Lydia Quentin's original target: "I saw her expression," was her succinct shuddering comment.

All Lamb herself said afterwards was: "Look what you've done. I've killed him. You've made me kill him," as she stood with her now empty pistol gazing with her huge mad eyes across the blood-strewn body of Beagle, still half supported by Amy, half dangling. And that could be taken either way. Just as Beagle's cry of "Don't shoot!" could have been an attempt to save himself rather than the Princess. But that way, of course, he would have pulled the Princess in front of him rather than vice versa. Wouldn't he? At all events, Beagle was not there to give his own version of it all since he had died very shortly after Lamb's attack, probably before the police actually reached him.

He did say or rather mutter something more as the heavily armed besiegers, at the sound of the shots, burst in from the roof, through the windows, burst in from everywhere, even out of the air, as it seemed to the two people left alive inside the house. Amy heard the word "Innocent" but that could have meant anything, including a reference to Innoright itself. The last words she could distinguish as Beagle still looked up towards her from the floor to which he had now sunk, pulling her towards him, his eyes beginning to glaze over, a main artery close to the heart hit, as it was found afterwards, were "Your Royal Hostage." And that once again proved nothing either way; only that Beagle still knew who Amy was as he entered the straight towards death.

Did the word "Hostage" mean that Beagle still understood what he had done? "My Royal Hostage" would have been a testimony to that. "Your Royal Hostage" on the other hand was probably only Beagle's confused attempt to pay Princess Amy her due with what turned out to be quite literally his dying breath.

# EIGHTEEN

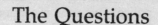

# The Questions

"The wedding will go ahead. As planned," said Jemima Shore to Rick Vancy, still holding the car telephone in her hand. Privately she thought it was amusing that the only truly important message that Rick Vancy had received while travelling in his car, had been taken by her, Jemima. This was because the profound shock—to Rick Vancy, let alone to the rest of the world—of recent events had had the unfortunate effect of making Rick take up smoking again. And he was currently lighting a cigarette—his fourth during the journey between Jemima's flat and the TUS office.

"I do not believe it!" Then: "I simply do have to have a cigarette." That was Rick Vancy's reaction not only when he heard of the traumatic course of the siege but also that Jemima herself had been in a certain sense involved. His reaction was in itself a mixture of outrage—what about her contract with TUS?—and admiration for the kind of upper-class British person whose contacts enabled her to be present somehow even at the dénouement of a British royal siege.

What she did not tell Rick about was the mixture of frustration, apprehension and excitement which had possessed her at the hidden police command post as she stood beside the rigid figure of Ione Quentin. In truth, the initial frustration of being a passive on-looker at the drama soon faded in face of her fears for the outcome. Admiring the extraordinary self-control of the police, given the exceptional nature of the hostage involved—up till the moment when the shots were heard inside the house—Jemima herself found it difficult to maintain an equivalent calm.

She knew that their calm was preserved in the interests of efficiency; perhaps if she had had some-thing to do beyond supporting Ione, she too might have found it easier to stop her thoughts dwelling on the awful possibilities of the siege ending in some innocent death. *Some* innocent death? Since Princess Amy was, it seemed, the only person who could be described as innocent inside the shuttered shop, she had to face the fact that it was her death or injury that she dreaded.

Jemima knew that she should follow the example of Ione Quentin whose excited speeches in Jemima's flat had been succeeded by a marble self-control. Even her use of the loud-hailer as directed by the police—"Lydia, no harm will come to you . . ." —might have been the work of a professional politi-cian used to addressing crowds. Was such discipline the product of a highly disciplined upbringing? For Jemima remembered that Ione's father, that father whom Lydia had much disliked for his severity, had been a well-known soldier. Colonel Q. Yes, that was it. The discipline might not have done Lydia much good, but it had certainly produced impressive re-sults in her sister.

Jemima only saw Colonel Q's elder daughter break down once as Lydia was led away by the police, her small figure muffled in some kind of blanket, jeans-clad legs just visible beneath it.

"Leelee," said Ione in a low voice. Then she straightened her shoulder.

None of this did Jemima choose to confide to Rick Vancy; for one thing she was still sorting out much of it in her own mind, as an orderly person goes through drawers tidying them one by one. That went for the dramatic end of the siege. And then her initial frustration at her own passivity was not something she wanted to share with Rick; let him believe she had herself played a prominent part in the end of the siege. . . .

"I just do not credit it," repeated Rick Vancy, and he shook his distinguished head, now subtly enhanced by an English hair-cut, even as Susanna Blanding wordlessly handed over her own packet of Marlboros. (Curt silently helped himself to one on the way, which must have been loyalty, since he had never hitherto been perceived to be a smoker.)

The reaction of the rest of the world was equally incredulous even if the manner of implementing that disbelief was not necessarily that of Rick Vancy. Now that the Press was released from its self-imposed silence and Major Pat was left to pay with those "exclusive" releases, the debts of honour he had incurred throughout that long summer night of negotiation, the floodgates were well and truly unloosed. Yet it was remarkable that for once even the most lurid headline could scarcely be accused of exaggeration. That was the trouble. On the principle of crying "Wolf!", the Press had presented the public with so many previous headlines all the way from PRINCESS: WEDDING SCARE (something vague to do with high buildings along the route), to PRINCESS: WEDDING

FEARS (a lack of American tourists to buy souvenirs), that even the blazing 30-point letters with which the *Daily Exclusive* led next morning: PRINCESS AMY SAFE— were somehow not quite as dramatic as the story itself, related in much smaller print beneath.

The staider papers, with more space at their command and a far calmer track record, had the advantage; it was generally felt, not only within the confines of the Times building, that *The Times* in its sonorous lengthy leader under the headline A BRIDE FOR ALL SEASONS had, for once, spoken for the nation more effectively than the *Daily Clueless*.

But that was all in public. Private reactions varied. Mirabella Prey, for example, put in a call to Prince Ferdinand (which he refused to take). So then she sent round a note to Cumberland Palace which contained some unwelcome phrases to linger in his mind, although the Prince only remembered them roughly afterwards. This was because he read the note through quickly, or rather read it half-through, then crumpled it and threw it away in that negligent way of his; except that now there would be no Taplow to unscrew the paper, only the impeccable and truly discreet servants of Cumberland Palace.

He did not therefore read as far as Mirabella's announcement of her future plans: life on a Greek or at least Greekish island with her Greekish admirer. The admirer was founding a wild animal sanctuary in her honour. This coincidental realization of the Innoright plans for Windsor Great Park, Regent's Park and other royal parks (if not generally perceived as such) was in fact broken to the world in general by Miss Mary of the *Daily Clueless* the next day.

"LOVE AMONG THE LEOPARDS! How too, too sweet," exclaimed Princess Amy on this occasion when she read Miss Mary's column. "I hope they *eat* her," she added generously.

Mirabella's phrases, roughly remembered, which haunted Ferdel in spite of himself went as follows: "So now she is a heroine, your little Princess. You will admire her and who knows, perhaps at last you will love her. I congratulate the little white mouse. How was she in the hands of the sexy photographer. . . . Often these so prim English girls . . ." It was at that point that Ferdel had crumpled the paper. He should have known better than to read anything penned by Mirabella: that ever maddening ability of hers to get under his skin. . . . However, he was no longer thinking of Mirabella now, there being plenty to think about nearer home, to put it mildly. And Prince Ferdinand was still wondering quite how he *could* put it, put it mildly that is. There was a question which was torturing him, to be frank, beneath the smooth and tender caring surface which he had exhibited ever since Amy's return.

It was not a question which affected his admiration. Admire her! Ye Gods, he admired her. The pluck, the spirit, the *endurance*, even including the last dreadful incident and the removal of her own lady-in-waiting's sister, to say nothing of his own chauffeur's son lying there in pools of blood. . . . Somewhere at the very bottom of Prince Ferdinand's horrified reflections was surprise that *servants*, royal servants should somehow feature so strongly in all this. (For he did not in the very last analysis distinguish between Ione Quentin, the lady-in-waiting, and Taplow the chauffeur: both were to him and perhaps finally to Amy—servants.) And how bravely Amy had handled all the rest of it, including even, with courage beyond any reasonable expectation, allowing a very short Press Conference to be held at Cumberland Palace!

"Otherwise, Ma'am," admitted Major Pat ruefully, "they'll never believe you're all in one piece."

"I jolly well am all in one piece, aren't I?" replied Princess Amy with a touch of new asperity in her voice, or perhaps it was sheer exhaustion. "Which is more than you can say for my sapphires. Did no one ever find that earring? Ione, now did you ask—"

But there was of course no Ione to ask. Amanda, the young secretary at the Palace who had been helping with the wedding arrangements, seconded to a more senior position, was, in Amy's opinion, simply not a patch on Ione in competence, knowledge or tact. So grievously in fact did Amy, in her first flustered moments of return, miss Ione's calming presence and all it meant in terms of security and comfort that for a long time she simply could not understand why it was no longer possible for Ione to attend her.

"But why *can't* Ione be here, Mummy?" she cried angrily, used to having her own ways in all things with the Duchess, an arrangement which generally suited them both splendidly. The willowy Duchess, wafer thin to the point of emaciation (Amy had inherited her father's tendency to *embonpoint*), could do no more than sigh; tears—hers—were clearly not far away. Of the Princesses Sophie and Harriet, the one knew herself to be too plain-spoken (in the circumstances) and the other too nerve-wracked like her mother, to do anything; they rolled their eyes at each other, those huge slightly exophthalmic blue eyes which all three sisters had in common.

It was Prince Ferdinand who softly explained: "My darling, you must understand: it is just not possible.

Poor Ione. We are all of us so sorry for her. But the sister, you know, she is—" How to put it? Yes: "In the hands of the police. Ione must rest at home. It is very difficult for her. She is, she *was*, devoted to her sister, and that this should happen to *you*! She is naturally quite shattered. Besides, it would not be—quite *suitable*, would it, darling?"

"In the hands of the police, is she? Well, I hope they keep her in their hands. I shall never forget her expression. Did I tell you, Amanda—" The thought of Lydia Quentin a.k.a. Lamb did at least distract Princess Amy from her lost sapphires—and her lost lady-in-waiting.

As for Princess Amy's decision—for it was finally her decision to go ahead with the wedding on the same date and with exactly the same arrangements (at least outwardly: what the police now did was their own business), that too was, as far as Prince Ferdinand was concerned, beyond praise.

It was not only the feeling of relief which such a decision gave to the nation as a whole: things could not be *that* bad, could not have been that bad, the poor little Princess couldn't be in that bad a state. Nor yet the commercially based relief of all those whose arrangements (and profits) depended on a given Royal Wedding on a given royal day: not least among these TUS and Rick Vancy of TUS, booked to leave for the Middle East immediately afterwards. But Ferdel himself had a deep-seated almost superstitious feeling that if the wedding did take place exactly as arranged, then his own relationship with Amy, that too would be restored to its original state. This relationship, which Ferdel believed would be the basis of a long and happy married life, was certainly not lacking in physical passion; all the same he knew it to be *au fond* more affectionate than passionate. If not precisely an arranged marriage, theirs was a marriage of convenience, great convenience. In such a relationship, affection was more important than passion.

But Ferdel could not forget one particular conversation with Amy following her release. In the immediate aftermath she had been almost totally distraught and in the course of her distraction had made, or at least begun to make, certain statements, highly frightening statements about her captivity, the import of which Ferdel had simply not dared think through at the time. The conversation came later. He would really like to obliterate the memory of it, as he wished to forget Mirabella's lethal phrase "the sexy photographer"; alas, he was unable to do so.

How odd to feel what must be jealousy for virtually the first time in his life! (In principle Ferdel considered jealousy a terrible waste of energy.) To feel it in this situation and to feel it on behalf of *Amy*! Of all women in the world. When he thought of all the other delightful creatures he had known and their composite behaviour, exotic, sensual, provoking, none of whom had managed to arouse his jealousy although many had tried. Ah well. Did jealousy perhaps come with age? Another horrible suggestion.

Amy had been encircled by Ferdel's arms when the disturbing conversation in question took place. It was when he allowed himself to say (and in retrospect that had been his mistake): "Amy, my darling, exactly what happened? You said such odd things when you first came back. He didn't— My God, my darling—" In his agitation, Ferdel found he was gripping both Amy's arms till she winced; he was also gazing at her most intensely.

A curious expression crossed Princess Amy's face. It was not that pop-eyed capacity for right royal indignation she had inherited from the late Duke, still less the air of sweet resignation characteristic of her mother, but seldom seen on her own very different features. No, Prince Ferdinand found it quite impossible to analyse the exact nature of Princess Amy's curious expression: in another older, more sophisticated, woman he might even have detected a very faint air of triumph there, but that was to be ruled out where Amy was concerned. Nor could Ferdel analyse quite why he found her look so disquieting, nor why some inclination of future trouble reached him, and from the direction he had least expected it. For an instant he was looking once more into the eyes of Eve, into whose beautiful and challenging eyes in one form or another he had been gazing all his adult years.

Of the two of them, Prince Ferdinand was the first to look away. After all, he had always known how to handle women, hadn't he? He gathered Amy more closely into his arms so that she nestled there.

"My little one," he said over the top of her head, "I'm going to protect you so carefully in the future. No harm will ever come to you," he added very firmly. "Thank God, no real harm has come to you."

Still Princess Amy, her face buried in his shoulder, said nothing. But then, come to think of it, what was there to say?

Elsewhere there were other questions in the air, some—but not all—of which received more satisfactory answers than that posed *malgré lui* by the anxious Prince Ferdinand. For his part, he never returned to this particular interrogation just as Princess Amy herself never enquired again after her lost sapphire earring. Since she had decided that never never in a thousand years would she wear those hateful *evil* sapphires again, the whole subject might be allowed to lapse; thus the Rasputin sapphires were locked away once more (minus one earring) waiting like Camus' plague for their next malevolent appearance on the European scene. The comparison was that of Susanna Blanding who alone among observers had appreciated the historic and superstitious significance of the jewellery adorning Princess Amy at the moment of her abduction.

One of the important questions posed elsewhere concerned the extent of the Innoright conspiracy and the fate of the conspirators. Innoright Overground, the parent organization, expressed itself properly appalled by the events of the abduction and hastened to disavow, root and branch, the behaviour of its cell. Files were flung open with wild-eyed haste, protestations of non-violence, appeals to the Innoright charter and the Innoright motto—Protection of the Innocent and Princess Amy *was* innocent—filled the air. It was nevertheless only a matter of time before Innoright, as its honest members sadly realized, went into voluntary disbandment.

Non-violence as a policy was hard to sustain in view of the death of the detective; and there were other details to take into account, deaths which not only bit into the very structure of Innoright but also demonstrated clearly that the criminal cell had in fact been closely involved with the central organization. The death of Monkey a.k.a. Edward James Arthur Monck MBE was one such example, which together with the revelations concerning his participation in the cell, caused the keenest anguish among the members. Generous and kindly, if some might say endowed with an over-managerial manner, Mr. Monck had after all been one of the founders of Innoright.

On the other hand, from another point of view, Monkey's death did answer one question: the question of whether he had been involved in the abduction itself as well as in its organization. Princess Amy was understandably unable to state whether he had actually driven the getaway car, but Monkey, in a carefully explicit note to the police, laid down his own actions; at the same time regretting the death of the detective and "the discourtesy to HRH Princess Amy."

Monkey gave much thought to the manner of his death: it was after all to be his last plan. When the news of Princess Amy's rescue broke, he considered at first a last meal in South Eaton Place, a fine Burgundy (but no meat-eating: dying was no time to desert one's principles) and a host of fine pills which he prudently kept by him. Many dreams were over, dreams of Lamb (what had become of her? Under arrest, poor child), dreams of a world made safe for the innocent, were over.

He would go to join Cynthia. As a Catholic of his own particular variety, Monkey did not rate such an action as a sin: once again—as with the detective's death—joining Cynthia was the end to justify it. Monkey was in the process of writing a last note of command for Carmencita—"Do *not* enter the library. E.J.A.M."—when the appropriate last plan was revealed to him. Cocking an eyebrow, at his most agreeably simian, Monkey destroyed the note. Carefully he attired himself in his City clothes, dark pin-stripe suit including a blue handkerchief in his breast pocket, an umbrella—and a bowler. The umbrella and blue handkerchief indicated postponement and the bowler signified after all the final abandonment of the Underground Plan; and with Monkey's death on the electric rails of the Underground just outside Sloane Square station, it could be said that the final abandonment of the Underground Plan had taken place.

Fox died, too, adopting the same solution as Monkey (which would have pleased the latter: at the last, Fox was obediently following his lead in a way that he signally failed to do on the night of the abduction). Fox's choice of death-place was Tottenham Court Road Tube station—Fox being aware that the lead of the costumes from Leaviss made it only a matter of time before the police reached him. All his emotions were by this time bound up in his dread of parting from Noel, which was how he viewed the prospect of long imprisonment. It was ironic that the dog Noel, who had nothing of his master's death wish, used his notorious cowardice to pull back at the last moment from the drop and thus survived the experience. So that Fox's last wish of a death together with Noel, like his wish for a free kingdom of the animals, was not to be granted.

The police did reach Mrs. Charity Wadham a.k.a. Chicken quite quickly, but Mrs. Charity Wadham made no attempt to kill herself. She saw absolutely no need. Chicken was reached via a number of routes: not only her appreciation of Ignazio Dorati but her condemnation of Zeffirelli's film on the stairs leaving the Royal Opera House was recollected by one witness, who had turned to look at her: the witness in question had particularly enjoyed the Zeffirelli film of *Otello*. Most telling of all, the abandoned saris were found wrapped round Chicken's score of *Otello*—a substantial mistake on Pussy's part but perhaps she had been unconsciously jealous of Chicken's paraded knowledge of the opera during its performance. What with Chicken's condescending remark concerning Zeffirelli and her score-book, she had certainly paid dearly for this knowledge. There were plenty of finger-prints there to identify Chicken with the score-reading Indian woman, even if one of Chicken's teaching associates to whom it had once belonged, had not recognized the score.

Two questions in all this remained unanswered. The identity of the second "Indian" woman, the masked "cruel" woman who had guarded Princess Amy, assuming that they were one and the same person, remained officially unproved. Chicken reso-lutely refused to say anything on the subject; in fact she refused to make any statement at all, refused a lawyer (one was assigned), refused to consider her defence and merely announced her determination of pleading "Guilty" and accepting her sentence what-ever it might be. Chicken was confident in herself that she would never talk, never break, despising Monkey and Fox for their abject solutions. How like men! Women were so much stronger when it came to the point.

Chicken gave no trouble on remand in prison, however; was pleasant, respectful, nice to the young girls who were her fellow inmates: even if they were not particularly nice back to her since she was held to have laid hands on Princess Amy, by now a genu-inely popular folk heroine. It was a consolation that the problems with her diet gave her opportunity to administer well-turned little lectures on the cruel treatment of battery hens. Vegetarianism proving a far more sympathetic subject, Chicken somewhat redeemed herself. Even in Holloway, thought Chicken, once a teacher, always a teacher.

The charges against Chicken were serious enough but she was not, so far as the police were concerned, on a charge of murder or even of conspiracy to murder since it was accepted that she had not been present at the incident in the Royal Box. So, one way and another, Chicken was confident of holding out, serving her sentence—for the cause. Setting herself up to be a model prisoner, one day she would emerge—and work for it again with equal determination, or perhaps even greater strength, forged by the iron years of martyrdom in prison. But she would not trust *men*—men like Fox with their ineradicable and fatal tendency to violence—next time.

So the question of Chicken's accomplice, of the sixth conspirator, for want of definite proof remained officially open.

That meant that Pussy—for the time being—went free. There was nothing specific to connect her with Chicken in the absence of the latter's hoped-for confession. The witness who remembered Chicken's disparaging comment on Zeffirelli's film had no recollection, and maddeningly was not even sure if Chicken had *had* a companion, although he admitted that the remark could hardly have been made to the blank wall of the staircase. Like Chicken, he had been in a hurry.

Princess Amy never saw fit to mention the characteristic smell of lavender water which had linked Pussy to her hated governess; along with many other details of that horrendous time, she had suppressed it. In any case, such olfactory evidence would surely never have stood up in a court of law. And Pussy had been careful to keep her gloves on during her period guarding the Princess.

No, the police wanted proper evidence to arrest Mrs. Pussy Moscowitz and in their patient way they were convinced that with time they would get it. In the meantime they were watching Pussy.

That left Pussy free, like the rest of the world, to watch the Royal Wedding. She could either watch it on television in the flat dominated by huge pictures of Caro-Otter or maybe, as Pussy put it to herself, with one of her malevolent smiles, she would take her place among the crowds: "To see how the little Madam is getting on."

Another question which remained unanswered was the question of the killer of Jean-Pierre Schwarz-Albert a.k.a. Tom. It was the subject of yet another conversation between Jemima and Pompey, this time in the Groucho Club where Pompey sat nursing a whisky and showing a gallant appreciation of the various literary luminaries by whom he was surrounded.

"Anita Bainbridge!" he exclaimed at one point, "I must tell my wife. One of her real favourites." Jemima thought it best not to intervene. Then more sombre matters occupied them.

"It's all very well the shouting and the cheering, and the gutsy little Princess—and my word, she is gutsy—but I've still got my case," complained Pompey. "Work to do. I can't fit my murder to Taplow, the photographer; the little costumier is a possibility, just as he always was, except that the hotel is adamant he couldn't have got where necessary with the dog. The woman they're holding for abduction, the teacher, Wadham, will say nothing except she's guilty of the abduction but that she abhors violence."

"Pompey—" said Jemima slowly. "There's another woman of course. I've been thinking about it, working out a theory. Testing something I said to you a long time ago. That murder and now the Royal Wedding still to come. Tell me about the police watch. Who are they watching?"

# NINETEEN

# Living Doll

The problem, Jemima speedily realized, was to find a language of lyrical freshness which had not been used before; or was not being currently used by all the other hundreds and thousands of commentators upon the Royal Wedding of Princess Amy and Prince Ferdinand. Since the problem rapidly proved insoluble (what could you say that wasn't almost audibly being said in other television studios close at hand?) Jemima decided not to try and solve it. Instead she gave herself up to the enjoyment of the occasion; or to be precise, wished to give herself up to it. It was still impossible to disregard completely, in one part of her mind, the implications of her last conversation with Pompey and she trusted that Pompey himself had not disregarded them. All this was, however, for another day—or she devoutly hoped it was.

In the meantime journalistic tasks, the very reverse of humdrum, awaited her in the more-or-less plastic studio erected by TUS on the roof of a building at an angle to Westminster Cathedral. TUS's studio-in-the-sky jostled with those of other famous American TV stations. On the narrow stairs which led up to the roof from the main building, a mock-Georgian office block, Jemima was amused to encounter other

British notabilities ranging from the truly notable to the notable-for-being-notable who would give their own confident Best-of-Britain commentaries to be beamed around the U.S. She hoped she could still count herself amongst them despite her recent sacking from Megalith.

Among historical experts, Susanna Blanding was there, of course, notebooks, red books and all; her role was actually to crouch beneath the semi-circular simulated studio table at which Jemima sat, bemicrophoned and be-earplugged (to receive what was another form of royal command—from the producer) along with Rick Vancy. And along with Curt. The latter's perpetually sleepy stance had been abandoned overnight for a bright-eyed look which was almost disconcerting; his eyes positively glittered with innocent enthusiasm, and preppy, Jemima supposed, was probably the right word for the clothes in which he was now attired. This alien image—if not to the U.S., but then Curt would not be seen on camera—was in marked contrast to Rick Vancy's studiedly quiet British attire and Jemima's own sharply elegant emerald-green Jean Muir jacket (all that would be visible of her, she devoutly hoped, since she was wearing training shoes for long-term comfort, which could hardly be said to accord with her tight black skirt and sheer dark stockings).

As usual, Susanna's own wardrobe did not bear thinking about. Taken all in all, her crouching position, with a noiseless electronic typewriter to tap out news flashes and hand them up from below to the team, reminded Jemima of that of a crusader's dog carved at the end of its master's tomb. It was by now quite clear that where Susanna was concerned Rick was the crusader.

For the time being, Jemima had better things to think about than Susanna's potential problems in this direction. Other wardrobes claimed her attention, notably that of the Royal Family about to come on view, described in a series of Press releases evidently composed by the various designers involved, and accompanied by illustrative sketches. Where the sketches were concerned, Jemima would come to see them as an endearing triumph of hope over experience; that is, when she got her first glimpse of the dignified but, dare one say it, ever-so-slightly dumpy incumbents of the dresses and compared them to the slim long-necked swans of the artist's imagination. At the same time the Keatsian language entranced her, words like azure and malachite abounded where, contemplating the reality, it was difficult not to conclude that humbler words such as blue and green would have done just as well.

Jemima found that her mind was still half distracted by those other nagging fears: but she *must* put them aside, this was not the time or place, if only because Jemima, not being a natural fashion journalist, knew that she needed all her concentration to interpret the Keatsian language to American viewers (waking up after all to an extremely early breakfast by U.S. time). At this moment the final Press release was handed to her from below by Susanna. This was the one everyone had been waiting for: *the* Press release, *the* sketch, *the* dress itself. . . .

The sketch now before her showed in effect an enchanting doll. On the evidence of this, Jemima had no difficulty in believing that Princess Amy bridal dolls would be bestsellers for many years to come. As for the fluttering Princess Amy blue bows (the traditional "something blue") which were depicted nest-

ling at the shoulder and somewhere in the endless
bouffant train (eighteen feet long: six inches longer
than that of the Duchess of York, the Press release
proudly proclaimed), those belonged perhaps more
to the world of the chocolate box. Jemima also had no
difficulty in believing that chocolate boxes, mugs,
plates, thimbles and so forth, depicting Princess Amy
in all her bridal glory, would also be bestsellers for
many years to come.

All the same, why shouldn't poor little Princess
Amy look like a living doll if that was how she
wanted to look? Given her ordeal, which had so
nearly ended in her being not so much a living doll as
a dead one. It was time to think again about her own
personal language of lyrical freshness. What about
some historical and artistic comparisons? Winterhal-
ter, Greuze, Gainsborough: these were names to
conjure with and she only hoped that Susanna
Blanding, somewhere in her copious notes, had had
the forethought to conjure with them.

Jemima gazed down at the little television monitor
flush with the desk before her. The only public
alteration to arrangements made at the instigation of
the police, was to have the bride leave from one of the
other royal palaces in The Mall, as other royal brides
had done in recent years, instead of from Cumberland Palace itself, which being sited in Regent's Park,
involved a far longer and less controllable route. The
crowds in The Mall were quite as deep as Jemima
remembered from shots of other weddings involving
members of the Royal Family closer to succession.
The abduction, however distressing for its subject,
had undoubtedly been good for business: that is, if
you had the temerity to regard the public attendance
at a Royal Wedding as a form of business.

She could see numerous placards being held up echoing the theme of the celebrated buttons: AMY MEANS I LOVE YOU, now occasionally altered to AMY MEANS I ADORE YOU, and there were balloons and here and there paper hats of Amy blue bearing the same message. Then there were some new-style placards bearing the allusive message: AMY NOT ANIMALS. Jemima learnt later that a few rash protestors had emerged bearing placards which read on the contrary: WE LOVE ANIMALS NOT AMY.

Regrettably if understandably, these small groups were manhandled by the crowd and forced to disband, their placards pulled apart: equally regrettably perhaps, there was little or no interference from the police during these scattered episodes. The police, standing with their backs to the route facing the crowds (an innovation at the wedding of the Prince of Wales), maintained an impassive stance. They were watching of course: watching not only these—the few—who proclaimed their animal rights' sympathies but watching for those who might share these sympathies without proclaiming them.

There were no Innoright posters, placards or buttons, no Innoright balloons or paper hats. The sad-eyed logo was signally absent from the proceedings. Pussy, having reached a decision to attend personally instead of making do with television—"to see the little Madam one last time for myself," as she put it—took care to wear nothing and carry nothing that might connect her with Innoright. Weddings of healthy young women generally made her feel physically sick with rage when she thought of Caro-Otter who would never have a wedding, but for the time being she knew she must subjugate her revulsion.

Pussy installed herself on a small portable seat near

the front of the crowd in the piazza of the Cathedral. It was not, to be honest, that she had arrived all that early to achieve such an advantageous position: just that Pussy, heavily pressing, was a difficult force to resist when it came to having her own way. Her present desire was to watch the wedding from a convenient spot at the bottom of one of the stands in the piazza, amid the crowds but not swamped by them, and she achieved it.

Pussy took out a plastic box of sweet pastries and proceeded to lick round the chocolate coating of one. She needed sweetness, and sustenance. Pussy, unlike some of those near her, did not offer to share her pastries with the policeman in front of them. Pussy, watched by the impassive policeman, and watching him, licked resolutely on.

Jemima, from her perch roughly above Pussy's head, studied the order of events and the official programme with its seemingly endless list of coaches and carriages and cars and mounted escorts and so forth and so on. (No official mention of armed escorts and so forth and so on, although one would imagine that in view of recent events the practice at recent royal weddings of substituting policemen for various bewigged coachmen on the boxes of the coaches would scarcely be abandoned at this one.)

"She killed herself!" exclaimed Susanna Blanding suddenly from her crouching position, holding headphones with which she was listening to the news flash. "Killed herself in prison. Lydia! How on earth did they let her? My God, poor old Ione, this will kill her, sorry, unfortunate use of language. Well, perhaps it's for the best. Think of the trial and all that. Which reminds me—"

Still sounding rather shocked, but ever dutiful,

Susanna began scurrying through her notes and the order of the procession.

"What have we here? Ah yes, do you have this, Jemima? Rick—it needn't bother you. 'The Hon. Amanda Macpherson-Wynne, Acting Lady-in-waiting to HRH, etc., etc., will travel in the second carriage in place of Miss Ione Quentin.'"

"I have that," said Jemima, thinking with pity, certainly no vindictive satisfaction, of the intense girl she had seen praying—as she had then thought—at the statue of St. Francis. Even if Susanna, in her practical way, was right, and death, self-sought death (and how *had* she managed to achieve it? Some dereliction of care there?) was the best solution to that particular tragic life, she could not mark the event, like any youthful suicide, without some pang of emotion for what once might have been prevented.

Poor Ione. As Susanna, her cousin, had charitably and percipiently said.

It was while the first cascade of roaring cheers came through on the monitor, greeting Princess Amy as she was drawn slowly in her coach out of the gates of the royal palace into the Mall, that Jemima, looking in her monitor as the television cameras raked the crowds now here now there, saw a face she recognized.

"My God!" she thought. "I don't believe it. How could they have let her? They were going to watch her. She's right there. I *saw* her."

Subsequently, Jemima's chief memory of the events which followed centred on the fearful and frustrating experience, comparable only to a nightmare which sometimes plagued her of swimming through mud, of trying to move rapidly through a crowd which was profoundly and determinedly stationary. Only the trainer shoes were helpful and seemed like an extraordinary piece of prescience.

"It must have been like Jean Louis Barrault in *Les Enfants du Paradis*," observed a film buff friend wisely afterwards. "You remember, looking for Arletty as the crowd all swirled, revelling in the opposite direction."

"This revelling crowd was not swirling in *any* direction," countered Jemima rather sharply, for she too had seen the movie many times. "That was the whole point. It was standing stock still and revelling if you want to put it like that, on its stationary feet and in its position which it had risen at dawn or even slept out all night to protect."

At the time it was the thought of that face in the crowd which impelled her forward, a killer's face, above all a desperate face, and she must get there, no time now for phone calls, no good to appeal to the many policemen on the route, certainly no time to appeal to a higher authority.

So that it was in fact at the exact moment, in the antiphonal rise and fall of the cheering, of Princess Amy's own arrival in the piazza, that Jemima managed to get within striking distance of her prey. And it was at the moment of arrival too, that Jemima, whose determined path beaten through the crowd had not passed unregarded, was herself seized by the authoritative hand of the law.

Jemima, pulled back temporarily from engagement with the person she had sought, was able to witness for herself the moment when Princess Amy, pointing the toe of her plain but immensely high-heeled white satin shoe, stepped gingerly out of her coach.

The flowing white train with its occasional blue bows was bundled out after her and then fanned out on the pavement before the Cathedral by the designer, energetically aided by the cooing little French bridesmaids, Amy's nieces. Beneath the soft white tulle veil gleamed diamonds—some respectable British tiara one supposed, in view of the dismal track record of the Russian sapphires. Amy's distinguished and ancient French grandfather, who was to give her away, eased himself stiffly out of the coach and stood for all his age erectly beside her, a tall figure compared to her tiny one.

Beneath the drifting veil, lifting slightly in the breeze, Princess Amy's expression was impossible to discern. More strongly than ever, Jemima had the impression of a doll, a doll at the centre of these hieratic ceremonies, but still mercifully a living doll.

"Let me go," cried Jemima, and then more forcibly: "*Stop* her." For one moment Jemima did succeed in getting free and ran a short way, elbowing amid the crowd, only to be grasped yet more firmly by someone in plain clothes who was evidently a policeman.

"She must go into the Cathedral," thought Jemima desperately. "Once she's inside, she's safe. Don't just *stand* there. . . ."

Still the Princess stood, poised, inscrutable, in her ivory tower of lace and tulle and diamonds, on the verge of taking the arm of her towering grandfather, but still half facing the cheering crowds on the piazza.

"I'll just have to shout, I'll just have to bellow," thought Jemima. "There's no other way. We're quite close. I hope to hell she can hear me."

"Ione!" she yelled.

Although Jemima's frantic appeal, half scream, half cry, had to reach the ears of Ione Quentin, now in the front row of the crowd, over all the other noise, the cheers, the chomping of the horses, the jangling of their bridles, the music now swelling from inside the Cathedral, reach her it did. It must have reached her, because Ione Quentin hesitated just one instant, still with the concealed weapon in her hand, and turned her head, as it were involuntarily, sideways.

One instant was enough. In that instant Princess Amy put her hand at last on her grandfather's arm and began to move gracefully and, thank God, inexorably into the interior of the Cathedral.

Behind her, and still quite unknown to the bridal cortège, Ione Quentin, former lady-in-waiting to HRH Princess Amy of Cumberland, collapsed in the savage grip of three policemen.

# TWENTY

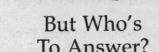

# But Who's
# To Answer?

Afterwards Jemima Shore's decision to abandon her post was much criticized—by TUS that is, and by Rick Vancy in particular. TUS behaved with what was considered by Jemima's agent to be a strange lack of moral fibre in trying to withhold her fee on the grounds that she had never actually commented on the wedding itself—not at the crucial moment anyway. Fortunately it was not for nothing that Jemima's agent, a girl in her twenties, was already known as the Dragon of Drury Lane (where her office was) and the matter, months later, was finally sorted out to the Dragon's, if not TUS's satisfaction.

Some of Rick's bitterness could probably be ascribed to the fact that TUS did not in the event find itself with only one presenter in the shape of Rick himself for the arrival of the bride. When Jemima precipitately and clumsily unhooked herself from her position, and fled the plastic studio-in-the-sky there was a short anxious cry from the producer: "Is she sick or something?" followed by the imperious command, "Cut the anchor." This sounded strangely nautical to English ears, along the lines of "abandon

ship." But it merely meant that the freelance British
cameraman hired for the occasion, who happened to
be Jemima's friend Spike Thompson, formerly of
Megalith, should swing away from the "anchor" in
the shape of Jemima and concentrate on the wedding
scenes below.

Spike, like the Dragon of Drury Lane, was in his
own way more than equal to the occasion. He swung
his camera neatly away from Jemima's seat, pausing
only to file away the notion of further financial claims
against TUS for services beyond the call of contract
(Spike Thompson's claims in this respect being a
legend in his lifetime, held by many of the mean-
hearted to be at least partly responsible for the recent
coup at Megalith). A minute later he had his camera
unerringly focused on the resplendent figure of Curt,
already installed, bemicrophoned and be-earplugged
in Jemima's place. So now there were two "anchors"
on the TUS desk again, if you preferred the more
exciting American phrase to the calmer British notion
of presenters.

The rest, as many at TUS (but not Rick Vancy and
not Susanna Blanding) would murmur with awe
afterwards, was history: British history. Where, oh
where, had the somnolent Curt acquired that intimate knowledge of every detail of the wedding
ceremony, that intimate command of anecdote about
every royal personage, that intimacy—one had to use
the word since a sense of intimacy combined with
pageantry subsequently became his trademark as a
broadcaster—with every facet of British history from
the Conquest onwards? By the time Curt's dazzling
reputation had been established, outclassing coast to
coast and rating for rating the laid-back style so
sedulously cultivated by Rick Vancy during his weeks

in Britain, it was far too late for Susanna Blanding's indignant cry from the depths: "None of this is in my notes. I do believe he's making it all up." A star had been born. For this at least Rick Vancy would always blame Jemima Shore.

Jemima Shore on the other hand would always blame herself for not being more emphatically direct to Pompey in their last conversation about Ione Quentin's responsibility for the murder of Schwarz-Albert at the Republican Hotel. Notions of opportunity came to her: she remembered seeing Ione Quentin leave the stage where Major Pat was holding forth at rather an odd moment in the proceedings, given her role in it all. She must have had the note delivered then, the note which drew Schwarz-Albert out of the Press Conference. Then she boldly took advantage of the royal arrival and the royal question-and-answer session for the killing itself, knowing full well how absorbed the general attention would be in the inner room. She had only to remember to remove the note from the body, and of course Ione had easy access to the "Royal" paper-knives, besides knowing in advance how sharp they were.

Notions of motive also passed through Jemima's mind. Who but Ione Quentin, who would, in her own phrase, "do anything" for her sister, had such a strong motive to eliminate the inquisitive Schwarz-Albert? The other members of Innoright could merely have ejected him, but Lydia's terrifying personal vulnerability, to say nothing of her royal connection, made her a soft target for Schwarz-Albert's machinations. Did he plan to use her for further information against her comrades? If so, Ione, who regularly went through her sister's things and even followed her, as she told Jemima, would have known. As Jemima had

pointed out intuitively to Pompey, the Republican
Hotel represented an opportunity for Ione—who had
the list of attendances at her command—an opportunity which might not come again.

With Ione, whatever her normal feelings outside
the influence of madness towards Princess Amy,
Lydia always came first. (Not that Lydia herself reciprocated those feelings: she had shown the total self-absorption of the mad—or the fanatic—throughout,
using her sister's royal position shamelessly without
regard to the consequences for Ione. She would never
even have known of Ione's daring deed on her
behalf . . . for Ione, as ever solicitous of Lydia's
welfare, would have kept her own counsel on that.) It
was Lydia towards whom Ione's thoughts turned,
not her royal mistress, at the moment of the abduction. That amazing conversation had given Jemima
the vital clue; just as Ione's conduct at the siege,
pondered over later, had brought Jemima to a full
realization of the cold-blooded indifference Ione
showed to Princess Amy's fate within the shuttered
shop—compared to that of her sister. So Jemima's
enforced passivity on that occasion had not been
wasted after all. It had enabled her to see that
someone capable of such indifference was in the final
analysis ruthless: in Ione Quentin's case, a ruthless
killer.

Perhaps Pompey was right and like the tortoise he
was, he would have reached Ione sooner or later:
after all he had his creative-writing witness from
the Underground who described the woman with
"burning eyes" threatening Schwarz-Albert. (Only
the burning eyes in question belonged of course to
Ione, not Lydia Quentin, as Jemima had surmised.)
But by that time Princess Amy might have been dead;

like Taplow, the photographer, and Lydia Quentin herself. As for the latter, Pompey had a few old-fashioned remarks concerning those who permitted, or at least had not prevented, her from committing suicide. The macabre detail that it was a long sharp pin, originally part of the Quentin tiara worn at the fatal Gala, which Lydia had secreted about her and with which she performed the opening of her veins at the wrist, did not make things any better in Pompey's opinion.

At least Ione, driven finally to craziness by her beloved sister's death, had failed in her last mad rash attempt.

"It would never have worked," Pompey comfortingly assured Jemima. "Though I grant you she shouldn't have been there in the first place—our failure entirely, so much police presence needed elsewhere, that was the trouble."

He patted her knee. They were seated in the Groucho Club again, Pompey confessing himself to have taken quite a fancy to the place, especially since Mrs. Pompey had recently approved all late home-comings from this particular quarter; the literary gleanings were to be her reward. Detective Sergeant Vaillant had dropped his superior there with some reluctance, or rather he had left him there with some reluctance; he meditated some off-the-record conferences with Jemima Shore himself one day—starting at the Groucho Club.

"There was a good deal of focus on the other one, of course," continued Pompey. "The big woman with the model daughter. But do you know all she did? Munched her way through a box of chocolate biscuits, then cried with happiness along with all the rest of them at the sight of the bride coming out of the

Cathedral. Finally queued up to see the wedding flowers inside the Cathedral after the ceremony. Even then they kept a pretty close eye, naturally. But what should she do then? Never looked at the flowers but went and lit a candle to some statue or other. Harmless as you please—if you call the saints and all that sort of thing harmless, which, I have to admit," concluded Pompey generously, "many do."

It was true. Pussy had not lit a candle since her own violent rejection of the Catholic religion years ago; but some kind of cathartic experience had happened to her as she watched Princess Amy, married at last, on the arm of her handsome husband, standing on the steps of the Cathedral, laughing and waving as the bells began to peal out overhead, joined, so it seemed, by all the bells of London. Not rage and bitterness but overwhelming sorrow swept over her; she wept not for happiness as her covert watchers had supposed but for loss, a loss which no anger could hope to assuage.

So Pussy lit a candle for her daughter Caro in front of the statue of St. Francis in Westminster Cathedral. Unaware of Lamb's suicide and thinking of her held in prison, she lit a candle for her too, another gesture of reconciliation towards those young women who could not really be held responsible for the death of her own daughter.

"You did very well, my dear, very well," Pompey conceded.

"And my instinct? What you call my woman's instinct and I call my rational good sense. Did that do well?" demanded Jemima; but she knew she would never win this particular argument with Pompey. A team . . . long might they remain so.

As for Ione Quentin: "A cool customer," was

Pompey's final verdict. "But she'll probably end up in Broadmoor. Given the circumstances."

"You mean—she shouldn't."

"No, no, that's the solution all right. She's totally deranged according to the prison doctor. By the way, it seems the mother, the Quentin mother, committed suicide. Started Lydia off on her particular course. Something very unstable in that family."

"And the famous father—Colonel Q, you remember him—was obviously a monster, at least where Lydia Quentin was concerned. What a recipe for disaster! Martinet for a father, depressive for a mother. Ione told me that Lydia wanted to have her father put down in revenge for the death of a pet dog that *he* put down, when she was quite small!"

"Now we know it was a recipe for disaster for both of them," pointed out Pompey. "Even if it took this particular crisis to bring out the craziness in the elder girl. But when she did go off her rocker, she still had all that lethal courage she must have got from the war-hero father. Talk about the female of the species—" But that did not seem a particularly profitable line of conversation to pursue with Jemima, so Pompey sighed and returned to the subject of Ione Quentin's future.

"'Given the circumstances' just meant being a lady-in-waiting—serving, servitude, perpetual attendance. Might begin to give you some funny ideas, I suppose."

"I have to say that the rest of them seem all right," murmured Jemima. But perhaps Pompey was merely ruminating on his own servitude, in horticultural terms at least, to Mrs. Pompey.

Others would have sweeter memories of the Royal Wedding than Jemima Shore. Major Pat Smylie-

Porter, for example, had some sweet memories, while shuddering away from what-might-have-been in every sense of the word, not only the demise of his royal mistress, but those secret hopes concerning Ione . . . but these were now repressed deep into his unconscious, as only Major Pat knew how to repress inconvenient and strong emotions. His sweet memories included not only arrangements perfectly carried out—and God knew what a triumph that was under the circumstances—but the particular way young Amanda Macpherson-Wynne, acting lady-in-waiting to Princess Amy, had carried out her new role, staunchly and discreetly. Major Pat intended to keep a fatherly, well a not entirely fatherly, eye upon young Amanda in the future.

The sweetest moment for Jemima herself came on her return to her flat from the Groucho Club following her drink with Pompey. She saw from the red light on her answering machine that there had been at least one call, and from the number registered on the machine itself, she discovered that there had in fact been a positive host of callers—or calls. The telephone rang again as she patted the purring Midnight, draping himself round her legs and arching his tail as one who had been unfed for weeks (a gross libel on Jemima's cleaning lady Mrs. B). Jemima decided to ignore the noise.

"A telephone that rings but who's to answer—" she hummed. But Cole Porter did not know about the 1980's solution of the answerphone. The noise stopped as the machine began to click.

Around Jemima literature concerning Royal Weddings, past and present, still proliferated while Princess Amy's radiant face, veil flung back, gazed up at her—in full colour—from the heap of morning papers. Most of the papers had chosen for their front page the balcony shot in which Prince Ferdinand— crafty foreign bugger or romantic hero according to taste—held Amy's hand to his lips and implanted upon it a deep deep kiss while gazing romantically— or craftily—into her eyes. It was a specially popular picture since the lip-readers, not present at the Royal Gala, had been out in force on this occasion.

What Prince Ferdinand said, looking so soulfully at Amy, was: "A dream come true."

A minute later Princess Amy, who could do no wrong, won even more hearts by exclaiming in rather a different mode: "Hey, Prince Charming, you're treading on my train!" And then she added, surely roguishly: "This is your wife speaking."

A good deal of pictorial attention was also paid to little Jamie Beauregard, who had revenged his defeat over the kilt by concealing his dirk in the beribboned tie of his page's knee breeches. He brandished it aloft in triumph on the balcony where his furious mother could not reach him: but for once this was a weapon which caused no one (other than the aforesaid mother, who would make him pay later), any anxiety.

Prince Ferdel's own comment: "I'd like to wring that boy's neck," although dutifully translated by the lip-readers was ignored on grounds of taste by all papers except the *Daily Clueless*.

"Marriage!" thought Jemima. "I wish them the joy of it." She picked up the papers and the notes and the family trees—all Susanna Blanding's patient work— and began to stuff them into the wastepaper basket. (She had an awful feeling that some of the numerous calls on her machine must have come from a sobbing Susanna, Rick having departed that morning for the Middle East.)

Feeling herself in a reckless mood, Jemima added: "And I wish Cass and Flora Hereford the joy of it too." The moment she had framed the thought, she realized to her surprise that it was true. She was free of all that. Weddings, marriage, royal or otherwise, were simply not for her.

Pity under the circumstances about the career, the TUS fiasco and the Megalith one which had preceded it. Oh well, there was always Midnight. . . . She would end her days as an unemployed spinster alone with her cat. That thought seemed to call either for tears or for celebration. Finding the latter preferable, especially since Midnight, an independent cat who liked to choose his own moment of embrace, had jumped out of her arms with an indignant mew, she routed out a bottle of champagne from the fridge. She realized wryly that it was the bottle given to her in tribute by a member of the Press on the day she had been sacked by Megalith and appointed by TUS.

Jemima had just opened the bottle when the telephone rang yet again. This time she decided to answer it. Susanna or no Susanna, what could she lose?

"Where are you?" cried the instantly recognizable voice of Cy Fredericks without any preliminaries. It was not only the instantly recognizable voice of Cy Fredericks, it was also the instantly recognizable voice of Cy Fredericks in a state of great agitation. "Didn't you get my messages? Where are you? Why aren't you *here*?" Then, virtually without pause, "Jem, my Jem, we have plans, wonderful new plans, most exciting plans, I can't wait to see you and tell you everything—"

"Cy darling, where are *you*?" But Jemima should have known better than to ask. Such a question, even at the calmest of times, had been known to cast Cy into a fearful state of uncertainty and these were definitely not the calmest of times.

"Miss Lewis," she heard him shout in the familiar manner. "Where am I? Miss Lewis, where are *you*?"

"I'm here, Mr. Fredericks," Miss Lewis's voice cutting in on the line had a soothing timbre which was equally familiar. "Mr. Fredericks is back at Megalith, Miss Shore," she continued. "There have been a few, er . . ."—discreet pause—"changes recently and in short Mr. Fredericks has been . . ."—another discreet pause—"reinstated."

"Only I'm now President," boomed Cy's voice, interrupting. "Tell her I'm President, not Chairman, President-for-life. We've all the time in the world. And tell her to get here as soon as possible." Evidently seeing no irony in his late statement, Cy Fredericks flung down the telephone, leaving Jemima alone on the line with the ever-helpful Miss Lewis.

"Can you possibly get him to wait till I finish this glass of champagne?" asked Jemima Shore Investigator.

# ABOUT THE AUTHOR

ANTONIA FRASER is the acclaimed author of several historical biographies, among them *Mary, Queen of Scots*, *Cromwell*, and *Royal Charles*. *Your Royal Hostage* is the seventh mystery featuring Jemima Shore Investigator; the earlier ones include the full-length *Oxford Blood*, *Cool Repentance*, *A Splash of Red*, *Quiet as a Nun*, and *The Wild Island*, and a collection of short stories, *Jemima Shore's First Case*. A television series based on the Jemima Shore mysteries was aired nationwide in 1983. In 1986 Antonia Fraser was chairman of the Crime Writers' Association.

She lives in London with her husband, the dramatist Harold Pinter.

# THE LATEST BOOKS
# IN THE BANTAM
# BESTSELLING TRADITION

Experience all the passion and adventure life has to offer in these bestselling novels by and about women.

---

Bantam offers you these exciting titles:

### Titles by Jean Auel:

# DON'T MISS
## THESE CURRENT
## Bantam Bestsellers

| | | |
|---|---|---|
| ☐ 26807 | **THE BEET QUEEN** Louise Edrich | $4.50 |
| ☐ 26808 | **LOVE MEDICINE** Louise Edrich | $4.50 |
| ☐ 25800 | **THE CIDER HOUSE RULES** John Irving | $4.95 |
| ☐ 26554 | **HOLD THE DREAM** | $4.95 |
| | Barbara Taylor Bradford | |
| ☐ 26253 | **VOICE OF THE HEART** | $4.95 |
| | Barbara Taylor Bradford | |
| ☐ 26322 | **THE BOURNE SUPREMACY** | $4.95 |
| | Robert Ludlum | |
| ☐ 26888 | **THE PRINCE OF TIDES** Pat Conroy | $4.95 |
| ☐ 26892 | **THE GREAT SANTINI** Pat Conroy | $4.95 |
| ☐ 26574 | **SACRED SINS** Nora Roberts | $3.95 |
| ☐ 26798 | **THE SCREAM** | $3.95 |
| | Jonathan Skipp and Craig Spector | |
| ☐ 27018 | **DESTINY** Sally Beauman | $4.95 |
| ☐ 27032 | **FIRST BORN** Doris Mortman | $4.95 |
| ☐ 27458 | **NEW MEXICO—WAGONS WEST #22** | $4.50 |
| | Dana Fuller Ross | |
| ☐ 27300 | **OMAMORI** Richard McGill | $4.95 |
| ☐ 27248 | **'TIL THE REAL THING COMES ALONG** | $4.50 |
| | Iris Rainer Dart | |
| ☐ 27261 | **THE UNLOVED** John Saul | $4.50 |

**Prices and availability subject to change without notice.**

Buy them at your local bookstore or use this page to order.

------------------------------------------------

Bantam Books, Dept. FB, 414 East Golf Road, Des Plaines, IL 60016

Please send me the books I have checked above. I am enclosing $_____
(please add $2.00 to cover postage and handling). Send check or money order
—no cash or C.O.D.s please.

Mr/Ms _____

Address _____

City/State _____ Zip _____

FB—2/89

Please allow four to six weeks for delivery. This offer expires 8/89.

# Special Offer
# Buy a Bantam Book
## *for only 50¢.*

Now you can have Bantam's catalog filled with hundreds of titles plus take advantage of our unique and exciting bonus book offer. A special offer which gives you the opportunity to purchase a Bantam book for only 50¢. Here's how!

By ordering any five books at the regular price per order, you can also choose any other single book listed (up to a $5.95 value) for just 50¢. Some restrictions do apply, but for further details why not send for Bantam's catalog of titles today!

Just send us your name and address and we will send you a catalog!